# best *laid* plans

## ERIN HAWKINS

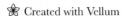 Created with Vellum

*To Eric for your unwavering love and support, and all those words of encouragement over the years… 'Just get it done'*

# BROOKE

"Where do you want it?" the masculine voice calls from the bedroom doorway. My hands continue their work, smoothing out the white duvet cover on the king-size bed in front of me before turning to see him standing there.

He's tall and lean, with muscle probably made from manual labor not from working out at the gym. I continue my perusal and notice his sandy brown hair is tousled, and I can see the beads of sweat forming on his forehead and temple, evidence from his efforts of hauling a seventy-pound nightstand up a full flight of stairs. The white t-shirt he is wearing is sweaty and clings to his chest, revealing the treasures underneath. And I can't help but notice the dirt smudges on his shirt match those on his ripped jeans as they hug his strong thighs. He's the perfect image for every woman's hard-working, furniture delivery man fantasy. I'm pretty sure that's a thing. Right up there with shirtless fire-fighters cuddling puppies.

When my eyes return to his face, I'm met with a sexy grin. *Oh, my.* He looks like a good time. Which I'm usually up for, when I'm not on a job. I return my focus to the room around me, because I'm a professional who does not get distracted by hot guys at work. Then, I glance at the walnut bedside table in his hands.

Where do I want it? That was the question, wasn't it?

"On this side, please." I point to the space by the bed, closest to the door.

As he moves past me, I watch the bead of sweat roll down the side of his face and am immediately thankful for the air conditioning in this townhome. And also, for visually-pleasing men who carry heavy furniture. Steve, one of the usual delivery men, hurt his back. He's in his fifties, overweight and balding. His sweat is not sexy. This personnel change is making my day. Sorry, Steve.

I'm a design assistant at Sue Allen Designs, and I love my job. Originally, Sue's business had been strictly interior design, but with the increase in new-build condo complexes and townhomes in the Northwest Denver area over the past two years, she branched out to staging models for builders. I've recently been put in charge of the home staging portion of her business, which is a huge deal, considering my degree is in communications, and I didn't have an ounce of design experience when she hired me three years ago.

"That's the last thing." He moves closer to me and I can smell his manly scent. I tamp down my reaction because, different time, different place, I'd be very interested.

"Great. Thank you."

"Do you need me to do anything else?" He's standing next to me now and his eyes lock on mine.

While he waits for my response, he lifts the hem of his shirt up to his forehead to wipe the sweat away and I get a glimpse of his six-pack. Jesus. That's a lot of muscle.

Hmm. I could think of a couple things. My brain suddenly has the most vivid vision of him throwing me on the bed. Down stuffing flying everywhere as he rips off my clothes and takes me hard. Then I envision the dirt and sweat-stained white duvet, and Sue walking in with the realtor while the delivery guy is mid-thrust.

"Um, no. I think I'm good."

He smirks as he pulls out his wallet and opens it to grab out a business card. He hands it to me with a wink.

"In case you're in need of any other services."

"Okay. Thanks," I drop my eyes down to the card, "Jake." I know he introduced himself earlier, but I was too busy staring at his butt for name retention. I tuck the card in my back pocket, smiling at him as we say our goodbyes.

Wow. Did I mention I love my job?

Okay, where was I—the table.

I pull a lamp with a glass base from the large bin at the foot of the bed, place it on top, then add a light gray lampshade and plug it in the outlet behind the table. Nice.

Next, I add a collection of throw pillows on the bed, then arrange a gray faux fur blanket diagonally across a bottom corner of the bed. One more glance around the room, and I smile at the transformation.

That's the best part of my job, watching an empty space become a furnished home that people can envision themselves living in. That, and hot delivery guys that make my vagina tingle.

It's almost three o'clock. The realtor will be here any minute, their open house is scheduled from three-thirty to six, likely to take advantage of the young professionals who call it quits early on Fridays and will be flocking to the neighborhood's trendy bars and restaurants for happy hour. A glass of wine is exactly what I need after a hectic week. I'm envisioning a glass of rosé, my couch and Netflix.

I move quickly to pack up my tools and carry the bin with all my stuff down the stairs to the main level.

I never imagined I would be staging homes for an interior designer. Tidy and organized are not words you would use to describe my apartment, but there's something exciting about arranging a space. I've always been into decorating, even when I was a kid, I liked to move the furniture around in my room. It wasn't a big room, and I always had to get Ellie, my identical twin sister, to approve the rearrangement. It was her room, too. But she always humored me. Not much has changed. There were only a handful of configurations, but I loved the feeling of having a completely different room. It was also the only motivation I had to actually clean our room, which was more Ellie's strong suit. We balance each other out that way.

"Brooke?" Sue's voice calls out to me just as I enter the living room. Her eyes register my presence. "Oh, there you are."

"Hi, I was just finishing upstairs." I take in Sue's outfit of the day. She is her job personified; an effortlessly appealing exterior without a lot of fuss. Her printed blouse and stilettos are perfectly coordinated, without being too matchy, her manicure and lipstick the perfect pops of color, and a chiffon neck tie around her neck, her signature piece, that like drapes to windows always makes her look flawlessly complete.

"It's gorgeous!" she exclaims, looking around the living room. "You were right about that art piece. The lighting in here really makes it pop."

I beam at Sue's praise. It never gets old. She looks around, examining my work.

For not having a design degree, I think I've picked up on a few things pretty well.

After years of odd jobs like bartending and dog walking—let me tell you, working a late-night bartending shift did not mix well with needing to wake up at six in the morning to walk a dog—I decided to put on my big girl panties and get a real nine-to-five job. Josh, Ellie's husband, recommended a temporary placement agency that his bank uses from time to time. After several awful placements, one at an insurance company answering phones, and another filing paperwork at an oil and gas company, I was sent to Sue.

At the time, Sue had just broken her arm skiing and needed a second assistant at her design studio. I started with fetching coffee, taking notes, and performing a lot of Sue's personal errands; dry cleaning, grocery shopping, anything and everything a woman with a broken arm couldn't do.

One day I was at Sue's house where I was waiting on a furniture delivery. She had just bought a beautiful Article leather sofa that felt like butter, off-white—really gorgeous. When the movers arrived and swapped out with the old one, I didn't like the way the new sofa fit in the room, so I rearranged...everything. Sue was initially shocked, and I was terrified that I might have overstepped and she'd send me back to temp agency hell, but ultimately, she was pleased and gave me some other design tasks around her house to see what I came up with. She liked those as well, and when she got an exclusive contract with a builder to design and stage all their new builds, she let me take a shot at staging their model homes.

I'm not into the interior design aspect of picking out flooring, countertops and cabinets, making bulk orders of tile and coordinating hardware finishes—that's all Sue and her staff of designers. My passion, I've discovered, is to choose which furnishings, art and accent pieces would look great, not only on site but also visually for listing photos, all to help entice buyers to purchase it.

"I'm going to do a quick walk through. I'll be right back. Oh, and Jeff will be here any minute, want to let him in and get him situated?" Jeff is the realtor with the listing for this townhome, as well as its four adjoining neighbors. Its three bedrooms and three bathrooms will likely appeal to a young family or an older couple who are looking to downsize but want spare bedrooms for visiting guests, such as their grown kids and maybe even grandchildren. I've furnished a few kids' rooms, and one nursery, for clients outside of the staging-to-sell business. There are so many cute ideas for kids' rooms these days, I wish I could do more. But, nurseries and kids' rooms are not part of the model staging I do for Sue's building contractors. All those homes need to be family neutral, meaning you don't want someone looking at the house who isn't going to have kids think the house isn't their style if they see a baby crib in one of the bedrooms. Some couples choose not to have kids, and some couples can't.

With that thought, I remember Ellie had her fertility appointment today. It's been two weeks since her latest embryo implantation and they were going to get results this afternoon.

"Sure thing," I comment while Sue heads for the stairs. I'm gathering the rest of the accessory bins from the dining room, and simultaneously looking around for my purse, when I hear the buzzing coming from on top of the sideboard. I have eight text messages. One from Sue letting me know she's on her way and asking if I need anything more from the warehouse. One from Sam, my best friend, continuing our conversation from this morning about where to meet for brunch on Sunday.

"Knock, knock." I look up to find Jeff coming through the front door with a case of bottled water.

"Hey, Jeff."

"Hey there, Brooke." He smiles warmly. Jeff is in his mid-forties, he's got salt and pepper hair, and one of the best smiles I've seen on a man. It's warm and captivating. If he wasn't a realtor, he'd probably kill it as a news anchor. He's also charming and funny, which I'm sure contributes to his ability to close deals. He sets the water down on the kitchen island and looks around. "Looks great in here."

"Thanks. I just finished up and Sue is upstairs doing a walk through."

He tears open the plastic wrap around the waters and moves to start putting them in the refrigerator.

My phone buzzes, catching my attention. It's Ellie.

I open her text and realize the other six messages were from her, ugh, how did I miss those? The first two seem normal, asking if I can come over, then if I can bring ice cream. The rest have misspelled words that apparently autocorrect couldn't even salvage, and rambling sentences that I can't decipher their meaning. What the hell was she doing?

I hope I'm wrong, but from the looks of Ellie's text messages, I think I can guess how the appointment went today. Knowing she's probably a mess right now, I let her know that I'm on my way, adding a few hugs and kisses emojis.

Sue's halfway down the stairs, raving about the art I put in the master bedroom, when I cut her off.

"I gotta go, Sue. I hope that's okay. Ellie had her appointment today, and well, you know how those have been going and I'd feel awful if I didn't go check on her. I don't think things went well. Again." I make a face. Sue knows the face. She's been along for this ride with me.

Ellie and her husband, Josh, have been trying to conceive for years. Round after round of In Vitro Fertilization with no success. The process is making my sister crazy —not only from the medication she has to take with each attempt, but the rollercoaster of emotions that it brings every time they think this will be the time, just to be let down again. They're on their third fertility specialist, have seen several reproductive endocrinologists and done at least six rounds of IVF. They've changed their diets to be more reproductively friendly, and Josh is not allowed in hot tubs or restrictive underwear. According to the doctors, everything checks out for their sperm and egg, but the embryo never sticks in Ellie's uterus.

She gives me a hug. "Go. I've got everything here. Maybe things will be better than you think." Her smile doesn't reach her eyes as she knows as well as I that's probably not the case.

"Where is she?" Josh doesn't even balk at my lack of greeting as I whiz past him through the front door he's holding open for me. He's still dressed like a banker in slacks and a button-down shirt, but his usually styled hair is messy, like he's been running his hands through it, and the look on his face is pure defeat.

"On the deck." Like I said, it's not the first time we've all been through this. Unfortunately, by now Josh and I know the drill. We're like medics assessing an emergency scene, applying pressure in the form of hugs, trying to stop the bleeding from Ellie's broken heart. Even through all the negative pregnancy tests, Josh has always stayed positive. There's something about this time that feels different, a sense of hopelessness in his otherwise usual optimistic outlook. Josh is a great guy and an amazing husband to Ellie. If their love alone could produce babies, they'd have ten kids by now.

Josh shuts the door behind me and I shift the paper

grocery bag in my hand to hang my purse on a hook by the door, then move quickly toward the kitchen, with Josh in tow.

I bought a few essentials that work well during times like these: wine and ice cream. Ben & Jerry's Chocolate Therapy, Ellie's favorite, chocolate ice cream with chocolate cookies and swirls of chocolate pudding.

The wine is for me.

In the kitchen I grab a wine glass and a corkscrew from the cabinet. Ellie's never been a big drinker, especially since she's been trying to get pregnant. I pour the cold, blush liquid into my glass, before pausing at the back door.

Through the window I see the brown, messy bun that belongs to my twin peeking over the top of a lounge chair. I take a big gulp of wine. I'm accustomed to this routine. The lead up to one of Ellie's doctor's appointments is usually two weeks of hope and excitement that this could be the time that everything works out. Those are the fun times where we dream of a little mini-Ellie, talk about names, and as an aunt I think of all of the museums and parks to take her. But that time is short-lived because once the usual test results are revealed, Ellie's spirit is crushed.

"How bad is it?" I ask Josh so I can prepare myself before speaking with my sister.

"The fertility specialist thinks it's Ellie's uterus. The sperm and egg are always good, it's the embryo just never sticks." He runs his hand over his hair, possibly attempting to calm it back down. "They told us we're wasting our money if we continue IVF." Josh turns his head with the last remark but I can hear the hitch in his voice.

My eyes close on a slow exhale. I feel so bad for them both.

When Ellie first told me they were having trouble

getting pregnant, I used to joke that she didn't need a baby because she was already mothering me. Her twin sister, a full grown woman with no direction in life.

I've kind of got my shit together now, but I'm still firm on the whole no marriage and family thing. Ellie and I have very different views on that. She wants a family to replace the one we lost, and I don't want a family for the very same reason.

Another gulp of wine to give me courage and then I reach in the grocery bag for the ice cream. I grab a spoon from the drawer before I leave Josh standing in the kitchen to join Ellie on the deck. Nothing prepares me for the sight of Ellie's red, puffy eyes. I'm about to offer her the ice cream when I notice an empty tumbler on the table beside her.

"Hey, sisss." Ellie's hand reaches for my arm to pull me down beside her on the lounge chair, but the weight of her hand on my arm causes the spoon to fall to the floor with a clatter. Once we're eye level, I notice her eyes are glassy from crying, but she also appears to be drunk.

"Hey, love. I brought your favorite, but it looks like you're trying something new tonight."

"I had some of Josh's scotch." Her mouth moves in a circle, trying to wrap itself around the word scotch.

She takes the pint from me. I move to retrieve the dropped spoon, but Ellie has already removed the lid and inserted a long finger right into the untouched surface. With alcohol not being good for women trying to conceive, Ellie hasn't drunk in years. Typically, ice cream is her indulgence of choice, drowning her disappointment in a pint of B&J's. This is not our usual routine.

We sit silently, Ellie eating ice cream, finally accepting the spoon I hold out to her, while I drink my wine. Ellie starts laughing. She sounds manic and it saddens and scares me a little.

"Isn't it ironic? We spend our teens and twenties taking birth control and worrying about getting pregnant, only to find out later that we can't even get pregnant."

Her wild hand gestures send a spoonful of ice cream flying, the glop lands on the wood deck then slowly sinks between the planks.

She hiccups, tears escape her eyes and suddenly I feel as helpless as Josh probably feels.

I don't want Ellie to be unhappy, but it is moments like these, where she falls apart a little and I try to hold her up, that I feel the closest to her—this time feels different, though, and I'm worried. Ellie's always been the twin that has life figured out. She knew she wanted to be a middle school math teacher when she *was* in middle school. And I still don't know what I want to be when I grow up. I love my job now, but I don't know if it's what I want to do forever. She knew Josh was the man for her, married him, her college sweetheart, and they are the cutest couple ever. And me, I dated a lot of guys in high school and college, but none of them were men I'd want to marry.

I'm mid-sip when Ellie stops shoveling in the ice cream. She sets the pint down on the table, her eyes wide with alarm, as her free hand lifts to cover her mouth.

She barely makes out an 'oh, god' before she's up and stumbling toward the hydrangea bushes where a moment later, scotch and ice cream vomit rains all over the unsuspecting plants.

―――――

With Ellie snoring softly in the comfort of her bed, I exit her bedroom, and pull the door shut behind me. Josh helped me get her downstairs, the joys of a 1920s bungalow being that the bedrooms are in the basement, and I helped her into bed, wiping off some of the vomit still clinging to her hair. It didn't take long for her to pass out and I just sat with her for a long while thinking of life and where we were at.

It's moments like these that the absence of our parents feels the greatest.

On my way back upstairs, I notice a light on in the last room on the left. The would-be nursery. When I push the door open the rest of the way, I see that the star projector lamp that Ellie bought a few years ago is on. It sits on an empty bookcase, next to the gray upholstered glider. Ellie is a planner through and through. Even though she's never had a positive pregnancy test, as soon as she and Josh started trying, she started planning the nursery. I had just started working with Sue, and I've always been the more creative one, so Ellie was excited to get my opinion. We talked about décor, what color to paint the walls, which was dependent on if they would want to find out the sex of the baby or not. The color swatches we picked out are still taped to the wall by the window. They even bought a crib. It's still in its box, leaned up against the far wall.

Even with every month that didn't produce a positive test, we continued on measuring and planning. I can't remember exactly when Ellie stopped working on it. It now sits empty and unfinished. A visual reminder of her and Josh's inability to conceive.

I switch the lamp off and close the door behind me.

Heading back upstairs, I find Josh in the kitchen sitting at the dining table peeling the label off his beer. I watch him from the doorway for a moment, realizing how much he's hurting, too.

"This isn't good, Josh. I've never seen Ellie like that."

Josh looks at me with sadness in his eyes. I don't think I've ever seen him look so defeated before.

"She's been so stressed out with all this baby stuff. Brooke, I don't even know what to do anymore to help her." He takes a swig of beer.

I pick up my wine glass off the counter and take a sip, only to dump the remnants in the sink a second later. I can't even stomach it right now. I hoped this time would have been different for them, or at least the same, where Ellie smiles optimistically and tells me it's going to happen the next time. But, it is way worse than I could have thought. What little my sister was coherent enough to tell me is her body is unexplainably not equipped to carry a child.

As a former houseguest, Ellie has me trained, so I rinse my glass and put it in the dishwasher.

"So, no more IVF?" I ask Josh, already knowing the answer.

"That's what they recommended. That's the medical advice." Josh looks at me with all sincerity, "Brooke, I don't want Ellie going through all she's been going through—I want us to have kids but this is too much on both of us."

"What about adoption?"

"It's an option, with a lengthy, grueling process, but you know what Ellie wants. I don't think she's ready to give up her dream of having a baby that is biologically ours."

My throat closes in on itself when I think about Ellie's determination to have a baby. Not just any baby, though I'm sure she would love an adopted baby as her own. She wants a baby that passes down her genes, the genes that our parents gave us. She wants to tell her baby about our parents and say you've got Grandma Diane's long eyelashes, same as ours, or Papa Jim's laugh, boisterous and contagious. She wants a piece of what she lost. And there's no way I can fault her for that.

When our parents died, my dad's sister, Margaret, came out from Iowa to help us with the funerals, to sell the house and figure out all the insurance and financial stuff that followed. She sorted and boxed up their belongings, putting the majority of what we decided to keep in storage, and donated the rest. After a month, she had to get back to Iowa and her own kids. She would check in on us periodically, but as time passed, we fell out of touch. It's not like we were little kids that needed to be taken in, but it was still a shock at twenty-one to suddenly feel the real-life burden of not having the parents that loved and supported us to turn to anymore. Ellie was far better at the adjustment than I was. Or at least she appeared to be.

I'm used to Ellie being the one with a solution to a problem. I feel helpless. But, I know if the roles were reversed, Ellie would figure out a way to help me.

"Josh, how can I help? I want to support you both." I sit in the chair opposite to him hoping there is something I can do.

"Man, Brooke, if I only knew." He takes another swig. "I've been thinking about taking Ellie on vacation, impromptu to somewhere warm and exotic, somewhere she's not thinking about babies. I don't know."

He is such a good guy, looking out for my sister. "That's a good idea, I can manage things here if you need. Just let me know how I can help."

There's more to say, I just don't know what it is, but I can tell that Josh isn't exactly in the mood to talk. He's in his own thoughts and needs time to process. I leave Josh staring at his beer bottle, and gather my purse to head home.

One thing is for certain, I'm determined to solve this problem for Ellie.

———

Back home in my apartment, I change into cotton shorts and a tank top after a hot shower, and grab a bubbly water.

Juggling my laptop and drink, I curl up on my sofa. When I'm staging a home, especially the modern, new-build condos that I've been working on recently, I have to keep the décor fairly neutral to make the space approachable to the greatest number of buyers. I add in a few pops of color here and there to make each space unique, but my apartment is a true reflection of my style, and my desire to be surrounded by color.

My apartment, with its dark blue walls that offset the vibrant pinks and greens of floral paintings and the fuchsia mid-century modern sofa, appeals to me. It has been my favorite project.

After I learned I wasn't allowed to have animals in my apartment, I took to collecting plants. I found a large tiered plant shelf at a thrift shop and painted it gold. I've got at least ten plants now, mostly succulents because they're low maintenance, and they can handle it if I forget to water them.

If it's Ellie's uterus that is the issue, maybe she could have mine. I don't plan on using it. It seems like a waste of a good uterus. If it's good, I mean. Maybe I have a defective uterus, too. Who knows?

I discover that it's not really a thing to exchange uteruses. Since a woman's uterus is not a vital organ, it's not commonly transplanted. Instead, couples struggling to get pregnant, in which cases the egg and sperm are healthy, can hire a surrogate to carry their baby. A uterus rental program. I've seen television shows and movies depicting this so I knew it was a thing. But when I see the cost to hire a surrogate, I nearly fall off my sofa. *Eighty thousand to one hundred fifty thousand dollars*. Not only is that sum insane, but why is there a range? Are there premium upgrades to a woman's uterus? I keep reading to find out the cost is dependent on where you live and the availability. That makes more sense. A chart informs me that in Colorado, surrogates charge about one hundred thousand dollars on average.

I trade out my laptop for my phone, and get sucked into social media. Instagram is like a portal to another dimension; it sucks you in so deep until you have no idea how to get back to where you came from.

But, it's also very informative.

There's a couple who just had a baby via surrogacy. She's an influencer so every detail of their journey is documented, along with all the products they use. I make a mental note to try the plant-based deodorant she suggests. It comes in a refillable case which is also good for the environment. Before I know it, I'm checking out pictures of her and her husband's vacation to the Bahamas. See, that's the problem with social media.

Flipping back to her Instagram story about the surrogacy, I see their photos and they look happy with their new baby so that's pretty cool.

She must have sold a ton of plant-based deodorant and energy drinks in order to pay for her baby!

I check my savings account which is growing steadily, but is nowhere near any substantial amount that would help Ellie and Josh. I wonder if people take out loans for this kind of thing? Like a thirty-year mortgage for a kid? It would be a bit depressing to still be paying off the loan that paid for your surrogate to have your baby when the kid goes off to college. Josh is money savvy so he probably knows about all of this. I wonder if I should ask him about it?

I grab my phone to text him then think better of it... it's two A.M. and maybe this is something you don't text. I can't pay for Ellie's baby but there's got to be something else that I can do for her.

With an idea forming in my head, I finally put down my phone and go to sleep.

# 3

## BROOKE

The next morning, I call Ellie to see how she is feeling. She's hungover, a rare occurrence, so she's hard to motivate, but I eventually convince her to agree to a shopping outing. I've got a few returns to make, impulse purchases that were not bank account friendly. Although I love them, I really can't justify another pair of Tory Birch flats.

I pick Ellie up around ten then we head to the Cherry Creek Shopping Mall. Ellie's not much of a shopper, so it's typical for most of her purchases on our shopping excursions to be influenced by me. I think back to the days when we would do our big back-to-school shopping trip with our mom every fall, and I'd always try to get Ellie to be interested in clothes that I liked, hoping to add more trends to our combined closet.

After we stop at Nordstrom to do my return, I steer us to the Everything But Water store to look at swim suits. If Josh does want to take Ellie on a beach vacation, she's going to need something other than the black one-piece she's been wearing for the better part of a decade. I really didn't know that swim suits could last that long. I'm also itching to try on the tie-dye bikini in the window.

Just as we're entering the store I hear a little boy say, "Look, Mommy. There are two of the same people over there."

I have to laugh. I get a fair number of glances, especially from the opposite sex, when I'm alone, but when Ellie and I are together it feels like there's a spotlight shining down on us. Sometimes I forget that we look exactly alike, especially to people who don't know us. Passersby who think we are carbon copies. Upon first glance, we are. It takes time to notice the subtle differences in our appearances and the way we dress. Ellie has a wider smile, and higher cheekbones, my face is more heart-shaped and I have a prominent freckle near my mouth. These are all observations from over the years, so it's impossible for a stranger to see the differences at first glance.

Once we're inside, I focus on finding suits that Ellie would like, but are also different than her usual basic black while Ellie follows me around giving disapproving looks to each suit I hold up for her.

"Trying swim suits on under fluorescent lighting while managing a hangover is not my idea of a good time." She sighs, rubbing her temples.

The saleslady comes over to gather the pile of suits I've collected. When she sees us, she smiles.

"We'll take one dressing room. It'll save us the back and forth." And, if I don't supervise Ellie, she probably won't try anything on. I'm trying to do Josh a solid here, and I need her to work with me.

She nods. "No problem."

When Ellie removes her clothes, I rear back at the sight

of the yellowish-purple bruises on her belly that the low-cut swimsuit does nothing to hide. She must see my face.

"Bruises from the injections."

I've seen them before, a while back when they were first starting IVF and Ellie was changing her clothes, but I honestly didn't think about it at all when I suggested trying on swimsuits. I feel bad now that I'm pushing this. Ellie doesn't say anything else, she just reaches for the first suit and pulls it on over her underwear.

As she tries on the suits, it appears I misjudged the size of her chest, and I have to send the saleslady out for new sizes in all the tops. We can now add Ellie's larger boobs to our list of differences.

"Did you get a boob job that I'm unaware of?"

"Fertility hormones. They'll go back to normal eventually."

Right. Because they're going to stop trying. Fuck. I am doing a horrible job of trying to distract Ellie from this topic. Obviously exposing Ellie in a swimsuit is not the best way to avoid observations about her post IVF body. Finally, we leave, me with a new tie-dye bikini and Ellie with a courtesy bottle of water from the saleslady. I guess this store really does have everything.

After we leave the mall, I decide taking Ellie to get ice cream will be a way to cheer her up, since shopping was a fail, and especially after her ice cream vomit in the bushes last night. It's like when you have a bad sexual encounter, you have to just get back out there because chances are the next one can't be as bad. All is going well, we've each gotten a double scoop cone at Ellie's favorite spot, Little Man Ice Cream, and suddenly two vans pull up to the curb, an entire little league team exits and soon it's a clusterfuck of kids. Which in hindsight is poor planning on my part. A sunny, Saturday afternoon in June just screams kids eating ice cream. I should have thought this through better.

There's this large metal slide, and there's a pack of kids just going up and down, up and down. Ellie is eating her salted Oreo ice cream while staring at the kids playing. I had hoped to get her out of the house and take her mind off the whole baby thing. Epic fail.

Things won't get better soon. Ellie teaches middle school math, and while it's summer and school is out, she picks up nanny and babysitting jobs for extra money, but mainly because she loves kids so much. If I got a three-month break, I would be sipping a cocktail by the pool, but that's the difference between Ellie and me.

"Do you want to walk around?" I offer.

"No, I'm good here."

She takes another bite of her cone.

This is not what I had in mind to keep Ellie's mind off her fertility issues. But I realize there are bound to be kids anywhere we go, especially in this neighborhood. It's a young family breeding ground, where all the young professionals morph into parties of three within two years of living here. That's why Ellie and Josh moved here. She thought it was a perfect transitional neighborhood.

"The doctor advised we not do another round of IVF. They think the shape of my uterus is problematic. That it's not a good environment for embryo implantation."

My hope had been to distract her from all the baby and IVF talk for a little while, but it's obviously weighing heavily on her mind. She's still trying to process it all.

"Yeah, Josh told me. In not so technical terms." I think he had called her uterus misshapen. Men. Eye roll.

Ellie nods. "Well, it doesn't really matter. Even if they advised me to do ten more rounds, we've spent so much money already, it feels like such a waste." She licks her cone.

Her comment gives me pause. I wasn't sure how to broach the subject, but she's giving me the perfect opening for my idea.

"What about a surrogate? It would still be your biological child."

Ellie stares at me for a minute before responding. "Surrogacy is an option. We've looked into that before, actually after our first try at In Vitro, but realized it was cheaper to do what we were doing, even with the emotional anguish it caused. I don't know how much you know about it but it's ridiculously expensive because of the surrogacy service fees for legal contracts and finding the right surrogate. Like a hundred grand or more. I know the surrogates go through intense vetting beforehand, but could you imagine putting your baby into a stranger's body and having no control over what is happening?"

Not revealing how much I did indeed look into it, I continue, "But would you do it if you had the money?"

"I think I would. Because I want our baby so bad."

Ellie has made good work on her ice cream, already taking bites out of the cone whereas I'm busy managing a drip situation that requires a lot of licking and some napkins. Even our ice cream eating is telling of our different personalities. Ellie's more of an ice cream fanatic, I'm more into baked goods. Like cake. And pie.

"I wish Mom was here. You know?" Ellie stops nibbling on her cone. "She always had the best advice."

I agree with her whole-heartedly that our mom was the best advice giver. She somehow always managed to stay unbiased, which I imagine would have been hard to not want to sway your child in one direction or another, whichever you personally found more favorable.

All the research I did last night on surrogacy comes to mind. There was a woman whose mother carried her child for her. That would be wild.

"She'd probably have the baby for you. Could you imagine?"

There's a pause while Ellie and I both take in the imagery of our mom pregnant at sixty years old. And then we laugh hysterically, because we know she would have totally done it. She was selfless that way.

I remember one time when she took Ellie and me to the zoo when we were nine. It was a cool spring day, but the sun was out and I was dying to wear a new dress that I'd gotten for my birthday. Ellie dressed dutifully in pants and a jacket, but despite my mom's warning, I wore the sleeveless dress, refusing to even bring in my jacket because it would ruin my look. The sky clouded over and there was a chilly breeze by the time we had reached the back half of the park. I was trying to pretend I wasn't bothered, but my chattering teeth and purple lips were hard to miss. Without a word, my mom took off her jacket and wrapped it around me. It was a simple thing, probably what any mom would do, but it made me realize all the little sacrifices that you make for ones that you love.

When our laughter subsides, Ellie's distracted again, this time by a little girl walking around with rocks from the landscaping that surrounds the patio. The girl—maybe two years old I imagine, I'm horrible at gauging kids' ages—she looks at us for a second and I imagine just like the kid at the mall, she's wondering why we look exactly the same. After a slight pause, she moves toward Ellie and without saying a word hands Ellie a rock.

"Wow! Is this for me?" Ellie's voice is way more enthusiastic than I would be about getting a rock. We're twins, but Ellie must have gotten all the maternal instinct genes. The little girl smiles at her.

"You." That's all she says.

"Thank you." Ellie smiles, there's happiness in it, but I also recognize a sadness, too.

And suddenly my insides squeeze and I think this can't be the way the story goes. This can't be the end of Ellie's dream to become a mom. If I had the money to give Ellie and Josh for the surrogate I would in a heartbeat. I don't even know if she would take it, but it doesn't matter because I don't have that kind of money. All I've got is me. And then the fuzzy memory of what I was onto last night clicks into place.

"What if I was your surrogate?"

Ellie's still clutching the rock in her hand when her eyes turn back to me.

"What?" She looks confused and suddenly I'm not even sure if this is what I want but I continue.

"Like you put your embryo in *my* uterus? No service fees. That would save a ton, right?" I'm on a roll now. "And it would be me. You wouldn't have the stress of wondering what some random woman is doing with your baby inside her."

Ellie's eyes shine with tears, and I think I have her.

"I don't understand. Why would you do that?"

"Because you're my sister! And I love you, and by default, Josh, and I want you both to be happy. And I would be an aunt, which I'm thinking could be pretty awesome."

"Brooke. You'd seriously do that?"

"Of course!" I'm super enthusiastic now. Although I'm not thrilled about the process: weight gain, going to the doctor all of the time, giving birth. But I put that out of my mind because I'm really good at focusing on the positive and worrying about the consequences later. "I have no use for my uterus."

"I don't think you know what you'd be getting yourself into. Obviously, I've never been pregnant, but from what I've read and friends who've told me, it's not exactly a walk in the park. Your body will change, you'll be uncomfortable, your emotions will be all over the place. It's a lot to handle."

What I think Ellie means to say without really saying is it's a lot to handle for you, and I agree—the body changes worry me. But she's been ready to jump into whatever wild rollercoaster ride pregnancy and motherhood is for years, so I understand she wonders if I have what it takes to grow her a baby. Because it's me. Wild, unreliable Brooke. A reputation that I've been battling back since college. Okay, maybe since I was born, but college for sure. And since our parents have been gone, Ellie's looked after me like the nurturing, emotionally stable person she is.

I understand her reservations, but I hate that she might think putting her baby inside a stranger would be more appealing than having her own twin sister as her surrogate. For once, I want to be the one that has a solution, and I want, need, Ellie to take me up on the offer, especially now that I put it out there. I mean, how many aunts get to tell their niece or nephew that they pushed them out of their vagina?

It sounds cool until I really think about what it would be like to push a baby out of my vagina. I'm pretty sure it would never be the same. Maybe I could start saving up for that vaginal laser treatment that tightens you back up again. I saw it on a *Real Housewives* episode. Those women are always in the know about that kind of thing. When I realize most of my information is coming from reality television, I decide to not mention that part to Ellie.

"I mean, Brooke, you eat pie for breakfast." I know where she's going…I'll have to improve my eating habits.

"That's a serving of fruit."

"What about dating? How would you date when you're six months?"

I give her the usual eye roll that is reserved for this conversation. But Ellie brings up at good point. Not about dating, but more about sex. I can go without dating; sex might prove to be more challenging.

"The same way I date now."

"But you don't really date now."

"Exactly. Besides, it's only nine months." OMG, nine months, that's a long time…but I can do it.

"Don't you want to find someone?"

"I'm only thirty, stop pressuring me," I joke.

Since she married Josh, Ellie's been hoping I'd find the one and change my tune about marriage and babies. Even through all of my protests, she insists I'll 'find the right guy.' I tend to gravitate toward guys that aren't looking for anything serious either. It works. And there's no hard feelings when either of us ghost out. There's no emotional connection, just hanging out and having sex. Low expectations are the key to not being disappointed.

"Brooke, you like Josh, right? What if you had someone like him? It's pretty great is all I'm saying. Having someone." Ellie raises her eyebrows, like she's half encouraging me, half scolding me for not agreeing with her.

Josh is hot in a nerdy, finance guy kind of way, and he's perfect for Ellie, but sometimes I wonder if she thinks she settled down too early. Didn't test drive enough cars before making her final purchase. She lost her virginity to Josh our freshman year and has been with him ever since. Guess she knew what she wanted. They're crazy in love, which is awesome. But, I'm more of a lease type of girl, not into big purchases, and I like the idea of a quick trade-in if a newer model comes along. I'm not into cars at all so I have no idea where that analogy came from, but it totally fits.

Ellie's a hopeless romantic and convinced that everyone should be coupled up and in love. Yet another personality trait we don't share. Telling Ellie flat out that I don't want to get married and have babies doesn't seem to work. So, I try a new tactic.

"Nine months isn't going to interrupt anything. It will give me more time to work on me. Figure out what I want."

I think she gives up, or at least moves on when her eyes suddenly light up, "With embryo implantation you can decide how many embryos to put in. What if we had twins?"

"Twins?" My eyes widen at the thought. Then my mind starts racing, wondering if she's thinking this would be some fun project to do together. Or, like those friend-ship necklaces, you keep one half and give the other away. "You'd keep them both, right?"

"Of course, silly." Ellie's laugh turns into a dreamy smile. "Wouldn't that be amazing?"

I want to share her enthusiasm, I really do, but it's just not contagious. At least not the being in charge of tiny humans part. I love that this could be a solution for Ellie and Josh, to have a baby, or babies. That I could help her in this way.

My abs are off in a corner crying at my betrayal. But I follow a personal trainer on social media that has like six kids and she looks amazing. I'll just pop out a baby, then *Body by Rachel* will whip me back into shape.

"It would be something." I nod. Honestly, even as an aunt, one is enough.

"But I can't ask you to do this."

"You didn't ask. I offered."

"I just don't think you know what you're offering." Ellie's smile drops, her face resigned now as she sadly watches the little girl who is picking up more rocks.

There's that look again. The look that makes me feel like Ellie's eight years, not eight minutes older than me. The one that tells me I've got another crazy idea that's not going to work out. Like when I filled the bathtub up with Kool-Aid so we could increase production output for our lemonade stand. Or convinced Ellie to swap clothes with me at a party so I could talk to a guy she liked for her, so then she ended up accidentally getting her first kiss from my drunk boyfriend. But I'm not a kid anymore. I'm an adult, fully functioning most days, and I want to help. We've only got each other. For once I want Ellie to lean on me, let me help her, if I can.

"You're right. I don't know what I'm offering. I don't even know if it would work or if I'd be a good candidate for surrogacy, but I want to at least try. Explore the option."

I watch Ellie for a response. She appears to be zoned out, but I follow her gaze to find her still watching the little girl, completely transfixed with this tiny human playing with rocks. When her mom calls, the little girl drops the rocks in the flower bed and toddles over to her. She offers the toddler a bite of ice cream, then follows it up with a kiss. The little girl climbs up in her lap, now content to sit there and eat ice cream, rocks forgotten.

Ellie nods, "Okay."

## 4

## BROOKE

"I'm going to have a baby," I announce to my best friend, Sam.

We're gathered at one of our usual Sunday brunch spots. The Way Back, located on Tennyson Street, the main street that anchors the trendy Berkeley neighborhood that I live in, located just northwest of downtown Denver, serves up the best cinnamon sugar mini donuts. They're the perfect appetizer when I'm in the mood for something sweet.

Sam lives in Uptown, a neighborhood east of downtown and it was her turn to come to me. True to its name, the Highlands neighborhood is located uphill from downtown and Sam, who refuses to drive anywhere that is bikeable, has barely recovered from her arduous bike trek when I spring the news on her. She's in mid-hair tousle, reviving her blonde wavy strands after they've been flattened under her helmet.

"What?" Her blue eyes widen as she pauses mid-fluff. "Wait, who's the father?"

The waiter brings the mimosas I already ordered,

grapefruit for Sam and orange for me. Sam's eyes narrow as I lift my champagne glass.

"I'm not actually pregnant. Yet." I take a swig of my mimosa. "You know Ellie and Josh have been trying to have a baby forever. Ellie can't get pregnant, so I'm going to be her surrogate."

I'm pleased by how easygoing and relaxed I sound when I say it. Because although it's something I've had circulating in my brain for a while, it's another thing completely to give voice to it. When I suggested it to Ellie yesterday, there was no hesitation. I want to help her and Josh, period. They're all the family I have, and I would do anything for them. But I've been so excited at the thought of having a possible solution to their fertility issue, that I haven't given any thought about what anyone else would think about it.

I've known Sam since college. We were randomly assigned as roommates in the dorms our freshman year. Ellie and I had decided to go the random roommate route so we could meet new people, you know, expand the eighteen-year clique we had going on. Ellie got Marie, a Tri Delta pledge that was messy and brought home random dudes, while I hit the jackpot with organized, stylish, fun-loving Sam. Other than the time Sam insisted *Love Actually* was the best holiday movie ever, when it's clearly *Elf*, we were a roommate's match made in heaven, and have been best friends ever since.

Sam is originally from California, the Bay area, but decided to stay in Colorado after college, moving to the Denver area as Ellie and I did. She's putting her fashion and merchandising degree to good use with the online boutique she has been running the last five years. With her online sales through the roof, Sam has decided to open a brick and mortar shop in the Washington Park area.

Sam just stares at me blankly, then says, "I'm confused. Why would you do that?"

"Ellie is losing her shit about not getting pregnant. The doctor just told her that the IVF procedures have failed because they think her uterus is misshapen and therefore not viable to carry a fetus. She needs a surrogate. Someone to carry her baby."

The look on Sam's face is a mixture of horror and confusion. But I can't really be insulted. Sam knows me, my penchant for one-night stands, partying and general life irresponsibility. But, she also knows once I set my mind to do something, like the majority of the men's lacrosse team junior year, that I stick to it. I don't usually set goals, but when I do they're pretty life changing.

"Okay, but, why you? Aren't there professionals for that kind of thing?"

The server arrives with the donuts, and I immediately dig in. I moan when the mixture of cinnamon and sugar hit my tongue. I can feel Sam staring at me, still waiting for my response.

"Of course, there are," I answer mid-chew, "but the cost is outrageous. Like a hundred thousand dollars. Not to mention that would be so nerve racking to have your baby inside of some random woman walking around doing who knows what."

"But don't professional surrogates know what they're doing? They would know what to eat and how to take care of their bodies for the baby. And I'm sure they're background checked. It wouldn't be some 'random' woman. If you're paying that much money there has got to be a contract and insurance." Sam continues on, giving me her thoughts on the situation and raising all the questions that I have already thought of but dismissed.

Honestly, I think Ellie and Josh could come up with the

money to hire a professional surrogate if they had their heart set on it. Even with Ellie on a teacher's salary, Josh has a well-paid job at the bank and she's told me they have invested well over the years. I threw out the cost and stress of an unknown surrogate, because as crazy as it sounds, I want to be their surrogate. It may be the only chance I get to have the experience of being pregnant. I'm not planning to have a kid of my own, because that would require being in a relationship with a guy that lasts longer than one night.

"And who's to say you don't have the same uterus issue?" Sam responds, which she's right, it could be possible, something to be found out during the evaluation process with Ellie's fertility specialist.

I pop another bite of doughnut into my mouth and chew.

"You have had a lot of sex and never gotten pregnant. Maybe your uterus is not baby-friendly either," she continues as I wash the donut down with mimosa.

"Yeah, I'll have to get checked out and all that stuff." I just leave it there because yeah, it could be a problem.

"Brooke." At Sam's soft tone, my eyes lift to hers. "Your heart is in the right place for wanting to help Ellie and Josh, but you really need to think about what it means for you to do this before you jump in. You know?"

I know what Sam is thinking. I have a tendency to commit to things before I think through all of the details. But, offering to help Ellie and Josh have a baby isn't going to be like when I joined a pet fostering program before I checked with my landlord about the pet policy. That was a lesson learned.

My eyes light up, remembering the article I read online, preparing soon-to-be mothers of the body's changes during pregnancy.

"And, my boobs will get bigger."

Just then, our waiter appears with our entrées. Eggs benedict for Sam and lemon ricotta pancakes for me. He asks if we need anything else before quickly retreating from our table.

Sam shakes her head, "You're insane."

After pouring syrup all over the fluffy stack of pancakes, I take a big bite and hum with pleasure. Sugary sweet breakfasts are my favorite.

"I really want to help Ellie. She's my twin sister," I say in between bites. "She's always been there for whatever crazy drama I was going through. She's family. And if the shoe were on the other foot, she would totally have my baby."

"So are Ellie and Josh on board with this?"

Ellie and I have spoken a few times since our ice cream outing, though we've not mentioned it to Josh yet…that should be interesting. "Yeah, she's game for it. Obviously, she has to talk with Josh. It'd be his baby inside me, too."

Sam makes another face like I horrified her again, "Weird."

"Yeah, I know, but it's not like I have to have sex with him."

Sam just stares at me as I think about how icky that would be as well. I like Josh but no, that would be gross. "Obviously," she says.

"I don't know. This sounds like a lot, a huge commitment, even though it is for family. Do you actually know anyone who has been a surrogate for someone? I mean, I can't imagine it's easy. The toll it would take on your body just with weight gain and I'm sure there's other areas that would never be the same." Sam looks at me very pointedly.

"Of course," I quickly respond, a little annoyed with her lack of support. "There's…"

I'm about to list off a few names until I realize they're all from television shows or movies. Huh.

Sam notices my pause and her eyebrows raise in response.

"Something other than a romcom movie you watched half-drunk on a Saturday night."

I watch Sam press her fork into an egg, and the runny yolk oozes from inside over her English muffin. I take another bite of pancake. This conversation isn't going the way I thought it would. Not that I expected Sam to jump up and congratulate me on being sister of the year, that's not what this is about, but after Ellie was initially skeptical and now Sam is looking at me like I've grown horns, it's a little defeating.

I decide she just needs some time to adjust to the idea.

"How's the boutique build out coming along?" I ask, changing the subject.

I'm so excited for Sam's boutique. She's been working hard to gain an online following for her shop and now she's realizing her dream of having a store front. And I've been helping her find cool display furniture that matches the aesthetic of her athleisure boutique.

"It's turning out great. Everything looks amazing so far." Sam sets her fork down and reaches for her mimosa. After she takes a sip, she continues, "But my contractor is a fucking nightmare."

"Really? Wait, didn't you hire your brother's friend?"

"Yeah, Luke." Sam makes a face, like just saying his name is enough to put her over the edge.

"How is everything turning out so well if he's terrible?"

"Oh, Luke's a great contractor. His work is top notch, but I'd never say that to his face because he's such an arrogant ass. He wants to argue with me about every detail. And he's always glaring at me for no reason. I really don't remember him being such a jerk when we were growing up."

Sam is normally so even keel. She does a lot of yoga and meditation. I've never seen someone get under her skin like this before, and I can't imagine someone not getting along with her, especially if they are a friend of her brother's.

Unless…my eyes narrow at her.

"Wait a minute. Is he hot? Is this like a sexual tension kind of thing?"

I watch Sam's face. Her cheeks turn rosy, and even when she says nothing, it's written all over her face.

"What? No." Sam's eyes bounce around like they're in a game of pinball, never quite meeting mine.

"Has he been showing you his power tools?" I start to snicker. "I bet he's really good at drilling. And screwing." I wiggle my eyebrows.

"Stop." Sam tries to say it with a straight face, but she can't help but laugh, too.

When we've composed ourselves, Sam says, "Yes, he's attractive. But Luke's not interested in me like that. He's supposedly doing me a favor, but I don't exactly know what his deal is." She tucks a strand of hair behind her ear. "Anyways, you need to come by this week to check it out."

"Oh, I will." I don't really know what else to say to that. I'm more curious now than ever how the boutique is coming along.

We finish our food, slam back our mimosas and grab our bags.

———

After brunch, Sam rides off on her bike and I head down Tennyson Street to check out the shops. The main street is lined with clothing boutiques, coffee shops and the cutest little bookstore that I love to frequent. I've never been described as a bookworm, I wasn't the best student in school, but in my adult life, I learned to love to read.

The summer I graduated college I think I read ten books in three months because I was so excited to finally be able to read something that wasn't assigned by a teacher or professor. My parents had been gone two years that summer, and I worked my way through a stack of books that had been on my dad's nightstand. I remember reading one book in particular, James Patterson's *Crossfire*, that must have been the one my dad had been reading right before the accident because there was a bookmark in it.

So many emotions went through me when I surpassed the page that he had marked. He never found out how the book ended.

I find myself on autopilot as my sandal-clad feet cross the street, and I pull open the door to BookBar. The aroma of coffee hits me when I enter and I breathe it in deeply. The small, independent bookstore is half bookstore, half bar that serves the essentials like coffee, breakfast sandwiches, baked goods, wine and beer. It's got comfy couches for reading in the book area, and tables with chairs in the bar where people work on laptops, hold meetings, or meet for a glass of wine. I debate getting a coffee now, it smells so good and I didn't have time to make any this morning, but then a worker lining up paperbacks on a shelf asks if I need help finding anything and I remember what I came for.

I'm unfamiliar with the section of the store that I'm looking for so the saleswoman's help is welcome. If I'm going to seriously pursue surrogacy for Ellie and Josh, I need more information about the whole pregnancy thing. I'm aware of the process that Ellie has been going through with IVF, which I've read is similar to what is required of a surrogate, as far as hormones that I'd have to take to prepare my body for the embryo implantation, but I'm pretty clueless about pregnancy in general. Some of my friends from college have had babies, but other than picking out a swaddle blanket or pair of fuzzy booties off the registry for their shower, I wasn't really involved with their experience. The only tidbit I recall is a night out a couple years ago with my friends Jen and Amanda, who'd had babies a few months before, and how they talked about their baby's poop all night. Sam and I danced, then I went home with a cute guy. Both Jen and Amanda moved to the suburbs and we haven't talked much since, but according to their Instagram accounts are pregnant with their second babies now.

The saleswoman leads me through the children's book section and into a small room at the back of the store where she stops in front of a book case labeled as pregnancy and parenting.

"Everything we have on pregnancy is here." She motions to a smaller section at the top. "But we can order any book, so let me know if you want me to look anything up."

"Thanks," I tell her before she retreats to the front of the store.

I take note that the parenting section is ten times the size of the pregnancy section. Maybe that's an indication that growing the baby is not the most challenging part of this process. All the hard stuff comes later. That's Ellie and Josh's part, and I will get to be fun Aunt Brooke.

I'm about to reach for a book when a title in the parenting section catches my eye. *Eat, Sleep, Poop.* Then the one beside it, *Baby Poop: What Your Pediatrician May Not Tell You.* There are at least a dozen different titles concerning poop culminating in one titled *Oh, Crap Potty Training*. I guess my friends weren't wrong, there seems to be a lot to discuss where baby poop is concerned. I make a mental note to put together a poop themed gift—books, diapers, and wipes—for the next baby shower I'm invited to. Fingers crossed, it's for Ellie.

I load myself up with *What to Expect When You're Expecting*, which according to my internet research is the pregnant woman's bible. And another one about eating right for your baby, because eating right for myself is hard enough. They don't have any books specifically about surrogacy so I take the other books up to the counter to check if they have any others they can order. On my way, I grab the new Tana French paperback. Her mysteries are my favorite. They're a heart-pumping workout I don't have to leave my couch for. I fan the book pages in front of my nose. I love the way books smell. New books, old books, library books and newspapers. One of my top five favorite smells in the world, right behind fresh cut grass and gasoline.

I set my books on the counter and Paula, the salesclerk, according to her nametag, begins tapping away on her computer to see if there are any other books to order. My bladder is starting to scream with the two mimosas I drank at brunch. Dang it, I should have gone to pee at the restaurant. I excuse myself and use the restroom while she continues her search. On my way back, I stop in my tracks when I see Gina, an obnoxious woman that teaches at the same school as Ellie, at the counter talking to Paula. Shit. I remember Ellie telling me she had just bought a house in my neighborhood.

Gina is actually a lovely woman, if you don't mind anything you say being repeated to the first hundred people she talks to. I know Ellie shared her fertility woes with Gina early on, because she is a mom and Ellie thought she would be a good person to talk to. Gina told people without Ellie's permission and Ellie has had to deal with all the looks of pity from people she didn't even want to share her personal issues with. I met her at a school bake sale once where she roped me into an hour-long conversation about heirloom tomatoes. She makes a mean double-fudge brownie, but Gina is the last person I need to see me buying pregnancy and surrogacy books. Thank goodness for the wall that juts out to separate the bookstore side from the coffee and wine bar, which is also where the bathrooms are located.

Gina's chatting up Paula and hasn't seen me. Hopefully it's not about gardening, or she'll be there all afternoon. Now would be a good time to get that coffee I wanted, so I make a quick turn to head back toward the bar. My about-face is sudden, which makes it impossible to see the person getting up from the stool at the counter until I'm smashed up against him. I don't have much time to get my bearings before I realize that there's something wet now between us. Once I take a step back, I can see the crinkled plastic cup, its lid askew and the contents, a frothy green smoothie type thing, oozing over the edge of the cup.

"Shit. I'm sorry."

There's a little on the floor, a little on me, but most of the damage is on him, and that's when I look up for the first time to see *him*.

Thick, dark hair, bright blue eyes, a jaw line that could cut glass. Wow. He's next level hot. I then notice he's dressed casually in khaki shorts and a blue golf polo, one that fits perfectly to showcase his broad shoulders, muscular arms and chest. Whatever this green concoction is, everyone should be drinking it. Green smoothie, it does a body good. I'm almost positive I've seen that ad somewhere.

He turns to set his cup back on the bar and it snaps me out of my preoccupation of ogling him and into action.

"Let me get something to wipe with."

There's a stack of napkins in a console along with coffee stirrers, so I reach for a handful and start wiping.

"I can get it."

His hands attempt to catch mine, but I'm too quick. I've got his shirt mostly mopped up but there's really no fixing this without good old-fashioned soap and water. I wad up the used napkins, toss them in the trash and grab a clean set, determined to not leave until he's at least not dripping green smoothie on the floor.

"Oh, wait, I missed a spot."

The thick green liquid has dripped, leaving a spot the size of a quarter near the front pocket of his shorts.

"Let me just…"

A firm, but gentle hand wraps around my wrist, holding me back before I can reach the rogue drop.

"I can take it from here," he says and the sound of his voice gives me goosebumps.

My eyes shoot up to meet his gaze. He raises his eyebrows and it finally occurs to me that maybe I shouldn't be rubbing down a stranger, even if it is under the pretense of cleaning up a mess I made.

"Sure. Right." Makes total sense that he doesn't want my hand inches away from his crotch. Message received.

I'm feeling a little embarrassed as he takes the napkins from my hand and wipes his shorts. I watch every move, of course. 'Cause I'm a weirdo.

"That will have to do," he says and I'm mesmerized by the tone of his voice.

"You look good." My eyes do a complete body scan,

culminating at his face. "I mean you look better than good."

His eyebrows do that raising thing again. The one where I'm sure he's thinking I'm a complete sociopath. His blue eyes light with something I'm thinking is amusement —it could be fear, but I'm thinking it might be amusement.

"Better than you looked with green smoothie on your clothes." What the fuck is wrong with me?

A glance over my shoulder tells me that Gina is still at the checkout with Paula. Ugh, I still need to delay. Then it occurs to me that I should pay for this guy's drink, since he's wearing half of his first one.

"Sorry, again." I lift my hands and motion about, "I've got ninja-like reflexes. They're a danger to the public."

He smiles. I like the way the skin by his eyes crinkles. He seems a bit older than I'm used to dating. I mean he's definitely not old, but he seems like a guy I wouldn't find out at the bar on Saturday night. Someone a little more put together judging from the Rolex on his wrist and the brown leather loafers on his feet. Loafers have never looked so sexy.

"I can see how they might cause problems," he comments and winks and I almost drop to my knees.

"Yeah, it's a curse." I reach in my wallet to grab some cash. "I'll pay for your smoothie. How much was it?"

"It's okay. I'll just finish what's left." He's wiped the outside of the cup off and resealed the lid.

Judging from his appearance, I'm completely aware that he could probably buy smoothies for the entire bookstore and not break the bank, but it's the principle. If I wasn't so clumsy and self-consumed in avoiding a gossip monger this wouldn't have happened. Maybe years ago I would have just said okay and bailed, but I'm a responsible adult now and am perfectly capable of cleaning up my messes.

"I want to pay you for the smoothie, it's my fault. How much?"

"Seriously, it's cool. I didn't need to drink the whole thing. I've got dinner plans later."

As I study him, I can't help but wonder what his dinner plans are. Or more so, whom they are with. I've already noticed he's not wearing a ring, but that doesn't rule out a girlfriend or fiancée. I bet she's pretty, has Pantene-commercial hair and shops at J. Crew. And he uses his firm hands to hold her wrists over her head while he thrusts into her hard. Lucky bitch.

All right, this guy is hot, but also a tad annoying. He doesn't want me to pay for his smoothie, but I'm resourceful. I look up at the board hanging on the wall and scan it until I find the smoothie column. Under gourmet smoothies, there's a flavor called green machine, it's just a hunch but I'm gonna say it was that one. Kale, romaine and parsley are the first three ingredients. He's basically drinking a salad. Holy shit, it's twelve dollars!

My mouth gets ahead of me, "You paid twelve dollars for a smoothie?!"

He looks sheepish for a moment but then responds, "Yeah, it's really good. Have you ever tried it?"

"No." I shake my head, then look at the five in my hand before reaching back in my wallet for more cash. Good grief. While I'm counting out my money, I glance over at the register. Gina is gone, and Paula waves in my direction. My fingers are counting and I come up short, I only have ten dollars in cash. My thoughts drift back to his body and I almost consider telling him I'll work off the extra two dollars, but that would be completely inappropriate, so I decide to call it a day.

My hand extends out the cash I have, but he just shakes his head and refuses to take it. He fixes me with a smile, but let's be honest, it's more of a sexy smirk.

"I'm Cole."

"Brooke," I respond, still extending the money in his direction.

"How about you give me your phone number instead and we call it even?"

Huh. I guess I was wrong about the girlfriend thing.

I'm moments away from spilling my digits, because I'm beyond curious if he would actually call, when I stop myself. Cole is gorgeous and obviously easygoing, with his casual response to the whole smoothie fiasco. He also gives me butterflies, and sweaty palms. But Cole is a distraction that I don't need right now. I'm focused on exploring the surrogacy option for Ellie and Josh.

"Sorry, my number is worth more than twelve dollars." I grin, knowing I'm being extremely cheeky.

I roll up the cash and tuck it into his shirt pocket, then turn on my heels to go pay for my books.

Good news, Paula found the book I needed. She places the order, to be shipped to my apartment, and rings up my other books. I Apple Pay and am out the door in no time. On my way out, I think I feel Cole's eyes on me, but I don't turn to look because if I do, I might march right back and give him my number.

"You're late." When I pass by the dining room, I find my sister, Carrie, setting napkins on the table. I ignore Carrie's eyeroll and lower myself to her belly.

"Your mom is a real stickler for time. Good luck with negotiating curfew." I lean in closer to whisper, "Don't worry, Uncle Cole knows all the tricks."

I rise up to full height, at last addressing my sister, whose expression has softened during my conspiracy with her unborn son.

Carrie and her husband, Kyle, used to live closer to downtown, closer to me, but moved to the suburbs after they had their first child. It's a thirty-minute drive on I-25 South to their house.

I adjust the collar on the button-down shirt that replaced my smoothie-covered polo, and can't stop my lips from twitching when I find myself thinking about Brooke, again.

After a late morning round of golf with some buddies from college, I'd stopped by BookBar for a smoothie, because no matter how hard I've tried to replicate it, their Green Machine smoothie always tastes better. That's where I found myself on the receiving end of her self-described ninja-like reflexes and half my smoothie down the front of my shirt.

After a quick side hug due to Carrie's enlarged front, she pulls away, taking the bottle of wine in my hand with her. I follow her into the kitchen where her husband, Kyle, is prepping a lasagna and my mom is chopping vegetables for a salad. With my mom's hands busy slicing, I gently wrap an arm around her collarbone, then drop a quick peck on her cheek.

"Where's Dad? And the girls?"

"Out for a walk," Carrie replies as she reaches for the wine glasses in an upper cabinet, "the girls were driving me insane."

I round the island and step in behind her to help. "What? Not those angels." I smirk knowing full well how rambunctious my nieces, four-year-old Annie, and two-year-old Sophia, can be. Especially Annie, she's Carrie's mini-me.

After an easy twist-off cap on the wine bottle, Carrie does a heavy pour.

"I'm going to assume that's for me?" I chuckle.

She takes a deep sniff of the burgundy liquid; her exhale is a sigh as she extends the glass to me.

"After this baby pops out, I'm drinking a whole bottle of Whispering Angel and no one is going to stop me." Carrie enjoys wine, but she's also due in a month, so I'm guessing she's just really sick of being pregnant.

"Wine?" I lift the bottle toward my mom and Kyle. She accepts, he declines, motioning to his beer on the counter.

I pour a glass of wine for my mom and move to set it on the counter by the cutting board.

"It's so good to see you." She says it wistfully, like it's been months.

"You saw me last Sunday at dinner."

"I just like to know how you're doing. How work is going. If you're seeing any special someone that you might want to bring to dinner."

There it is. I can't help but smile. My mom is nothing, if not predictable. She needs to know what is happening in her kids' lives like she needs a decaf coffee after dinner every night.

I take a drink of my wine.

"Good, busy and no." My standard responses to her typical line of questioning. The answers to the last two have always been in direct correlation to each other. Work is busy; therefore, my personal life is non-existent. I haven't brought anyone to a family dinner since I was in medical school, and that was mostly a study session with a meal break.

I'm an OBGYN specializing in Maternal-Fetal Medicine, which means I work with women who have high-risk pregnancies, whether it be from a mother's pre-existing condition, such as high blood pressure or diabetes, or a chronic health problem, a risk of early labor or bleeding, or a birth defect that has been identified and requires treatment before birth. Also, women expecting multiples.

After medical school, internship and residency, I completed my Maternal and Fetal Medicine fellowship at University of Colorado Hospital and started my own practice. That was three years ago, and with the addition of more physicians and staff, I'm finally at a point in my professional life where I can take a breath. Have some fun. Date. Start a family.

My mom smiles and takes a drink of her wine. She knows that I want to find someone. She and my dad got married in college, and they had me before he finished his residency. He's retired now, but was a family physician for forty years.

Kyle pops the lasagna he's been prepping in the oven, then turns to give me a guy-hug. You know, the light embrace with a few solid pats on the back. "Good to see you, man."

"Looks like you're in charge here tonight." I motion toward the oven.

Kyle leans in and on a whisper says, "I'm not in charge, I'm just the worker bee, while the queen oversees the hive. You know what it's like with this one."

"I'm right here." Carrie smirks, watching our exchange. "I can hear you."

"I didn't think hearing was one of the enhanced senses during pregnancy." Kyle looks at me for confirmation, but I just shake my head and try not to laugh.

"It's not. You guys just have no sense of what a whisper is," Sis retorts.

"Huh." Kyle places a kiss on my sister's neck, then grabs his beer. "I'm going to go turn on the grill."

Kyle then turns and says to me, "Come on out after your interrogation." Then kisses her neck again, "Love you, boo."

Once he's gone, Carrie sighs at his shenanigans, slides herself onto a barstool and turns her attention back to me. "Let's run it back. Why were you late?"

"I'm not late. Dinner hasn't even started." I motion toward the oven where the lasagna just started baking. "Wait, why is Kyle turning on the grill?"

"He loves grilled garlic bread." My sister rolls her eyes lovingly, then motions with her hand for me to answer her question.

"If you must know, I had to change clothes. I bumped into a woman at the bookstore."

My sister makes a face, and I realize my explanation might have come out a little odd. She's now imagining me picking up a woman in a bookstore on my way to our family dinner. Which, I actually tried to do and failed miserably.

"She ran into me and dumped my smoothie all over my shirt," I clarify.

"Ahh." A sly smile spreads across her lips. "Was she pretty?"

At this question, my mom's head pops out from behind the refrigerator door where she's been returning the remnants of unused vegetables after finishing the salad.

I don't know if pretty would justify her description. Brooke's shoulder-length dark brown hair, big, expressive green eyes, the way her full, pink lips pouted when I refused to take her money. Pretty wasn't enough of a descriptor. Gorgeous and intriguing, definitely.

When she leaned in to wipe my shirt down, I could see down her V-neck shirt where her more than a handful, perky tits were covered in a nude lace bra. The short skirt she was wearing showcased her long, toned legs. Then there was all the rubbing she was doing to clean up my shirt. It gave me a chance to check her out. When she went for my shorts, I had to stop her. I didn't need the semi I was starting to sport to get to full mast. It was the gentlemanly thing to do. She also had this quirky thing about her. She was nuts, but in an endearing way.

Maybe it was arrogant to ask for her number, but it's been a while since I actually pursued anyone.

I don't tell my mom and sister any of this because what does it matter? All I got was her name and a smirk before she high-tailed it out of there as fast as she could. I just stood there, dazed as she walked off to pay for books and left. Maybe it was the fact that she had me feeling something, more than just a stiff dick, that put me back on my heels. It was a completely random encounter, and yet I left it feeling a longing, like she took something with her when she left. An energy that made me want to draw closer to her.

I'm losing it. I've been working too much for too long. I just turned thirty-six and other than a rock solid career, and a nice apartment, I don't have much to show for it.

"Yeah." I shrug, trying to sound indifferent when I answer. It must have been convincing, because Carrie moves on quickly.

"Oh, do you remember when I was telling you about my prenatal yoga instructor, Lori?"

I'm struggling to remember the exact conversation, but I play along.

"Sure. What about her?"

"Well, you're both single and I think you might have a lot in common with the whole women's bodies and babies thing, so I mentioned to her that I'd see about setting you up. Maybe for coffee, and you can see how it goes?"

I don't love the idea of my sister playing matchmaker, but I know her heart is in the right place. She wants me to find someone because she knows that's what I want. And the way to find that person is to meet new people, get out of my office and go on dates.

She's about to press me further when my nieces come bounding into the kitchen with my dad in tow. I scoop them up, one in each arm. Holy hell, they're getting heavy.

After exaggerating the amount of effort it takes to return to an upright position, I playfully tease, "You two are getting so big."

"No, you're just getting old." My four-year-old niece, Annie, wraps her arms around my neck.

"UnCole," Sophia, the two-year-old, adorably combines Uncle and Cole into one name, "you old."

Kids, they tell it like it is. When I rage a tickle war on them, Annie scrunches up her nose and giggles uncontrollably. It's moments like these that I wonder what it would be like to come home to a kid or two. A beautiful wife to tuck the kids into bed with, then have my way with her once the kids are asleep.

I'm happy for my sister and Kyle. But, she's four years younger than me, so it's also hard to watch her have these milestones—getting married, two amazing kiddos, and about to have another—without a bit of jealousy. It's just me. Not that everything has to go in chronological order, but sometimes I wonder if I'll ever have it. Or if I've spent too many of the years working where my focus should have been on something else. Looking for the right partner, working on my own family.

I catch my mom watching me with them and it's not hard for me to read her thoughts. She's got two grandkids and another on the way, it would be easy for her to be satisfied, but she's greedy, and I get it, because who wouldn't want more of these in their life?

I set the two giggling munchkins down and they immediately scamper off to play, their high-pitched squeals echoing down the hallway.

"Inside voices!" my sister yells. I fight back a laugh at the irony of her demand.

My dad drops his hat on the island, then gives me a hug. "Those two wear me out. What are we drinking, son?"

I pour him a glass of red, which he accepts before sitting down on the living room couch.

"Okay, lasagna's in the oven, salad is ready." Carrie moves around the kitchen as she checks items off her list. "Oh, will you take this garlic bread out to Kyle?"

With a plate full of garlic bread in one hand, and a glass of wine in the other, I manage to maneuver the sliding glass door out to the patio where Kyle is sitting in a lounge chair watching the girls, who have now decided to bless the outdoors with their screams, and chase each other around the yard, until they abruptly stop and decide to play 'lost treasure' in the sandbox.

When Kyle sees me and the garlic bread, he hops up to take it from me, "Thanks, man."

He throws the bread on while I sit and sip my wine. We catch up, as much as guys do, talking about sports primarily.

Minutes later the food is ready and we all gather around the dining table. We catch up on Carrie's recent doctor appointment, everything is looking great and the baby is measuring perfectly. My mom tries to pry potential baby names from Carrie and Kyle, so that she can get a jump on ordering a monogrammed blanket for him, while the girls recite silly names for the baby, like Chicky Pickles and Tootie Butt. Kyle updates us on the large commercial development project that his company just broke ground on, and my mom and dad inform us about their upcoming trip to Italy that was specifically scheduled around Carrie's due date as to not interfere with meeting their grandson.

"Cole, how's work?" my dad asks as he refills his wine glass.

"Good. We've got another new OBGYN, she just started two weeks ago, so I'm finally starting to feel like I can lift my head above the water. Work days aren't as long and now with four of us, I'm down to one on-call weekend a month."

"That's great, son. Those long hours take a toll. I'm glad you've been able to find a balance."

Annie chews a bite of lasagna, then turns to me.

"Daddy said you were a v-v-agina doctor. Do vaginas get sick?" She looks really concerned.

Her mother's eyes go wide and it's all I can do to hold back a laugh.

"Fagina! Fagina!" Sophia chimes into the conversation.

"Seriously, Kyle?" Carrie shoots daggers toward her husband, but he just shrugs.

"She asked what kind of doctor he was. I was looking for a simple response."

My mom perks up with a sly grin. "Do any of those vaginas have potential to give me more grandchildren?"

Carrie just about falls out of her chair, "Mom! This is not appropriate conversation for the dinner table."

My mom just shrugs. "I just thought since we were on the topic."

When I meet Carrie's horrified eyes, I can't help but laugh out loud.

My dad takes a sip of his wine, trying to take the conversation in a different direction, "Anybody catch the Rockies game last night?"

My mom starts gathering plates up. "I'm going to go put on a pot of decaf."

# BROOKE

I'm only a few chapters in to the *What to Expect When You're Expecting* book and to say I'm a little freaked out is an understatement. I'm actually on chapter four because the first two were about conceiving and I don't need to know anything about that. That's what the turkey baster is for.

I'm pretty fascinated by a woman's body, and what it can do. But it's also a lot of weird science stuff that just sounds a bit scary. The surrogacy book I ordered arrived on Tuesday. It talks about the process, hormones that are used to prepare the surrogate for implantation and the emotional impact of surrogacy, like growing a baby in your body that isn't yours and how that can cause attachment to the child. This is all natural, cause and effect, and at first, I'm bothered by that but then I think I'm going to rock this surrogacy thing because I will be more than happy to hand over the baby to Ellie and Josh. And it's not like I'll never see the kid again, I mean I'll be his or her aunt…

On Wednesday night I made dinner at Ellie and Josh's house. I brought groceries and made taco salad, the one of the few things I know how to make that doesn't come out of a box or the frozen food section. Ellie seemed to be in good spirits, she drank a margarita and we played Uno.

The three of us talked about exploring the option of me as their surrogate. She'd filled in Josh this weekend and he seemed kind of unsure about it all but as usual, if Ellie is into it then he'll support her. That's just the kind of guy he is.

Turns out Ellie had talked with her fertility specialist and set up an appointment for next week to see if I would be a good candidate. Things are getting real and I can tell Ellie is excited, but also trying to not get her hopes up. I mean, things may not work for me either—I could have the same poor plumbing as my twin and I'm afraid I'll disappoint her. They've been going through this process for so long, I can't imagine what it would be like if it doesn't work out.

But it feels like this is the last option for them to have a biological child. It's exciting and stressful, so I'm trying to not think too much about the appointment and enjoy the weekend. After we finish the last game of Uno, I get up to say bye to Josh and head home. I can see he's still rebounding from all they've been through. He's sitting in front of the TV, beer in hand, eyes unfocused, obviously in deep thought. Once again, I assure myself that I'm doing the right thing.

Saturday morning, I pick up bagel sandwiches and coffee from Leroy's then meet Sam at her boutique to check out the progress. I've seen the space mock-ups, and we've been working on the interior design together, so I know her vision. Sam is right, Luke's craftmanship is flaw-less. He's building most of the retail displays from scratch. Everything is turning out great. When I ask where Luke is, because of course I want to meet the man that is making my best friend come unhinged, she tells me he'll be there later. I'm disappointed that I didn't get to meet Luke, so of course I threaten to show up unannounced sometime this week. She just shakes her head and laughs at me.

We part ways so we can shower and get ready for the Rockies game we're attending this afternoon. Sam loves baseball, and she typically drags me to a few games each summer. She grew up with two brothers who played baseball all the way through college, her family basically lived at the ball park when she was growing up, and I go because I like to look at men's butts in their tight baseball pants and work on my tan.

When I get home, I'm excited to see the Amazon package waiting for me. The other night I was doing more research on surrogacy, and stumbled onto an advertisement for a fake pregnancy belly. I'm having the most anxiety about my body changing with the surrogacy and thought it would be a good way to give myself a glimpse of what it will be like to have a baby bump.

I hear Sam call out as she enters my apartment.

"I'm in my bedroom," I respond. A moment later she's in my doorway.

"I got the low-sodium seeds because I know you don't like—" Sam stops midsentence when I turn sideways.

"What the hell is that?" She points at my midsection, where I am now, according to the size chart in the prosthesis box, four to six months pregnant.

"A baby bump. I thought I'd try it out for a day. You know, research."

Sam laughs. "Wow. I don't know what's going to be better entertainment. The game or watching you with that thing on."

After trying on four shirts I finally find one that will completely cover the fake baby bump. It's weird to look at myself in the mirror with this on. Obviously, I have none of the other symptoms that come with pregnancy so it's cuter than the hard-hitting reality that a human could be growing inside me. At least for now, let's see how the day goes trying to maneuver around with this thing.

"It's kind of cute," I tell Sam and she just snorts.

"It's eighty-eight degrees out, let's see how long the cuteness lasts."

I start to think about if it were real and I become an aunt. I'm kind of into that because I'll get to spoil the kid and do fun aunty things without the responsibility. I don't even know if it's the responsibility part of having a baby that freaks me out, or if it's knowing that a baby would be someone to love and care for, and worry about. I just don't need that kind of pressure.

Sam drags me from the mirror and we grab our purses and head for the bus stop that will take us downtown. I nearly trip up the stairs getting on the bus. The driver is concerned, but of course, all Sam does is laugh.

"Are you sure you want to do this? It's not that you're a klutz but you're not the most graceful person alive."

The belly has its perks. When we get on, two guys exit their seats so that Sam and I can take them. They might have given us the seats to be chivalrous, but I'm going to give credit to the bump. As Sam takes the window seat in the crowded bus, I smile smugly at her, then take my seat.

I soon realize that with all my outfit changes and belly arranging, not once have I attempted to sit down with it on. Once I'm seated, my fake stomach just sits there—in the way.

Twenty minutes later, we exit at the Coors Field stop. Under normal circumstances the five-block walk would be nothing, but I can already feel the extra weight as my thighs start to burn with the effort to keep up with Sam's energetic pace. I think nature is really onto something with a pregnant woman's weight gain being more of a gradual occurrence rather than instantaneously. Once we get into the stadium, it's packed! Walking around with an extra six inches in the front of my body is not an easy task in a crowd. And we've another half-mile walk around the stadium before we climb the steps to our cheap seats on the rockpile.

"Let's grab our beers first. I'm going to get a pretzel, too, what are you having?" Sam turns to find me fanning myself with the free program book they were handing out.

"Yeah, beer for me and I'll get a hot dog, too—let me buy this because you got the tickets."

The line is long and while we wait, a group of women ask me how far along I am, what the baby's name is and all kinds of other things. If I were really a mother-to-be I'd be so into this conversation but I don't want to encourage them so I tell them everything is a surprise. Sam just smirks quietly next to me.

Finally, it's our turn and we place our orders, though when I ask for a beer at the concession stand, the woman working the counter looks at me funny, and it takes me a minute to realize that she thinks I'm *actually* pregnant. Of course, she does. Because who would be walking around with a fake baby bump? I just laugh like I was making a joke and order a lemonade instead, wishing I had brought a flask of vodka so I could enjoy a drink without everyone's judgy eyes. Though it does give me pause because that's nine months without alcohol of any kind…there are a few things I need to think through I'm realizing. This pregnancy is going to affect my lifestyle more than I was thinking.

But no one can deny me a Rocky dog, the footlong hotdog they serve at Coors Field. I charge everything and

Sam tells me she's going to go up to the seats while I head over to the condiment stand so I can load up my dog with relish and mustard. A cute guy appears on the opposite side of the island and our eyes catch over the pumps and he smiles. I smile back. He's cute. His brown hair is on the longer side, cut in a hairstyle that I thought only Zac Efron could pull off, but this guy is doing a pretty good job. He's probably younger than me, maybe mid to late twenties. I like younger guys, when they're not trying too hard they can be easy and fun. I think back to the smoothie guy from the bookstore, which I hate to admit he's been on my mind all week, and wonder what he would have done if I would have given him my number. Maybe I should have given him a shot. He was older, but that doesn't necessarily mean he wanted to get married and have babies. He looked like he might be mid-thirties and if he's gone this long without taking the family route maybe he doesn't want to.

Before I can take my analysis any further, I catch Zac Efron's brown eyes staring at me while he pumps ketchup into his French fry cup.

"Hi," I say, smiling widely, curious as to what he's up to.

"Hey," he responds with a lift of his chin. "How's it going?"

"Great." My dog is loaded up, so I grab a straw from the dispenser and poke it in my lemonade. "Gorgeous day for a game." My lips encircle the straw and I take a long suck of my lemonade. It's a bit sugary for my taste, but the straw is a nice prop to have.

I like flirting and casual hookups. It's fun and easy, no commitment involved. I'm really good at keeping my feelings at bay and I just enjoy the time together—I think I'm probably a guy's dream that way.

"Yeah."

Fry guy's eyes drop to my lips and I know exactly what he's thinking. I am, after all, sending out the vibe.

"I'm up in a suite with some friends." His eyes flick back up to mine. "They didn't have fries so I came out here to get some."

I smile. "Fries are good." If he likes my straw action, I bet he'd love to see me eat this hotdog. "But I'm a fan of Rocky dogs."

"That's a big hotdog," he comments, his eyes locking onto mine. Yeah, he gets it. "Listen. This might be forward, but do you want to join me in the suite?"

"Oh, that would be fun!" I gather up my Rocky dog and lemonade so I can move around to his side of the condiment island. "I'm here with a friend. Another girl. She's in our seats watching the game. Do you want to wait here while I go get her?"

While I'm talking, something in Zac's eyes changes. He was smiling and giving me sex eyes one minute, and the next he's looking at the fake bump, in shock. I nearly laugh at his reaction but what he says next gives me an odd feeling.

"Actually, it's my buddy's suite," he motions over his shoulder and starts to walk backwards, "and I forgot he had some other friends coming. I'm sorry."

I'm not going to lie, it's a hit to the ego. Although I can't blame him. He's just looking for a fun time, and he probably thinks I'm on the hunt for a baby daddy. It's a little much for a summertime Saturday afternoon. Suddenly I'm wondering why I wore this damn thing anyway. *Because it's going to be real soon and you wanted to see how it felt.*

"Oh, okay."

"Enjoy the game."

He's out of there so fast, somehow, he manages to kick up dust on the concrete floor.

"You, too," I call, realizing he's already taking the stairs four at a time.

Me and my bruised ego make our way back to the seats. Sam is there, eyes glued on the game that's already started while I was making eyes with Zac, with a cold beer in her hand. Before I'm even seated, the story falls out of my mouth.

"I was just rejected by a guy because I'm pregnant. Fake pregnant." I'm like stunned at how much it hurt me. I've been rejected before so why is this such a big deal?

"How do you know it was because you're pregnant?" She puts the word pregnant in air quotes.

"I was standing on one side of the condiment cart and he was checking me out, flirting with me. He even asked me to come over to his buddy's suite, but as soon as I moved around the cart and he saw my bump, he backpedaled. Uninvited me, us. You were a part of it, too."

"Thanks. Glad to know you weren't just going to ditch me." She smiles with a wink—she knows I'd never do that, we're BFFs.

I turn my focus to the game and take a big bite of my footlong hot dog. That guy has no idea what he's missing out on. French fries, pfft. I talk as I chew. I'm very lady-like.

"So that's how it's going to be? I get no action with a baby bump?" Not a complete surprise but it's confirmed now.

"Maybe he was vegan and that footlong wiener freaked him out. It's sure starting to bother me." She makes a face.

I wash my food down with lemonade, and Sam takes a sip of her beer.

"You never know, you might be able to find a guy with a pregnant woman fetish."

"Really? Is that a thing?" I humor her.

"I think it's a biological urge, for men to see a woman swollen with child."

"Even if it's not their child? That doesn't sound right."

Sam shrugs. "No, I've heard of it, really. People are weird."

"I think Ellie would freak out about some random guy's dick poking around near her baby's head."

"The baby's inside your uterus, it's not going to get poked in the eye by a penis." She eyerolls me like I'm some idiot, but honestly, I had to think for a second.

"Well look who's been catching up on her reading." I smirk, giving it right back. It's a wonder sometimes that we're that good of friends. We tease each other like sisters, and always push the other to do things outside of their comfort zone. Like I make her get a bikini wax and she drags me to hot yoga.

"I glanced at the book while you were adjusting that thing." She points to my belly, which is starting to sag on one side, making it look lumpy. Partially my fault as I've been pushing it from one side to the other to sit more comfortably. The extra weight from the bump only makes the hard-wooden bleacher seats of the rockpile seating section worse. And, where I would normally be enjoying the exposure to the sun, the fake bump is like a furnace on the front of my body. I can feel the sweat sliding down between my boobs, and see where it is soaking through my purple shirt.

I take another big bite of hotdog and a glop of mustard and relish lands on my shirt, right on top of the fake bump.

Sam laughs while I wipe myself up. This day is really

getting on my nerves and I just want to get home and rip this thing off.

Then Sam asks, "So, you'll go on a sex hiatus, I guess. Is that going to kill you?"

Sam has a point; it's not going to kill me. I enjoy sex, but I'm not going to *die* without it. That's what vibrators are for, right? But, as long as I know there's going to be a dry spell, there's no harm in enjoying myself while I have the chance.

"We should go out tonight," I suggest.

"Really?" Sam's like me, always up to have a good time.

"Yes. I'm going to have a real one of these soon," I pat my fake belly, which has started to slide a little to the left as my sweat has reduced the prosthetic's stickiness, "and I just discovered they're not man magnets. And I want to drink a real cocktail," I raise my lemon-flavored sugar water, "and find a hot guy to make out with."

———

My hands smooth over my flat stomach and the stretchy black material of my form-fitting mini-dress that covers it. After the game I was a sweaty mess. It's nice to be back to my normal state. During the seventh-inning stretch I peeled off my bump, deciding that stadium seats were not designed with pregnant women in mind and I had enough practice for one day.

Sam and I arrived at Lustre Pearl, a cocktail lounge in the River North Art District near downtown around nine, two hours later I'm thinking this isn't going to happen tonight.

"Should we go somewhere else?"

Sam dances around me, "No, this is my song!"

The guys that I've talked to tonight are not really what I had in mind for my 'last meal' as Sam keeps calling it. I mean if it were your last meal, would you demand filet mignon or settle for chicken fingers? There's a cute guy who I keep making eye contact with across the dance floor, but I think he might still be in college, and I'm not really in the mood to be the older woman tonight.

It's not like I'm going to be pregnant tomorrow, there's still time, but as I look at the scene around me, people laughing and dancing, their arms swaying to the music with one hand clutched around their cocktail while the other arm waves freely, I wonder if this is the right approach.

I open one of the three dating apps on my phone and start to peruse, hoping there is someone there I can swipe right on. I'm considering a personal trainer with a beard when Sam grabs my phone out of my hand.

She waves it around as she dances.

"Hey! I was just about to swipe right."

I try my best to pout but really, I'm not that upset.

"You're trying too hard. Just let it happen."

Sam tucks my phone back in my clutch then pulls on my arm to make me stand.

Then, we decide to dance, because who needs a guy when you've got Beyoncé?

W e danced for an hour before Sam was ready to call it a night.

After I tuck Sam into her uber, I decide I'm not in the mood to go home yet. I'm not tired and I feel restless. Something that a quiet apartment will not cure. The hook-up thing didn't happen tonight, but that doesn't mean I'm not going to indulge. My eyes catch the neon sign across the street, and I can't help but smile at the comfort it brings. I cancel my uber that hasn't arrived yet, then do a quick scan left and right before I do my best attempt at a quick jog in my tight dress and heels.

A moment later I'm pulling open the door and the tiny silver bell fastened to the top of the door frame announces my entrance. In contrast to the dark street, the inside of the diner is almost blinding. The lights bounce off every surface, as if I've just entered a Mr. Clean commercial. I nod at Bruce who is wiping off a table. He's got the bald head and earring, just not the muscles. My heels click on the black and white tiled floor as I make my way to the counter where Carla's familiar face smiles in greeting.

"Well look who it is."

"Hey, La."

I slide onto a mint green leather stool in front of her. Five years ago the diner was updated by new owners. Wanting to retire, the old owners sold their classic greasy spoon diner to an established restaurant group that turned it into a yuppie hangout, complete with a menu overhaul and shiny new interior. The only thing remaining from the diner of my childhood is Carla. And her pies. But, that's enough.

"You done for the evening, or just getting started?" she asks.

It's typical for me to stop in after a night out. I always get a little nostalgic when I've been drinking. The diner and Carla are pieces of my childhood, a time that Ellie and I spent here with our parents when life was simple and a milkshake or a piece of pie could fix anything.

"I'm here to eat my feelings."

"That bad, huh?" Carla's thin lips pinch together, and I can tell her signature pink lipstick has faded since the start of her shift. Her short hair is wavy, light blonde, almost white, but she's added pink tips since I saw her last. It's very Cyndi Lauper-esque. Carla is in her fifties, but I swear she actually looks younger now than she did when I was a kid. Maybe it's the uniform change, denim and t-shirts replacing her vintage waitress dress. The few wrinkles around her eyes and lips are the only giveaway that she's been here for twenty years.

"Nothing a piece of your peach pie can't fix."

And when I say pie, I mean the world's best piece of pie. Marie Callender's got nothing on Carla's famous peach pie.

Carla's lip twitches. I can't tell if she thinks I'm being funny or dramatic. Her eyebrows draw in.

"Wish I knew you were coming. I would have reserved you a piece."

I smile at that, imagining a large piece of pie with a toothpick flag stabbed into its layers, my name scrawled on the label.

"That's sweet. I'll just take the biggest piece you've got."

"Sorry, hon, I just sold my last piece to that young man."

Carla nods her head toward the end of the counter. My head immediately turns in that direction to find a guy sitting a few seats down from me. My sole focus had been on pie and I hadn't even noticed someone sitting there.

My eyes narrow as I study him. His thick, dark hair, the five o'clock shadow on his jaw, the large metal watch on his wrist. The blue scrubs he's wearing make me wonder if he's a doctor. Maybe a nurse. I don't want to sound sexist. Men can be nurses, too.

I don't know if it's my lingering buzz from the drinks at the bar, or if I'm just that desperate for pie, but something has me moving out of my seat and toward him.

As I get closer to him, I can't help but think that he looks familiar in some way. It's one of those moments where you know you've seen a person before but you can't quite place where.

I watch him, fork in hand, as he presses it down into the tip of the pie. The peach filling oozes out the sides as the flaky crust breaks from the rest of the pie and gets scooped up by his fork. I can practically taste it. When he brings the fork to his lips, I feel my mouth open in anticipation of the sweet deliciousness that is about to enter his mouth.

Whether he heard the click of my heels as I approached or he sensed me near him, his fork stops short of his lips, then returns it to the plate before he turns to look at me. With a full view of his face now, it clicks. The piercing blue eyes, strong jaw and perfect smile. It's Cole, the bookstore guy that I spilt green smoothie on. I'm still not over that. Who pays twelve dollars for a smoothie? I don't care what's in it, that's ridiculous.

I'm glad to see he's come to his senses and is eating three-dollar pie now.

In the bookstore, I recognized that he was hot, but I wasn't focused on him in that way. I was busy avoiding Gina and then ordering the books about surrogacy. When he asked for my number and I said no, it wasn't because he wasn't worthy of it. The exact opposite, in fact.

He's not the usual type of guy I go for. If I'm being honest, he looks like he has goals. And a 401K. And possibly lives somewhere that he doesn't share with the other members of the band. He most definitely is not in a band. But, if he was, he'd be the dreamy lead singer that all the girls go crazy for.

But, now he's here at midnight, eating pie and looking sexy as hell in blue scrubs.

He stares back at me and I can't remember if I said anything or if I've just been standing here staring at him like a creeper.

I watch as he slides his plate six inches to the left, in the opposite direction of me.

"I haven't forgotten about your ninja-like reflexes."

## 8

## COLE

Now that I've addressed her, she slides onto the stool next to mine.

"They are memorable."

A smile spreads across her face and I can't help but smile, too. She's gorgeous. Her long, chestnut brown hair is styled in waves, and she's wearing more eye makeup than she was at the bookstore. I should keep my focus on her face, but my eyes drop lower to take all of her in.

Her tight black dress hugs her breasts, the low cut garment giving me an excellent view of her cleavage, and with her legs crossed, the hem of her skirt rides up revealing long, toned legs that end in the highest heels I've seen since med school when I did a rotation at the ER and a girl came in with a broken ankle.

"Are you going to eat that?"

She motions toward the plate in front of me, then leans forward, propping her elbow on the counter, so she can rest her chin in her hand.

"Are you going to watch?"

"Yup. You're eating my pie, so I'm going to sit here and watch you."

"Your pie?"

She shrugs, making her dress inch up even further.

"Well, I come in here most Saturday nights and get a slice of Carla's peach pie." She motions over to the waitress who is filling up a man's coffee cup at the end of the counter. "You took the last piece."

"I see." My gaze drops down to the peach pie I have yet to taste. After my shift at the hospital, I was supposed to go home, shower and meet some guys out to play pool, but instead I found myself taking a detour to the diner that everyone at work recommends. Get the pie, they said, it's amazing! Now, I'm not sure it's just the pie I'm interested in.

Don't get me wrong, if she was an old lady, or a drunk guy, this would have gone another way. Well, maybe I could spare a bite for the old lady.

I reach over the counter to a stack of rolled silverware, pull on the paper tab to unfurl the napkin and pull out the knife. She watches me, curiously, as I cut the pie down the middle, then lift the extra fork in her direction.

She smiles and her fingers graze mine as they wrap around the stem of the fork. When she leans forward, her dress hem reaches a new height, one I imagine continuing until I can see between her pretty thighs.

She swivels toward me, her knees sliding along the outside of my thigh, as she attempts to get closer to the pie plate, and I'm officially hard. Eating pie in a diner at midnight with a boner. My friends are right, I need to get out more. Or stay in more. Whichever would allow my dick to get action from something other than my own hand.

"Hey, that's not halfsies. Yours is bigger," she says.

"Halfsies? Is that a technical term?"

"Yes. It's very important to know the lingo when nego-tiating pie with a stranger." Her words slur a little, she's really cute.

"We're not really strangers, are we, Brooke?" Her lips quirk to the side when I say her name, as if she wasn't sure I'd remember it, but is pleased that I do. "I seem to recall you getting pretty handsy at the bookstore. I'm Cole," I remind her.

"I know." She smiles again.

"And that's my finder's fee." I point to my piece of pie that is barely bigger than hers. If at all.

"What?"

"I get more because it was my pie, and although preschool taught me to share, I don't particularly like doing so." I reach for her fork in a mock suggestion that I'm rescinding my pie share offer. She rears back, grasping the cutlery with both hands.

"No backsies."

I raise my eyebrows.

"More pie negotiation terms?" I tease.

"Exactly."

She reaches forward quickly and takes a bite. It's the sexiest thing I've seen in a long time.

"So how often do you negotiate for pie? Is this a regular occurrence?"

"My first time." She smiles around a bite. "I'm pretty good, huh?"

"You're something."

"So, what's with the scrubs?"

"I'm a doctor." I motion over my left shoulder in the direction of Rose Medical Center down the street. "I just got off a shift."

"Oh, good. I thought you were just one of those people

who wear them for fun and I was going to feel really bad for you."

"I'm glad that's not the case." When the bite of pie finally hits my tongue, I'm regretting sharing with her. It's phenomenal, and I'm mad at my dick for making me share. She must have known I might have second thoughts because her half—and no matter what she thinks, it was half, because I've got precision knife skills—is almost gone.

"What about you?" My eyes roam over her dress, the question of her appearance evident.

"Oh, this is my 'fuck me' dress." She takes her last bite of pie, then slides her fork slowly through her lips to clean it off. "You know, when you go out and want to send out a vibe." She motions the length of the dress, which takes about one second. "Do guys have clothes for that occasion?"

She makes me smile. She's also making me hard.

"I think guys want their entire wardrobe to 'send out the vibe.'"

Brooke laughs and the sound is intoxicating.

"I don't know. The scrubs aren't really giving me the vibe. Maybe you need a stethoscope? A white coat?"

I finish my last bite of pie and set my fork down on the plate. I lean back and study her. If I stood up right now she'd be getting more than a vibe.

"It didn't work tonight?" I ask her.

"Let's just say it was doing its job a little too well for my liking, sending out vibes to all the wrong guys." She laughs lightly, then her knees slide along my thigh as she swivels her stool in my direction. "Besides, it wasn't a complete fail. It got me half a slice of pie." She smiles. "Speaking of, what did you think of it?"

"It was delicious." I slide the empty plate a few inches away, "Definitely worth the stop."

"Carla makes all the pies from scratch. You better tip her well, I already know you spend twelve dollars on smoothies, and this pie has to be so much better than that green sludge."

She's got me there.

Having already paid for the pie, I reach for my wallet, pull out a twenty and slide it under the empty plate. Brooke moves off her stool, again her knees making slow, seductive contact with my thigh.

After thinking about her all week, I can't just let her walk out the door, again. Even though she rejected my phone number request at the bookstore, tonight feels different. She seems more relaxed, less distracted.

And Jesus that dress she's wearing should be illegal. I'm thirty-six, my nights of going out and partying are well behind me. I've been working non-stop for years and haven't been on an actual date in the same amount of time. I know what I want now. To find a partner to settle down with and have a family. I'm not interested in casual hookups that are going nowhere.

But, I've got to do more than what I've been doing, which is an endless reel of work, sleep, workout then work all over again. I'm finally in a place where I can take a breather and I should have some fun. And Brooke looks like fun. Not to mention I am insanely attracted to her. There's a chemistry between us that I felt at the bookstore, even when she was busy cleaning up smoothie and turning me down. Something tells me she might not reject me this time.

Brooke stands and I follow suit. She's tall, at least for the moment with the stilts for shoes that she's wearing, and just inches away from me. Her green eyes are fixed on mine. I watch her tongue peek between her lips, wetting them slightly.

"Bummer your dress didn't work out."

"Yeah, it's too bad," she says with a barely contained smile.

The pie was delicious, but something tells me it won't be the sweetest thing I taste tonight.

## 9

# BROOKE

After excusing myself to the restroom, I call Sam and leave her an erratic voicemail about the sexy doctor I just shared pie with at the diner, then wash my hands and dry my armpits with a paper towel. I probably should have done that in reverse order, but it doesn't really matter—*if* I sleep with him, I'm not going to see him again. This encounter has one-night stand written all over it. Witty pie chat, exchange of first names only, it's perfect. Although, I should text Sam a picture of his ID in case he's the kind of doctor that dissects women and keeps body parts in jars in his refrigerator. I think I saw that on *Dateline* once.

I don't know what's gotten in to me tonight. I usually don't make a habit of telling strangers I'm wearing a 'fuck me' dress, but tonight the words just flowed freely without any embarrassment. I wonder if he thinks I'm a slut, or a hooker. Oh, shit. Maybe he thinks I'm walking the streets, and just taking a break for pie. The 'fuck me' dress thing sounded funny in my head, but now I'm wondering if I've made it awkward. I should have made it clear that I don't expect him to pay for it, that I'm just looking for a casual, one-time hookup, free of charge.

I think the liquor has definitely gotten to my brain and I take a deep breath and pull open the door. I can see the counter from the restroom hallway and it's empty. Oh, shit. I should have been clear. A simple, wait here, I'll be back and we can have sex, for free, would have been good. Was he freaked out?

The door to the men's restroom opens and Cole steps out.

"Oh, hi. You're still here," I state the obvious.

I step back a foot to give the man some space. He definitely looks more intimidating without green smoothie all over his shirt. Had he been that tall and broad-shouldered at the bookstore? I don't think I'd noticed him in that way with the whole green smoothie debacle and my anxiety about running into Gina. Even in my five-inch heels, Cole —that's right, he does have a name—towers over me. His shoulders are broad and for how baggy I thought scrubs were supposed to be, Cole's scrubs fit snuggly on his thighs and chest.

The color brings out the blue in his eyes. Since we've been talking tonight, one thing I've noticed about Cole is the different smiles he has. And how they all make me flustered. There's the full smile that makes the skin next to his eyes crinkle, like when he's laughing. The no teeth, humor in his eyes smile when he seems amused but not quite chuckling. And then, there's the sexy smile, which is more of a smirk, where the left side of his lips lift up higher than the right. I'm not really sure what he's thinking when he's got that sexy smirk on his face, but that's the smile he's giving me right now. My low belly pulls and I can feel my arousal dampen my panties. Yikes, by the time he actually touches me it's going to be a slippery slide down there.

"I didn't want to miss what comes next," he says.

"Yeah?"

The diner is open twenty-four hours, and with it being so close to the trendy downtown bar scene, it's starting to fill up with the post-bar crowd searching for a late-night snack before they call it a night. Carla is taking orders out in the dining room and Cassie, another waitress, has appeared to help with the influx of diners.

He steps closer and I can smell him, masculine, a hint of aftershave, but even more I can feel his warmth, the heat pulsing through his body, and it makes me shiver.

When his lips lower to mine, my body melts against his hardness. His kiss is slow, exploratory, and I love the way his five o'clock shadow scrapes against my chin. One large, firm hand slides over my hip, pulling me closer until our bodies are aligned, his other hand finds its way to the base of my neck and gives the smallest squeeze, making me putty in his hands. My hands start their own exploration, the thin material of his scrubs leave little wonder about the chiseled body underneath.

Okay, wow.

There's a moment where I think I could just make out with this guy all night, forget sex, this is really hot. But then, Cole's hand slides to the hem of my dress, his fingers caress the inside of my thigh, just inches from what is quickly becoming my damp center, and I decide sex should not be forgotten. I'm optimistic that Cole is the guy I've been looking for. The last sex before I get pregnant with Ellie and Josh's baby. And if his deep kisses and firm hands are any indication, sex with Cole is going to be amazing.

Carla's throat clearing in the background pulls me out of my Cole-induced sexual trance, and we break apart on a gasp. My eyes widen and we both suppress a laugh. We are officially like horny teenagers who suck face in public.

The ones that make out after school at a park or bus stop because they don't have anywhere else to go. The good news is we're adults and we have options like our own apartments and beds.

Cole comes in close again, his lips trailing kisses down my jaw, until they are right next to my ear.

"Come home with me."

Check, please.

## 10

# BROOKE

Cole seems like a good guy, not a serial killer, but I still have Carla take a picture of his driver's license before I leave with him. He watches me with a small smile on his lips when I inspect his ID before handing it back to him. Cole Matthews. And he's a donor.

We walk to his apartment, which he says is only three blocks away. But three blocks in heels is not easy. First my day starts with a damn fake belly and I can barely maneuver about and now I'm teetering on high heels when Cole grabs my hand to steady me. He doesn't let go, which is fine and we're holding hands now. I remember in middle school holding a boy's hand for the first time at the movies. Both our palms got so sweaty, but you didn't want to be the person to let go, so you both just sat there in the movie theater with palms dripping, eating popcorn with the other hand. But Cole's hand isn't sweaty. It's warm, and firm, and completely envelopes mine. I'm trying to think of the last time I held a guy's hand when Cole maneuvers me to the front of a building. I wasn't sure of our destination so it takes me a moment to recognize where we are.

"You live at The Glass House?" I don't know if I'm impressed or annoyed. Both, really.

"It's close to work. And it's got a great gym," Cole responds casually.

There's nothing casual about The Glass House. Especially, the cost of living here.

The Glass House is named aptly for the fact that the upper two-thirds of the building are all windows, with a floor plan designed to give every condo's living area floor-to-ceiling windows. The lower third is surrounded in red brick, an attempt to blend into the surrounding neighborhood at street level. It's the tallest building, located just outside of the downtown area, and boasts unobstructed city and mountain views, especially from the higher floors.

I've toured a condo here with Sue, taking notes for a potential project, and it was outrageously luxurious. The owner was obnoxious and kept saying the word avant-garde like it made him important. The owner went with another designer. Sue was relieved because he was a whack job, and she was not looking forward to working with him.

I lean backwards, trying to get a view of the upper part of the glass building, but Cole must think I'm teetering again because his hand grips mine tighter. He doesn't even let my hand go when he reaches in his pocket for his wallet to swipe his key card to enter the building. He holds the door open for me and we enter into the lobby.

White striated tile floors create an aisle straight toward the concierge desk, with plush sitting areas flanked on either side. Rectangular tier light fixtures hang above each sitting area, giving it a modern vibe. In contrast to the light-colored flooring, the walls and ceiling are covered in mahogany wood. The wall behind the concierge desk is white marble stones arranged so it gives a three-dimensional look. When I was here that day with Sue it was bustling with residents coming and going, packages being delivered and tours being conducted. Now, at nearly one o'clock in the morning, it's deserted, except for the man at the concierge desk. Cole acknowledges him with a wave, then guides us to the elevators, where he scans his key card again and pushes the button for the nineteenth floor. There are twenty-three total.

"So, city view or mountain view?" I inquire.

"Both." Cole's blue eyes light with amusement, and I think he's invented a new smile. Lips only, half amused, half sexy smirk.

I just shake my head because somehow this guy manages to be cocky and humble at the same time.

When the elevator closes, it's the first time we've ever been alone. It's oddly calming, like the outside world has shut off and it's just us. That, and Cole is idly tracing slow circles against my palm with his thumb while he casually leans against the elevator wall looking like a sexy television doctor. It's making me horny and sleepy at the same time. I wonder what other sexual voodoo magic he knows.

The ride is quick, not enough time for me to break the seductive trance his thumb has placed on my body and maul him like I really want to.

Before I know it, we've exited the elevator and are standing at Cole's apartment door. He punches in a code on the keypad and opens the door, then, after turning on a lamp at a console table, he holds the door open for me to enter first. My first order of business is to ditch my heels in the entryway, my arches immediately thank me as they begin melting toward the hardwood floors.

Cole drops his keys and wallet on the console table by the door.

"How long have you lived here?" I inquire as I let myself wander down the hallway toward the living area, curious to see his apartment layout, furniture, and most of all, the view.

"About four years. I bought it after I finished up my residency."

The apartment has an open floor plan. Its modern, black-cabinet kitchen with white quartz countertops has me nearly salivating as I take a lap around the island. A small dining area still manages to hold a dining table for six and it all opens to a large living space furnished with a leather sofa and concrete coffee table. It's clean and modern. The ceilings are at least ten foot. It's impressive and I haven't even seen the view.

I'm vaguely aware of Cole's activity in the kitchen behind me when I finally reach my destination.

"Oh, wow." Just as I expected, Cole's living room is made up of floor-to-ceiling windows. What I wasn't expecting was the fact that his apartment is a corner unit, allowing the windows to wrap around to the adjacent wall. The corner view is of downtown Denver, completely lit up. I can see Union Station, with its orange letters lit up above the main terminal, the Spire, its needle alight above the rest of the skyline, and the cash register building, which has to be over a mile away but looks to be within arm's reach. It's too dark now, but it's obvious his apartment faces west and during the day there would be a breath-taking view of the Rocky Mountains. The sunset views would be incredible, too. Too bad I won't get to see any of them.

"Nice view," I throw out before moving back toward the kitchen where Cole is filling up a glass with water.

As I approach, Cole's eyes don't even glance toward the windows, but instead are performing a slow perusal of my body, until his gaze finally locks with mine.

"I sure think so."

Cole's lips shift into that sexy smile of his, and my body immediately responds. My panties are embarrassingly wet now, and I wonder if I'll be able to remove them before he notices.

I watch him take a drink of water, his eyes never leaving mine as he tips the glass up. The sexy way his throat constricts as he swallows. When he's done, he extends the glass out to me. Cole's upper lip is wet now. I want to lick it. Instead, I accept the glass, take a long sip, then set it back on the counter.

"Do you want anything more to drink?"

I shake my head. That's not what I'm here for.

He's so close now, just like in the diner, I can feel the warmth radiating off him, and it makes me shiver with anticipation. Cole's firm hands begin a slow ascent up my arms. His long fingers wrap around the backs of my arms, his finger pads caressing the sensitive skin there. I already know what Cole's kiss feels like. At the diner his lips were firm, unyielding. And hot. Everything about that kiss is why I'm here.

My body feels spring-loaded, like it's at the start line waiting for the gun to go off, but Cole is taking his sweet time. Apparently, he's not running the same race I am. I feel the need to move faster. I don't want to think, just feel, and with Cole staring at me with his intense blue eyes, my mind is starting to run wild.

Cole slides a firm hand behind my neck, his thumb caressing my jaw. Just when I think I might go insane, he finally lowers his mouth to mine. This kiss isn't like the one at the diner. It's less frenzied, slow and languid, and the gentleness of it makes my chest squeeze. It feels like something more.

Cole's other hand drops to my hip, his fingers sliding to the curve of my ass before pulling me closer. I immediately feel the press of his hard length into my stomach. The urge to reach into his pants and pull him out is strong. I have to remind myself that this is going to be the last time I have sex for a while, so I should relax and enjoy it. But I'm finding it impossible to slow my heart rate, to take in breaths that don't sound like I'm recovering from a 100-meter sprint. I'm hot and needy, and all this caressing is making me impatient for the main event.

Sliding both hands to my hips, Cole lifts me onto the counter. The cold, hard surface bites at the back of my legs, but as soon as Cole's hand slides between my thighs, I'm oblivious to anything else but the shiver of pleasure his touch brings. His lips drop to my neck at the same time he slowly thrusts one long finger inside me.

"Do you know how hard I got watching you eat pie?"

Cole's words cause me to clench tightly around his finger. I reach out to palm him through his scrubs, the thin material making it easy to feel every inch of him. And there are a lot of inches there to feel. His lips move along my jaw, finding the sensitive spot right below my ear, the five o'clock shadow on his jaw causing the most delicious scrape against my skin.

The heel of Cole's hand is aligned perfectly with my clit, adding the exact amount of pressure I need. When he adds a second finger I'm pretty much done for.

"You feel amazing, and I'm not even inside you yet."

His words push me over the edge. My hands grip his biceps as I explode around his fingers. If his dick is half as magical as his fingers, I'm in for a real treat. Under normal circumstances I would have no issue having a quickie right here on his kitchen island, but if this is my farewell to sex for the next nine months or so I want the real deal—Cole's naked body hovering over me.

"Bedroom?" I suggest.

## 11

## COLE

When I detoured to the diner, instead of going home after my shift, I had no idea that my night would end like this. What I remember most from our encounter at the bookstore, besides the way Brooke insistently tried to scrub the smoothie off my shorts, were Brooke's long legs, and how I wondered how they'd feel wrapped around my waist.

I decide I don't want to wonder anymore. My hands slide over Brooke's hips until I'm cupping her ass to slide her off the counter. Her thigh muscles squeeze my hips. Through the thin material of my scrubs I can feel the warmth of her.

"Everything okay?"

"Um, yeah." Brooke lowers her eyes between us. "I'm trying to not get your pants wet."

I was already so hard for her, but with Brooke's mention of her arousal, my dick is fucking throbbing. Her eyes lift back to mine, her teeth working her bottom lip as she waits for my reaction. She can't see my dick swell, so I show her how much I like the idea of her wetness covering me by pressing my hips forward until our bodies align.

Her eyes are green and so expressive. I can't wait to watch them when she comes.

I walk us back to my bedroom where I turn on a bedside lamp. I want to see everything. She can't possibly be too modest with the way she's dressed and the words that come out of her mouth. My arms slowly release her to the ground. Her dress has ridden up, it's practically a tank top now. My hands finish the job. Brooke obliges by lifting her arms up. She's wearing no bra so I'm greeted by round, perky tits with small pink nipples. I can't help but slide the pad of my thumb across one. Brooke bites her lip and moans at my touch. I can feel her arching into me, wanting to feel more.

Her hands reach for the hem of my shirt, but I start moving us backward until her legs hit the bed. She sits on the bed, then attempts to reach a hand inside the waist-band of my pants before I press her backward with my body.

"Lie back."

Her hair splays out across my bed and I just take a moment to stare at her. She looks amazing laid out underneath me.

"This would be so much better if you were naked."

She reaches to pull the drawstring on my pants, but I press her arms above her head with my hands. Brooke makes a sound which I take as annoyance at my slow pace. I think if it were up to her, I'd already be deep inside her, but it's not up to her so she needs to relax.

My lips lower to hers and she meets me hungrily. I explore the softness of them, molding them with mine, before finally dipping my tongue in to taste her. She tastes like peaches and desire.

Her hips are grinding up into my pelvis, trying to get friction. It's like she doesn't trust me to make it good for her. Like she's got to start working toward her own orgasm in case I don't give it to her. And she's in a hurry to do it. I'm not interested in making this quick, so she needs to relax and let it happen.

I press my pelvis down to keep hers from rocking. My lips trail down her jaw to her ear.

"I want your shirt off."

I trail kisses down her neck before I lean back and pull my undershirt and scrub top off. Brooke's eyes roam over my naked torso before finding my eyes again. When I lower back down on top of her, she sighs as our bare chests meet.

I spend a few minutes licking and teasing her nipples until I can tell she's getting antsy again. My lips place kisses over her ribs, then the flat plane of her belly as I make my way down. Then, I'm right there. I bury my nose in her crotch. Fuck, she smells good.

"What are you doing?" Brooke lifts her head off the bed to look at me. She looks horrified. "Did you just smell me? Down there?"

"Yes. Is that a problem?"

"Um." She wrinkles her nose. "No. But we can just skip this part."

She waves her palm over where my head rests between her thighs.

"I don't want to skip this part."

"Well, I never get off this way, so it's a waste of time."

I want to laugh. She's really cute.

"Okay. Well, maybe I want to lick you. Maybe this is about me, not you." I enjoy eating pussy, but this is most definitely going to be about her, she just doesn't know it yet.

"So you *like* licking pussy?" She almost looks offended. I might as well have told her that I like drowning puppies.

I tug on her hips, pulling her to the end of the bed which forces her upper body to fall back onto the mattress in a humph. Then, I spread her legs and smile. Brooke is bare, so everything is on display. I love what I see. She's pink and glistening with arousal. My dick throbs just looking at her. I hook her knees over my shoulders, then give her a long, slow lick up the middle. Her legs tremble when I suck on her clit. She's so wet, and her pussy tastes so sweet.

The pie I had tonight was something I don't normally indulge in, but Brooke's pussy? It would be on the menu every night.

I spend the next few minutes licking and sucking, finding a rhythm that she likes. Because no matter what she told me before, she's enjoying herself now. When she's writhing on the bed, I thrust a finger inside of her.

"Oh, god."

"Cole," I remind her.

"More, Cole. I need more."

Another lick and suck, then I'm adding a second finger. Her hips rock with the rhythm of my fingers. Her hands are wild, her fingers pulling hard to press my face closer. I suck the tiny bundle of nerves and hook my fingers inside of her.

Brooke's orgasm hits, her muscles milking my fingers even before she announces on a gasp, "I'm coming."

Her words are an afterthought as she rides her orgasm. I don't miss her content sigh as her breathing returns to normal.

Fuck, she's pretty. My dick aches looking at her flushed skin and seeing how wet she is. How ready she is for me. I rub my palm down my hard length over my scrubs. I'm so ready for her it's almost painful.

Brooke's eyes open, but her eyelids look heavy. Drunk from her orgasm, her words come out in a jumble.

"That was...yeah...wow, okay."

It takes a minute for her to recover. But as soon as she does, her eyes open wide and immediately focus on my hand. She props herself up on her elbows, intent on watching me.

With a quick pull of a drawstring my pants are on the floor. I watch Brooke watching me, her eyes intently focused on my crotch as she wets her lips. When I pull down my briefs, my dick springs out, and Brooke's eyes widen.

## 12

## BROOKE

Cole has a big dick. For a moment, I just stare at it in amazement. Finally, I move to sit up so I can wrap a hand around his length. Even when I grip him tightly, it's a struggle to get the pad of my thumb to touch my other fingers. I stroke him a few times, watching as Cole's eyes become hooded, and a low growl escapes his lips. My thumb moves around his crown, spreading the pre come that has accumulated there. I bring my lips to him, giving the head of Cole's dick a slow lick. As soon as I make contact, Cole makes a hissing sound, his dick jutting forward searching for more.

I lick and swirl my tongue against his head trying to get used to his girth. When I finally slide him past my lips, it takes extra stretch to keep my lips tucked over my teeth. I can't take all of him, that would require surgically expanding my throat, so I use my hand to pump him where my mouth can't reach.

"Fuck, Brooke. Do you have any idea how hot you look with your pretty lips stretched around my cock?"

Cole's words give me a feeling of feminine power. That

I'm in control. I have power over this sexy man. It makes me more confident, and it makes me wet.

Just when I'm starting to get into the dick sucking zone, Cole gently cups my jaw, using his thumb to press against my cheek as he slides out of my mouth.

"What..."

Cole's muscular body leans over me until I'm forced to fall flat on my back.

"Hey, I wasn't done."

"I want to be inside you when I come."

"What if I wanted to make you come with my mouth? Why do you get to be in charge?"

I realize it's silly to argue about how he comes, but it's the principle, am I right?

Cole's mouth moves into the sexiest smirk I've ever seen. That smirk should be patented and marketed; women everywhere would be helpless against it.

"Do you want to be in charge, Brooke?"

Cole's blue eyes scan my face as he gathers my wrists in his hands and eases my arms above my head. His hold is gentle, and I could easily move out of it. With his body pressed against mine, I can feel his hard length sandwiched between us, pressing on my stomach. The weight of him, both his body and his hard cock, feels delicious against my skin. My body responds with a rush of liquid heat between my thighs. I like the feeling of him holding me down, pressing me into the mattress and feeling him everywhere. If that means he's in control, I can live with that. I want more of that.

He keeps one hand on my wrists while the other hand snakes down my body until it's between my thighs. This time when his fingers slide inside me, Cole doesn't stroke me, but uses them to stretch me from side to side.

I'm so wet and I'm dying for more friction.

"More." I rock my hips up into him, hoping he'll take the hint and thrust his fingers inside me.

Cole presses his thumb onto my clit, but it's not what I want.

What I like about random hookups and one-night stands is there's no time to be self-conscious, you need to get what you want because there are no second chances. Leaving satisfied or unsatisfied usually depends on how well one's needs are verbalized.

"Cole, put your dick inside me."

Still, it's important to be polite.

"Please." It comes out whinier than I had intended.

He chuckles at my demand, but he seems like he's going to oblige, moving off me to grab a condom out of his bedside table. My body feels chilled with him gone, but then he's back and I relish his heat. My hands explore his chest as Cole tears open the condom packet. I don't miss that it's a Trojan extra-large. My sex clenches with anticipation of what is to come.

Cole rolls on the condom and positions himself at my entrance. His head nudges inside and I can already tell it's going to be a snug fit. When he thrusts into me, I can't help but clench down at the intrusion. A breathless ahhh leaves my lips. I haven't been a virgin for a long time, but there's something about his size that makes me feel like sex is new. Like it's my first time, not my last, at least for a while.

Cole's jaw is clenched and I can tell he's fighting to not move while I adjust to his size. I tell myself to relax, and take a few deep breaths. He starts to move, slowly in, slowly out. The friction I had been craving is there. It's already the best sex I've had and I haven't even come yet. Cole lowers himself back down on top of me, his arms bracketing my head.

"You feel amazing. So fucking tight."

His lips lower to mine, a soft kiss that turns hot and needy in no time at all. Our chests are pressed together, my sensitive nipples relishing the drag of his chest with every thrust. Our lips tangle, Cole's hands are everywhere, sliding along my jaw, my neck, my waist, until he's cupping my ass to change the angle so he can thrust in deeper. I feel my orgasm building. I want to come, but I also don't want it to end. I try to hold off, but the thrust of Cole's dick and the expert roll of his hips wins out in the end. When my orgasm hits, it's like a tidal wave. Cole stills for a moment as my muscles clamp down hard on him, milking his cock deep inside me.

After my orgasm subsides, Cole lifts up off of me, and hooks his arms under my knees, lifting my ass off the bed. His gaze drops to where we are joined and I can tell by the dark look in his eyes he likes what he sees.

"You're going to be sore tomorrow. When you sit down, you're going to remember how it felt to have my cock buried deep inside you."

With my lower body angled up this way, I can see where he's moving in and out of me, too. I'm so wet now, I can feel myself dripping down the crack of my ass. The sound of our breathing mingles with the slick suction sound of Cole sliding in and out of me. I'm completely caught off guard when I feel another orgasm building. I'm actually kind of annoyed. Is this guy for real?

Cole must sense it, too, as he speeds up his thrusts, then moves a hand over to stroke my clit.

"I can't…"

"Yes, Brooke. I want you to come all over my cock." His voice is low and husky, my body obeys its command.

"Oh. My…" My orgasm nearly knocks the wind out of me. I'm pulsing around Cole, when I feel his release pulse inside of me, too. His jaw clenches, his lips part and a bead of sweat runs down the middle of his chest. I have a strange desire to lick it. Holy shit, he's gorgeous.

Cole leans back over me. Supported by his hands, he lowers to kiss me. A slow, languid movement of lips and tongues. He's still hard inside me, and it takes a lot of effort not to rock my hips. How can I possibly want more? I orgasmed four times. This is unreal. He's like a purple unicorn. He can't possibly be real.

"You're perfect. That was perfect," he whispers in my ear before rolling off me to go dispose of the condom.

I'm confused. One minute he's whispering filth in my ear, the next sweet nothings about how perfect I am. Jesus, man. Pick a lane. I'm much more comfortable with the filth than I am with the sweetness.

When Cole comes back from the bathroom, I take a moment to enjoy the view of his body. Hard, muscular planes, but it's a lean muscle, not bulky. When he catches me watching him, he smiles and winks. There's another one to add to the collection of Cole's many smiles. The relaxed grin.

Cole gently lifts me so he can pull back the covers, then slides me underneath. He crawls into bed next to me, sliding one arm around my waist to pull me to his body. For anyone who thinks sex with a stranger is awkward, I think post coital with one is more so.

But Cole doesn't think it's awkward because he's asleep in two minutes flat, whereas I lie there for another thirty thinking about what just happened. Amazing sex. Okay, really amazing sex. It should be exactly what I need to float me for a while. Nine months to be exact. This is what I was looking for. To go out with a bang. There was something different about this, though. I got what I came for so why am I feeling unfulfilled? Like there's something I'm miss-ing. My mind wanders for a minute before I start fantasizing about more sex with Cole, and I realize maybe this wasn't what I needed. It was too good. Dangerously good. The I want to do it over and over again kind of good.

Cole rolls onto his back with a heavy sigh, releasing me from his grasp and I take the opportunity to get the heck out of there.

## 13

# BROOKE

"**Y**ou snuck out?" Sam looks incredulous. "After the sweaty, passionate, mind-blowing sex?"

She pauses for effect. "With a gorgeous doctor that lives in a luxury apartment?"

"Um, yeah. That's what a one-night stand is."

I pound the side of the ketchup bottle, and it releases a huge glop onto my plate. We're at Steuben's, a brunch/lunch spot with a retro vibe, in Uptown near Sam's apartment. Sunday brunch became a late lunch when I texted Sam that I needed more sleep this morning. What can I say? I was tired from all of yesterday's activities.

"Huh. I would have gone back for seconds. At least a morning-after romp. Those are the best. You don't even have to be completely awake yet. Everything is still juicy down there, no foreplay, he just slides right in."

Sam looks pointedly at my French fry currently mid-dip into my ketchup puddle, and I scrunch up my nose at her description.

"That's graphic."

I don't tell Sam that I was tempted for seconds, and that's the exact reason I left after Cole fell asleep. I didn't want to leave, instead I wanted to slide over his hard body and wake him with his cock in my mouth. It was a perfect one-night stand. The sex was amazing. Almost too amazing. Cole was perfect. Almost too perfect.

I set down the fry, and take a drink of my water. The cool liquid helps to calm the wave of heat that rushes over my body when I think about my night with Cole. He was right, I am sore today. And it's a delicious reminder of what happened last night. How good it felt to be filled with him. Up until last night I didn't understand how people could be controlled by sex. Need sex, want sex, be addicted to sex. My sex life has been made up of guys that I could take or leave, depending on my mood and level of desire. With Cole, I'm pretty sure if I hadn't snuck out, I would still be lying in his bed, letting him have his way with me. There was a connection that I couldn't even explain and as much as I wanted it, it frightened me a bit, too.

My body is satisfyingly sore, just like Cole hoped I would be, and shifting in my seat only reminds me of how full I felt with him inside me, how his touch made me feel alive and wild. There will definitely not be a repeat. It would be dangerous to my sanity.

On the other hand, I do feel bad that I snuck out of his apartment this morning. But what was there to do? Say thank you over a cup of coffee? Have the awkward morning-after discussion? It was fun, just what I needed, and I want to leave it unmarred by the morning-after awkwardness. Plus, I never want to be the girl that's still around when the guy just wants me gone. He should be grateful that I'm not clingy and trying to tie him down.

I slip out of my jacket and lift my hair off the back of my neck.

"No, it's best this way." I shake my head. "Now it's a memory I can fantasize about when I'm bloated, gassy and no one wants to get near me."

Sam takes a sip of mimosa.

"So, what happens next?"

"Ellie and I are going to meet with her doctor on Wednesday. They're going to ultrasound my uterus and make sure I'm a good candidate. Maybe run some tests."

"And you'll be pregnant soon?"

"Depends on how everything goes." I dust the French fry salt off my hands. "Ellie would love an April birthday. Same month as Mom's and Dad's."

Sam sets her champagne flute down.

"You know you don't *have* to do this. Ellie would understand."

Of course, she would understand. Ellie's the reasonable one. Even when she was on the fertility hormones with her sixth round of IVF, she was very rational and easygoing.

My eyes dart around the restaurant patio before finally meeting Sam's. Her stare makes me feel uncomfortable, like she can see right through me. See my hesitation. It's unnerving. But, she also knows that once I've made up my mind to do something, it's pretty much full steam ahead.

"Of course, but I want to do it. For Ellie. And Josh. They're my family. And helping them start their own family is a win for me, too. I get to be an aunt. You tell me all the time how cool that is."

I've got Sam with that one. She smiles and I can tell she's thinking of her own nieces and nephews. Both her older brothers have kids and she's pretty smitten with them, especially the youngest of the group, Stella, who's eighteen months and has the blondest hair, it's nearly white, and curly. Sam's always sharing cute videos of her cuddling the family dog, or pointing at things and speaking unintelligible words.

"Yeah, it's pretty awesome."

"So, it might be weird and uncomfortable and scary but I really want to try."

Sam nods, "Okay." Then she smiles. "It's going to be a wild ride."

**14**
_____

## COLE

B y Wednesday I've had three restless nights of sleep and I'm tired as fuck. The fact that Brooke snuck out of my apartment early Sunday morning after our night together has been weighing on my mind. At first, I thought it was just a bruised ego that had me in a funk. Did she not have a good time? It had been a little over six months since I'd had sex, a drunken hookup at a buddy's destination wedding back in December, but from where I was positioned, Brooke was enjoying herself. As the days have passed and I've gotten more irritable about the situation, I've started to think there is more to it. I had fun with Brooke and I thought our connection was more than a one-night stand. There's no question I'm attracted to her, but I also enjoyed our banter, her contagious laugh and the way she made me feel hopeful.

I had planned to wake her with my dick, make her come again, then take her to breakfast, but I woke up to an empty bed. No sign that she had even been there other than the pillowcase her head had been on smelled like her shampoo, vanilla and mint, and the faint nail marks she left on my shoulder.

After I analyzed Brooke's exit, I went for a run, then scrambled some eggs. The rest of my Sunday was my usual routine of golf with my college buddies, then I stopped by BookBar for a smoothie, hoping to run into Brooke there. I had no clue if she frequented that bookstore or if it was a one-time stop. If she lived nearby or on the other side of the city.

I left with my full smoothie intact and no sign of Brooke. Later at dinner with my family, Carrie was pushing to set me up with her yoga instructor again. The week before I had definitely been open to it. But now, after having had an amazing night with Brooke, I don't know what to think. It's not like we're dating. Shit, I don't even know her last name or where she lives, let alone a phone number to reach her. But I can't stop thinking about her, which makes it challenging to think about going out on a date with another woman. I've never been able to juggle multiple women like some of my friends have. Even when I was dating casually, not looking for anything serious, I found it difficult to see more than one woman at a time.

I'm reviewing a patient's chart in the hallway when Lois, my OB nurse, approaches me. Lois has been with me since I opened my practice, and working in the nursing profession for another thirty years before that. She's no-nonsense, can clear a group of chatting nurses from twenty feet away, and still manages to comfort freaked-out patients with a soothing voice. She's tough as nails, with a heart of gold.

As she approaches, I notice her scrub top has cats all over it. Upon closer inspection, it's cats with bodies shaped like avocados, the pit located at the stomach region, with the word 'avocato' printed all over. Only Lois can be taken seriously while wearing that scrub top.

Lois's short dark hair has a few more grays than it did when we started working together. Her small, dark-framed reading glasses are currently pushed to the top of her head.

"All right, what's her name?"

I look down at the file in my hand. "Sarah Thomas."

Lois shakes her head.

"Not the patient, the woman you've been moping around about all week."

Lois and I work well together, with mutual respect, to provide our patients with the best care possible. But, when she gets a spare moment, she loves to put her two cents in about my personal life. Mainly that I need to get one. She's been married for nearly thirty years and her youngest child, of four, just finished their first year in college, so she has a few things figured out.

"I haven't been moping." My eyes narrow at Lois's observation. Usually, I find Lois's insight to be helpful professionally, but right now her perceptiveness is irritating when it's directed at me. "I don't mope."

"Mmmhmm." Lois purses her lips.

I didn't share anything about Brooke with the guys on Sunday. Two of our golf foursome are married with young kids, the third is engaged and although we're good friends and have talked about relationships in the past, it would have been difficult to explain what the situation is with Brooke when I don't even know. I didn't tell my mom or Carrie about Brooke because I didn't need them analyzing every detail of the situation, and because I really don't want to share anything about my sex life with them. They'd probably try to hire a private investigator to track her down. There's a thought. Maybe I'm overanalyzing it all. My hope for a relationship and having a family is making me rush into things, want to commit to the first woman that I find interesting. And I do find Brooke interesting. Sassy and quirky and sexy, too. I didn't know all those things could go together so well. The sex was hot, but I also felt like I connected with Brooke. It didn't feel like two strangers fumbling their way through a one-time hookup. I want more time with her, to get to know her, and a repeat of everything we did Saturday night, but now I have no idea if or when I'll see her again.

I'm frustrated with the situation and maybe that's making me a little irritable.

"The best ones are worth the trouble, eh?" Lois winks at me, then takes the file out of my hands.

I decide to put Brooke out of my mind, and do what I do best. Work.

## 15

# BROOKE

By the time Wednesday rolls around, I'm exhausted from restless nights and reoccurring sex dreams about Cole. My work days have been mostly filled with client meetings with Sue at the helm, and my focus tends to drift to a continuous loop of daydreams where his hard, sweaty body thrusts on top of me and his dirty words fill my ear. I'm pretty sure I'm worse off now in the pent-up sexual frustration department than I was before I slept with him on Saturday night.

For once, I'm actually excited to put on a paper gown and have a stranger insert a speculum into my vagina. I'm hoping this appointment will refocus my attention onto the task at hand, helping Ellie and Josh to start a family.

The one thing I didn't expect was to have such fantastic sex that now I'm going to have to wait nine months to do it again. I think I might die.

Ellie's fertility specialist is located in a medical complex near downtown. When I enter the building, I find Ellie waiting in the lobby for me.

She threads her arm through mine and gives me a

squeeze. "You are amazing for doing this. What would I do without you?"

She's smiling, but I think she knows she might have less craziness in her life without me.

"How are you feeling? You're sure about this, right? I want you to be absolutely sure—I'd die if something like this came between us." Ellie has been texting, calling, asking this all week. Almost as if she's not sure now. Well, I'm almost sure—no, I'm sure. *Damn Cole.*

I don't mention my lack of sleep, my out of control libido or the fact that the chocolate chip cookie I ate for breakfast is making my stomach ache. My body's not exactly a ringing endorsement for you to put your baby inside me.

"I'm great!" My smile is a picture of enthusiasm.

I let her lead me to the elevator and up to the fifth floor. We don't have a long wait before my name is called, thank god, because their waiting room's reading material is lacking, only medical journals and magazines with babies on the front.

The nurse does all the basics, temperature, blood pressure and I get my blood drawn, but she tells me not to use the restroom until after the ultrasound, something about a full bladder making the pictures clearer. All I know is I've had two cups of coffee and my kidneys are floating.

Other than the fact that I feel like I might pee all over the doctor's hand, the ultrasound is actually pretty cool. I've never seen inside my uterus before, it's fairly enlightening to come face to pixelated screen with the organ that like clockwork, makes me bleed for seven days of every month. It's like learning a vulnerable secret about a frenemy and realizing that they're really not out to ruin your life. That, or my full bladder is making me hallucinate and think weird thoughts. Dr. Yang, Ellie's fertility specialist, finds each ovary and fallopian tube, then switches off the machine.

"Brooke, everything looks excellent." I watch Dr. Yang pull off the giant condom-like wrapper that was on the ultrasound stick, and it makes me think of Cole and his huge dick. *Now's not the time.* "Your uterus is pristine. It looks promising for an implantation attempt."

Dr. Yang smiles at me. That was probably the only compliment I will ever hear about my uterus, so I thank her.

I turn to smile at Ellie, who is almost on the verge of tears. I reach for her hand.

"Hey. You okay?"

"Yeah. I'm so happy." She wipes a tear. "It's just a little bittersweet, too, you know?"

"I know." I wish uterus transplant was a thing. I would trade with Ellie in a heartbeat.

I squeeze Ellie's hand while Dr. Yang pulls out some paperwork. She goes on to explain the surrogacy process, the hormones that would be involved to prepare my body for the embryo implantation, the resources available to help surrogates and their intended families through the process, not only physically but emotionally. Ellie asks a thousand questions. She's obviously done more research than I have.

"If you decide to move forward, Brooke, you'll need to stop your oral birth control, but condoms would still be used to prevent pregnancy. Do you currently have a sexual partner?"

I almost ask her to define 'current' but think better of it. Besides, Cole is in the past.

"No. It's just me and my vibrator."

She gives me a half smile, while Ellie looks mortified.

"Orgasms aren't an issue, are they?" I ask.

"No, Brooke, having orgasms during this process is completely safe," Dr. Yang comments.

Oh, good. I can give up dick, but I don't think I can give up orgasms. I'm grateful that they are not mutually exclusive.

"Then, I would start you on fertility hormones to prep your body for the implantation and increase the chance of a viable pregnancy," Dr. Yang explains as she hands me the paperwork outlining the procedure, then stands.

"I know this is a lot to digest, if either of you have any questions, please give me a call. Brooke, you can get dressed and use the restroom."

"Thank you, Dr. Yang." Ellie stands and gives her a hug. "We'll be in touch."

Dr. Yang exits and Ellie rushes over to envelope me in a hug. Ellie's hug is somewhat like a python's might be, firm and tight, squeezing you until you can't breathe.

"Thank you, Brookie." She sniffles, then squeezes impossibly tighter. "There's no one in the world I would want to do this with, but you."

My eyes well up. Not many times in our thirty years have I felt that Ellie really needed me for something. Most of our lives it's been me needing her help to get out of a jam, or her taking charge when I had no clue what to do. It feels good that I can finally be the one helping.

I squeeze her back, but then my bladder reminds me that it might rupture.

"Ahh, I have to pee so bad."

Ellie pulls away laughing. "I'll let you get dressed."

I'm sliding on my skirt when Ellie glances at her watch.

"Oh gosh, it's later than I thought. I really need to get going. I'm taking Max and Sadie to the pool this afternoon."

Max and Sadie are the kids that live next to Ellie and

Josh. Ellie babysits for them from time to time, and during the summers when school is out, she typically watches them a few times a week. Their mom is now pregnant with baby number three so Ellie has been trying to get them out of the house during the afternoons so she can rest.

"We'll talk later." She grabs her purse off the chair and turns to me. "Will you be okay leaving on your own?"

I refrain from rolling my eyes at her, I know she hates it, and I'm trying my best to not change the loving atmosphere in the room. "Yes, I will be fine."

"Okay, don't forget the paperwork."

Ellie drops a kiss on my cheek, then she's out the door. Putting my shoes on is extra stressful due to my bladder screaming the whole time, but finally I am dressed and rushing out the exam room door to find the restroom. After the longest pee in history, I emerge feeling refreshed.

I'm headed for the checkout desk when I remember I left the paperwork in the exam room. Ugh. I hate when Ellie reminds me to do something, like she knows I will forget, and I'm a thousand percent sure that I won't forget, but I still manage to, you guessed it, forget.

I'm two steps down the hallway, heading back toward the exam room, when the sight of *him* has me screeching to a halt. Cole.

Walking down the hallway toward me, with a white doctor's coat over his slacks, button-down shirt and tie, is Cole. He's looking down at the clipboard in his hand, writing something as he walks. Forget the whole doctor thing, writing while walking, this guy has skills. He hasn't noticed me yet. A million thoughts run through my head. Does he work *here?* I know he's a doctor, but we never got to the specifics of what kind of doctor he is. This office is specific to women's health and fertility, so he must be an OBGYN. Oh, god, he looks at vaginas all day?

If he's professionally studied the female anatomy, that explains a lot. Finding my G-spot was like his super power. Memories of our night together come rushing back to me. His long, groping fingers, wet tongue, and skillful cock. Man, if I thought memories of sex with Cole were driving me wild, seeing him in a white doctor's coat is only going to add to the fantasies I've been having about him.

"Ms. Ryan, you forgot your paperwork." I turn around to find the nurse from my exam walking toward me from the opposite direction Cole is. She's got the paperwork in her hand and she's waving it at me.

"I'm glad I caught you." She smiles while handing me the paperwork, which I quickly fold and shove into my purse.

Yes, that's exactly how I feel. Caught.

"Have a great day." She moves quickly down the hall and away from what I anticipate will be an awkward reunion in about two seconds.

"Brooke?"

I turn to find Cole staring straight at me, he has closed the distance between us and he doesn't look happy.

## 16

# COLE

"Oh, hey." Brooke's green eyes are like saucers. She sounds easygoing, but the way her hands fidget with the strap of her purse tells me she's anything but.

"Hi." The single word comes out sharper than I wanted it to. "What are you doing here?"

"I had an appointment."

I nod. "Okay."

Brooke doesn't need to elaborate. I'm a doctor and sensitive to the fact that we're in the hallway of a fertility clinic, so I don't push for details that would make her uncomfortable. I know many women that start to look into freezing their eggs when they're in their late twenties, early thirties. It's actually the best time to do it.

With my specialty in Maternal-Fetal Medicine, I receive referrals from Dr. Yang and Dr. Summers' clinic all the time. Many women with fertility issues can have high-risk pregnancies. And patients using IVF to conceive often times become pregnant with multiples, also putting them in the high-risk pregnancy category. If a patient that Dr. Yang or Dr. Summers is treating becomes pregnant and it is a high-risk pregnancy, they will refer them to me, or as of recent, our new MFM specialist, Dr. Applegate. Typically, a separate appointment is set up at our clinic, but Dr. Summers requested that I meet with her patient in tandem today.

After a long perusal of my lab coat, Brooke finally lifts her gaze back to mine.

"Dr. Cole Matthews." She reads off the embroidered letters on my white coat.

We just stare at each other for a moment. Brooke's cheeks flush pink and I wonder if she's thinking about our night together.

If I start reminiscing, I'll have a boner at work, so I tamp down the unwanted thoughts and focus on the fact that Brooke is right here in front of me.

We're right in front of the fertility clinic's nurses' station and currently have the attention of two young nurses. I don't want Brooke to leave, but I don't want to have this conversation in public.

Making sure my voice is loud enough for our audience to hear, I tell Brooke, "Let's discuss your file in my office."

Brooke's eyes do a quick side glance toward the nurses' station, then back to me. "Uh, okay, sounds good."

I start to move, Brooke follows a step behind me.

"Wait, so you don't work here?" Brooke motions behind us after I've led her down the hall and through the reception area.

I turn to face her while we wait at the elevator bank.

"No, I'm on three."

"Oh."

When it arrives, Brooke and I enter the elevator, and I punch the button for floor three.

We stand silently, a torturous trip down two floors.

Brooke is chewing on her bottom lip. She looks pensive, but sexy as hell. I will myself to not push the elevator stop button and haul her against me.

Although it's a complete surprise that she's here, it's a good one. Seeing her has my mood lifting. My thoughts drift back to Saturday night. I was exhausted from a twelve-hour shift and with tasty pie in my belly and an explosive orgasm, I slept the hardest that I have in a long time. The last three nights I haven't slept at all, I've spent them replaying my night with Brooke, the way she smelled, the way she tasted, the sweet sounds she made when she came.

The Brooke that I see now doesn't seem as sure of herself as she did on Saturday night.

That Brooke was a firecracker. The way she kept offering pointers on how to please her. Like she'd been with a bunch of idiots who need a road map to find a clitoris. Lucky for her, I'm an expert in the female anatomy. She didn't get far on her tutorial before she realized I wasn't going to need her notes.

I smile thinking about how fast she came on my tongue. The look on her face when I tilted my hips at just the right angle to find the sensitive spot inside her, then continued to thrust into her over and over until she screamed. Then I woke up to an empty bed.

Maybe I'm giving myself too much credit. Maybe it wasn't as good as I thought it was. I've been working so much there's been no time for a personal life and maybe what I thought was exceptionally fantastic sex was just a mediocre Saturday night for her.

I think about what I want to say to Brooke because thinking about what I want to do to her is dangerous. She's in a fitted t-shirt, and a skirt that falls right below her knees, her long hair is in loose waves, and she has nowhere near the amount of makeup that she had on Saturday night. She looks fucking perfect.

On the fourth floor, a mom and her two kids, who likely just visited the pediatrician down the hall, get on. The kids are sucking on lollipops while the mom types out something on her phone, all oblivious to the tension in the back of the elevator.

I shift closer to Brooke under the pretense that the little boy is waving his sucker around like a sword and I don't want to end up with sticky pants. My arm brushes against hers, the material of my lab coat prevents our skin from touching, but the hitch in her breath alerts me to the fact that she felt the connection. She smells amazing. Fuck. This is inconvenient.

When the elevator stops on three, I move us forward by placing my hand on Brooke's lower back, then guide her purposefully down the hallway, through the reception area, then past Lois and her raised eyebrows, and into my office. It feels like I haven't taken a breath since I saw her. My only goal is to get her alone so we can talk. I know I'll get the third-degree from Lois later, but it'll be worth talking to Brooke without curious eyes.

Brooke doesn't look like she wants to talk, she avoids my stare by moving to the far side of the room to examine my book shelf. I watch her for a moment, not sure what to say either. Maybe it's just a bruised ego that has me looking for answers, wanting her to explain why she snuck out after our night together.

"You told me you were a doctor." She waves the female reproductive system model from my shelf in the air. "But I didn't know you were this kind of doctor."

When she attempts to place the model back on the

shelf, the baby inside the model's uterus pops out. I take this moment, while Brooke is distracted by trying to put the baby back in, to cross the room and stand behind her.

She's still struggling with the plastic baby when finally, I take the model from her, and place it back on the shelf.

## 17

# BROOKE

"We didn't exactly do a lot of talking." Cole's voice is low, his warm breath on the back of my neck sends a wave of lust to my core. Visions of Cole bending me over his desk and roughly taking me from behind have me turning to face him.

I don't know why, but his words make me blush. I had gone back to his place for sex, and with no numbers exchanged, I didn't think I would see him again. That was the plan. Part of me forgets that I don't really know much about him. Then, I remind myself that was exactly the point. It was just supposed to be sex, nothing more. But the way Cole is looking at me tells me he isn't pleased that our night ended the way it did. I don't know that following him to his office was a good idea.

He's studying me now, a small smirk on his lips. Images of those same lips all over my body pop to the front of my brain, and I'm wondering if the wetness between my thighs is from the ultrasound lube or if it's from the way Cole's looking at me.

"That's true." I lick my lips, my mouth suddenly dry. "I like your coat."

What? I'd cringe at my horrible conversation skills, but he's still staring at me and that wouldn't make me look any less nuts. So, I own the word vomit that is coming out of my mouth and smile confidently.

Cole sets the clipboard down on his desk, the metal clattering against the glass desk top. My body must sense that the closer this man gets to me the weirder I act, so in its quest for self-preservation, when Cole moves toward me, my feet instinctively move backwards. A few steps later, I'm against the wall, a Brooke sandwich, me between Cole and a wall.

"You know what I like, Brooke?"

Cole's masculine scent washes over me, and I no longer have to wonder if it's the ultrasound gel soaking my panties. His blue eyes are laser focused on my face. I have forgotten to breathe, and I have to take a deep breath to calm my burning lungs.

"No." I shake my head, in case he missed the throaty whisper that came out of my mouth. "What do you like?"

"When I sleep with a woman, I like her to be there the next morning so I can fuck her again then take her to breakfast."

"Oh."

"I thought we had a good time," he smirks, that hot as hell sexy smirk of his, "no, I know we had a good time. Am I mistaken?"

"No, it was great. You were great."

Cole's breath is warm on my neck when he lets out a deep chuckle. His lips are near my ear.

"Should I remind you how great it was?"

Yes. Please, yes.

A sound I can't even describe releases itself from my throat involuntarily.

Wait, no. This was not the plan. It was supposed to be one time. I'm supposed to follow what the paperwork says. Did the doctor say I could have sex before the whole embryo injection thing? Wait, we're not going to have sex in his office. That would be…oh god, Cole's hand slides under my skirt and it's really hard to focus when his palm starts to caress my inner thigh, his long fingers inching their way toward my center.

"I've been thinking about your warm pussy pulsing around my cock."

"Is pussy a technical term?" Trying to keep my cool, I throw Cole's words from Saturday night back at him, but he just smiles. "It seems like pussy would be a dime a dozen around here." My words are challenging, like I don't believe in his world of seeing vaginas all day that mine is that unique. Is it weird that I want it to be? To him?

"Brooke, you have an exceptionally gorgeous pussy."

Cole's finger slides over said pussy, and I try to stifle my moan, but his lips swallow it up anyway. I open up to him, letting his tongue tangle with mine. My hands dig into his thick hair, and I immediately remember how I pulled roughly on the same strands when he sucked my clit Saturday night. The feel of Cole's lips on mine is like a sigh of relief I didn't even know I was holding in. I want to fight whatever this is, but for the moment I'm just lost in this feeling with him. The way his body presses into me, his lips on mine, his hand under my skirt. With long strokes, his finger slides up and down my center, moving my wetness up to my clit. My brain has stopped functioning, my body is in charge now.

"You're so wet, I wish I could fuck you right here." I can feel his hard length pressing into my stomach. He slides two fingers into me, and my knees buckle, but he's holding me up while he works me over. His fingers thrusting in and out while his thumb circles my clit. My hands tighten around the lapels of Cole's white doctor coat, holding on for dear life.

"Cole...I need...oh god..."

"What do you need, Brooke?"

His lips are leaving a trail of kisses down my neck, as his fingers thrust into me hard. Shit, he's really good at this.

Before I can form the words, my orgasm moves through me, a wave of pleasure unfurling from my lower belly, that rushes down my legs like an electrical current. My whole body feels like a limp noodle, and I'd likely be a puddle on the floor if Cole wasn't holding me up.

He holds me there for a minute, whispering sweet nothings about how he loves watching me come, and how hard he's going to be all day thinking about my wet pussy, how he's never going to be able to be in his office and not think of me, my hips rocking as he finger-fucked me against the wall.

Holy shit. That was amazing. And it is amazing to be lost in him, until I open my eyes and am reminded that we're in Cole's office. Cole's once perfectly-styled hair is now wild from my roaming hands, he looks even sexier than he did before, just slightly disheveled. His white coat is creased where my hands had been gripping it.

My gaze settles on Cole's, his blue eyes are relaxed, his smile is sexy, showing off his perfect white teeth.

"Don't move. I'll be right back."

With a final kiss to my jaw, Cole slowly releases me, then crosses the room to an adjoining bathroom on the other side. In his absence, my mind returns to reality.

The reality that Cole, who I've discovered is a gynecologist, just fingered me in his office in the same building as the fertility clinic where I just found out my uterus is pristine and a good candidate to carry my sister's baby. This shouldn't be sexy, and there shouldn't be orgasms involved. I'm here for Ellie, to help Ellie out so she can start the family she's always wanted. A sinking feeling washes over me, taking all the orgasmic feelings with it. I'm doing it again, I'm making it about me, letting my impulsiveness derail carefully thought out plans. I need to end this, whatever this is, with Cole.

If I see him again at the clinic, it might be weird, but it will only get weirder if I keep hooking up with him.

I lower my head back to the wall and stare at the ceiling. The water turns on in the bathroom and I imagine Cole thoroughly scrubbing his hands, like he's preparing for surgery. Proper hygiene is so sexy.

Cole is trouble, a kink in my plan to help Ellie. She needs me right now and it's a year of my life, compared to the years of buoying me along during my tough times. Now that I'm finally adulting, helping Ellie start a family is what I need to do. *Want* to do.

The appropriate thing to do is tell Cole that I can't see him anymore. Or whatever it is we're doing. It's not him, it's me. Blah blah. Ugh. I'm not good at this kind of thing. Something tells me that speaking those words while Cole is staring at me with his gorgeous blue eyes while wearing his sexy doctor's coat is going to be impossible. I push off the wall, my post orgasm legs take a moment to operate at full strength, but once they're stable, I rush out the door, leaving Cole and his sexy smile behind. Once again.

In the elevator, my phone buzzes, my daily alarm to remind me to take my birth control. The birth control that I need to stop taking in order to get pregnant with Ellie and Josh's baby. I rummage around in my purse, my fingers finally settling on the hard-plastic pack. The elevator opens to the lobby and I find my target, a trash can by the automatic glass doors. I stride over confidently, and without hesitation, my fingers release the birth control pack from my hand.

"**W**ait, wait," my friend, Evan, pauses before he takes a swig of his beer, "this is the same girl? And she left your ass again?"

I immediately regret telling Evan about Brooke. About the fact that she snuck out after our night together and ran off after our surprise rendezvous at the clinic. He's laughing so hard he nearly starts choking. Yeah, he's never going to let me forget this.

Evan is my best friend from high school. We started playing lacrosse together when we were ten, and eventually we were co-captains of our high school team. He went to culinary school on the east coast, lived in New York for years working his way up the restaurant chain, and recently relocated back to Denver to open his own restaurant. It's nice to have him back in town, even though I haven't seen him much lately with his restaurant opening. But, the fact that Carrie is best friends with his sister, Erica, makes it easier for us to sync our social calendars with minimal effort.

It's been three days since I fingered Brooke in my office

and if I wasn't already confused about her ditching me after sex last Saturday night, her disappearing act at my office this week pretty much sealed the deal that she's either nuts or unavailable.

We're gathered at Erica's house for a barbeque. Her two little boys and my nieces have devoured cupcakes and are now high on sugar, chasing each other around the yard with squirt guns. While their wives chat in the shade on the patio, Kyle is restocking beer in a cooler, and John, Erica's husband, is manning the grill.

"Wow, man. This happened to you?" Evan shakes his head. "If a woman is running from you, how do the rest of us even stand a chance?" He looks thoughtful. "I think you're pursuing the wrong woman. Do what I do, instead of going after the woman that is hard to pin down, you go for the woman who is practically tripping over herself to fuck you. Less work."

I've done that before. Gone for the woman that was easy and available. That's what I've been doing while I focused on my career. The problem with that kind of relationship is that I always found myself with women who no matter how honest I was about not wanting a relationship, would always get upset when our hook-ups didn't progress into something more.

Now, I want to put in the work. There's something about Brooke that makes me want to figure her out. I don't know her that well, but I have the desire to. Without a referral from a doctor at the fertility clinic, I have no access to her file, assuming she has one, and even if I did, I want Brooke to be the one to give me her number. I've stopped by BookBar the last two Sunday afternoons, hoping to see her again. It's getting really pathetic.

I'm taking a swig of my beer when I notice Carrie on her way over to us with a pretty redhead in a green dress following just steps behind her. Sometime during my conversation with Evan, she must have arrived.

"This is my brother, Cole." I can't help but notice her emphasis on the word brother. "And his friend, Evan. Evan is Erica's brother. Guys, this is Lori."

Immediately I recognize the name and I recall back to the conversation Carrie and I had a few weeks ago about her setting me up with her yoga instructor. I had completely forgotten about it until now.

Lori smiles brightly and shakes both of our hands. Carrie hints not so subtly that she and Evan should refresh the drinks, and then they're gone, leaving Lori and me to talk.

"It's so nice to finally meet you," Lori beams. "Carrie's been telling me about you for months." Her hair color is unique, almost a reddish blonde. She's pretty, with bright blue eyes and a perfect smile.

"You, too," I agree, but feel like a jerk when I can't remember anything that Carrie has said about her. The only thing I know is she's a yoga instructor, so I ask her about her job and she easily chats for twenty minutes before taking a breath.

"Sorry, I get a bit carried away with the yoga talk. I'm really passionate about it. And, it makes me happy."

"That's great. You should love what you do." I take a swig of my beer.

Lori sips her wine and we continue making small talk until John announces the burgers and hotdogs are ready. I sit between Evan and Lori, who actually seem to have more in common, and are basically talking over me. My distracting thoughts of Brooke make me a poor conversationalist. So, it comes as a bit of a surprise when Lori stands to leave for a yoga class she has to teach in an hour, but asks if I can walk her out.

"Sure."

As I'm standing to leave the table, Evan elbows me in the ribs and I can't tell if it's a friendly jab or a territorial one. We exit the back gate and walk until she stops in front of her white Toyota Prius.

Lori turns to me. "It was nice to meet you."

"Same."

"Would you like to grab dinner sometime?"

Although I didn't exactly feel the world turn on its axis when Carrie introduced us, there's a part of me that realizes this is what needs to happen. My goal is to date. To put myself out there. Going to dinner with Lori would be exactly that. It might also help me move on from Brooke. I have to admit it's an ego boost that she is asking me out and sexy that she has the confidence to do it.

"Yeah. I'd like that."

## 19

# BROOKE

Ever since I got my own place and moved out of Ellie and Josh's house, I've become accustomed to knocking when I come over. I used to live here and I still have a key, but figure after all the years of me living here, they deserve their privacy now. But, when my hands are full of grocery bags to cook dinner and no one is answering the door, I figure my key use is warranted.

"Ellie?" I slip off my sandals by the door and proceed down the hallway toward the kitchen. When I get to the doorway, I find Ellie and Josh there. Their casual 'hey' seems forced. I think Josh just zipped up his pants, and I'm pretty sure Ellie's shirt is on inside out. They were totally just having sex in the kitchen. Possibly on the table where we're going to eat dinner, no less.

I scrunch up my nose. I think I can actually smell sex in here. Gross.

I'm getting a killer bicep workout with these grocery bags, so when Josh moves to take them from me, I gladly accept.

"You guys remember I was coming over to cook dinner, right?" I look between them.

"Yeah, of course." Ellie pulls her loose hair back into a ponytail.

After setting the groceries on the counter, Josh moves back to kiss Ellie's temple.

"I'm going to go change out of my work clothes."

She smiles up at him lovingly, "Would you wipe off the patio table after? I think it'd be nice to eat outside."

Yeah, so we don't have to think about what just happened on the kitchen table.

"Of course." He drops another kiss, this time on her lips.

When he's gone, Ellie turns to me.

"Josh just got home."

"Does he always greet you with his dick?" I waggle my eyebrows.

She blushes, "Was it obvious?"

"Uh, yeah, I think I was only a few seconds shy of missing the big finish."

We both laugh as she moves to start unpacking the groceries. She's positively giddy, which should be the norm after having sex with your husband, but I know all the rounds of IVF and failed attempts to get pregnant have put a strain on their sex life. She hasn't shared specifics, but I know it's been challenging to find the intimacy in something that has become so clinical. I'm glad to see them in a good place.

"What'd you do today? Besides have a quickie with your husband on the kitchen table."

I'm happy for Ellie and Josh, that someone is getting some action, because right now, my vibrator is working overtime. I started the oral hormone medication a few days ago and I'm starting to feel the effects. I'm achy and tired, yet my sex drive is off the charts. If this is a preview of what pregnancy might be like, I'm a little nervous I've bitten off more than I can chew.

Ellie smiles and hands me a glass casserole dish from the cabinet. "I watched the girls next door for a few hours this morning, then cleaned the house. How was work?" She volleys back to me.

"Good. I just finished staging the model for the Highlands Place Apartments on 38th. It turned out amazing."

Ellie uses the can opener to remove the lids of the canned goods, then slides them on the counter to me when she's done.

Chicken taco casserole is my favorite dish that my mom used to make. Besides my taco salad specialty, it's the only thing that I can make because it involves dumping canned ingredients, cream of chicken soup, Rotel, and condensed milk, into a dish. I buy the precooked chicken because I have no idea how to cook chicken, and no one needs to get E. coli poisoning, then its sprinkle cheese and crushed up nacho cheese Doritos on top.

My mom grew up in the Midwest where her mother made a lot of casseroles. Hot dish is what they called them. Throw everything in, heat it up and voila, hot dish.

I haven't really shared my new raging hormone status with Ellie. The point of me being her surrogate is to alleviate stress, so I'm not going to burden her with all the details.

"That's great. Have you seen that cute furniture delivery guy again?" She wiggles her eyebrows. "Has he taken off his shirt yet?"

I'd nearly forgotten that I told her about the hot delivery guy. It feels like so much has happened since then. I haven't even thought of him since that first day, because I've been thinking about Cole instead.

Cole, the guy I've sworn off for the next nine months…I'm not sure how I feel about that. Not that he'll be waiting for me or anything. He's a gorgeous doctor with a skilled cock after all, a hot commodity in the world of single women.

"No, but he's definitely nice eye candy to have around." I continue the conversation with Ellie even though my mind has reverted to its happy place. Thinking about Cole.

His lips, his hands, his cock. It's all great material when I touch myself, but it's not nearly as good as having him touch me. Feeling his palm slide up my inner thigh, his lips against my neck, his tongue licking and tasting me. We only had sex once, but every moment has been imprinted into my memory, like a movie reel I can watch over and over. Also, I'm creative, so I have mixed in a few fantasies to change it up. My go to is Cole bending me over his desk and fucking me from behind. He's got one hand on my hip, the other hand on my breast, holding me in place as he thrusts into me hard. My hands grip the edge of his desk as I press my ass into his pelvis, meeting him thrust for thrust.

"Whoa there, killer. I think you're good."

I look down to find that I've completely smashed the hell out of the Doritos bag. While they're supposed to be crushed, they're not supposed to be obliterated. Whoops!

I pour them into the dish, stir, then add a layer of the crumbs on top.

"Are you okay?" Ellie lifts herself up onto the counter beside me. "How are you feeling with the hormones?"

"Like a fucking lunatic. Is that normal?"

"Unfortunately, yes." She gives me a sympathetic smile, then adds, "You'd tell me if you were having second thoughts, right?"

"Of course!" I busy myself with picking up the empty cans and rinse them out in the sink.

"Brooke."

I turn to find Ellie watching me, her green eyes filled with emotion. We're identical twins so it makes sense that sometimes when I look at her, I see a version of myself, but then there are these intense moments where I feel like our minds connect. Like Ellie is infiltrating my thoughts. Like we're one person.

The last thing I want is for Ellie to worry that I'm not committed to being her and Josh's surrogate. That she's bracing herself for disappointment and heartache once again. Since Ellie and Josh have been on this journey to conceive, I've been helpless as I've watched them get negative test results, disappointing news over and over. What I'm going through with the heightened hormone levels, Ellie has done six times. I have a new appreciation for how resilient she is and how badly she wants to become a mother to her biological child. I want more than anything to give Ellie hope again.

"It's just different than I thought. That's all. But I've got this."

Ellie slides off the counter and wraps her arms around me. When she pulls away her eyes are brimming with tears.

"Ugh. I don't know what's wrong with me." She wipes at her eyes. "You're the one taking the hormones."

She sniffles, and I pull her in for another hug.

"Maybe it's our twinpathy."

Ellie laughs. "Right. That must be it."

When we were younger, I was convinced that Ellie and I had telepathic capabilities. Ellie, not so much. I think it's all that logical math swirling around in her head. Ellie's all if A plus B equals C, then B can't be psychic capabilities. Or something like that.

After dinner, I'm loading dishes in the dishwasher when Josh enters the kitchen.

"Let me help you with those."

One thing I learned when I lived with Josh and Ellie is that Josh takes pride in being able to fit as much in the dishwasher as possible but not so much that the dishes and utensils don't get clean. He immediately swoops in and starts to reconfigure the dishes already loaded in order to optimize the dishwasher space. He's basically playing a game of Tetris with plates. I can't help but smile. He's such a nerd. I hand Josh the last plate, then reach for the dish towel to dry my hands. I watch with my wine glass in hand, and after some more rearranging, he finally seems satisfied with its placement and closes the dishwasher. He takes a wet dishcloth and starts to wipe down the counter. I also know that when Josh is under stress, he cleans. Ellie is similar, so needless to say their house is usually spotless.

"So, how's everything going?" Josh asks.

"Good."

He folds the dishcloth and hangs it neatly over the edge of the sink, then faces me.

"When Ellie first mentioned your offer to be our surrogate, I thought she was crazy."

"Gee, thanks." I try not to sound offended.

He shakes his head. "No, not because of you. I was hesitant because I didn't want her to get her hopes up. I just want to protect her, you know? She's everything to me and I can't stand to see her hurting."

"I know," I say softly. Ellie's everything to me, too. That's why I want to help them.

"And I have no idea what I'm supposed to be doing in this scenario. Guys don't get to experience pregnancy, but at least they get to be supportive and beside their partner for the journey. I always imagined giving Ellie foot rubs while she sat on the couch eating the ice cream that I went out in a snow storm to get."

"That's just amateur. You should have already had the ice cream on hand."

We both laugh, then.

"I have no idea what this will look like either, but I want both you and Ellie to be a part of the journey."

Josh nods, "If you need anything, I want you to know that we are here for you and you shouldn't hesitate to ask. And, if you aren't sure you want to go through with the surrogacy, we will understand. I want you to be sure."

"Okay."

Josh nods thoughtfully, then peeks through the kitchen window, keeping an eye on Ellie in the back yard watering her small planter's box garden.

"I'm planning on surprising Ellie with a trip to Glenwood Springs next month. I've got a cozy bed and breakfast booked and massages already scheduled. I figured it would be a relaxing trip, soaking in the hot springs and doing some wine tasting, something to take her mind off everything." He glances out the window again, then, "I was hoping you would help by packing her a bag so I can make it a total surprise."

I smile, but there's an unexpected twist in my belly. It makes me pause and I can feel my face fall as I identify the feeling. It's the feeling I get when I see families out to dinner together, a mom and her daughter shopping in a store, an older couple touring a townhome I've staged.

I've been around Ellie and Josh long enough that I'm used to their affection and the sweet things they do for each other, but something about Josh's protective nature regarding the surrogacy coupled with his thoughtful planning of a trip for Ellie is making me feel strange. It's making me think about what it could be like to have someone to lean on and make plans with. My mind involuntarily draws up an image of Cole and my brow furrows at the unwanted thought.

Josh must read my face as disapproval.

"Do you think it's a bad idea?"

"Oh, no," I shake my head and smile reassuringly, "she would love that." And I mean it. Ellie will be overjoyed. And she deserves it after all they've been through the past few years and especially in the last month with coming to terms with the thought that she can't get pregnant. I'm happy that Ellie has Josh to love and support her.

I want all those things for Ellie, but there's a small part of me that is starting to wonder if I might want those things, too.

## 20

# BROOKE

**M**y hand shakes as I attempt to apply eye liner. I have a doctor's appointment later this morning where I'll find out if I'm ready to schedule the embryo implantation. After my conversation with Josh last night, I'm feeling a bit anxious. He wants me to be one hundred percent sure about being their surrogate. I get it. The last thing I want to do is disappoint either of them. But who can ever be that sure of something? I'm usually leaning strongly in one direction and then just go with it and hope for the best. But, I couldn't exactly tell Josh that.

That's only half my issue. Honestly, I'm more apprehensive about running into Cole again. After two failed attempts to keep my hand steady, I toss the eye liner back in my bag and reach for my mascara.

It's been two weeks since Cole fingered me in his office. I've managed to avoid the fertility clinic, having Ellie pick up the oral hormone prescription I've started taking as part of the process to get my body ready for the embryo implantation. I can't speak for my uterus, but my body is ready for something, and that something would be SEX. The hormones are making me horny. So horny. I actually humped my pillow last night and came in two minutes flat. That satisfaction lasted about an hour and then I was back to my lust-filled state for the rest of the night. I twisted in my sheets, my mind conjuring images of Cole, his sexy smile and strong chest, and my fingers attempted to replay the scene in his office, but it wasn't the same. I wanted his touch, his deep voice in my ear. And more than that, I wanted more of *him*. More time to explore the connection that I had felt. I've had good sex before, but what I felt with Cole was beyond sex, and that was absolutely terrifying. That thought cost me even more sleep.

I'm in my closet now, and struggling with what to wear. My hands linger on the skirt I was wearing when I saw Cole at the clinic. For a guy I had sex with once, Cole is sure taking up a lot of space in my mind. There are the sexy time thoughts and then there are thoughts like whether or not he's finished that James Patterson book on his nightstand, has he been thinking about me, too, or has he been sharing pie with someone else? Then even more thoughts start to swirl around in my brain. What if I wasn't attempting to get pregnant with Ellie and Josh's baby? Would I have stayed at Cole's place that night? Would he have gotten my phone number? Would we have gone on dates, and be spending quiet nights cuddling on the couch watching Netflix? Making plans to meet each other's families and vacation together? I shake those thoughts from my head before they can take root. That's not me. Even if I wasn't pursuing the surrogacy for my sister, snuggles and hand-holding wouldn't be what I want out of a one-night stand. So why can I imagine doing them with Cole?

I don't even know much about the guy, other than he's an OBGYN with magic fingers. I have to repeat my mantra. He was a one-night stand. End of story. I shake my head and move past it to a pair of pants. Pants will be better. No easy access.

———

If Ellie thinks I'm acting weird, she doesn't say anything. I mean it's not like I'm ducking behind plants or anything. I really did think I dropped my lip gloss behind the large potted ficus in the waiting room. We make it to the exam room without any Cole sightings. His practice is on three so I'm relying on the chances that he'd be at the fertility clinic to be slim. Dr. Yang is chipper as ever and I kind of want to punch her in the throat. Either that or start humping the exam table. When she pulls out the large ultrasound wand, I nearly moan with pleasure. What the hell is wrong with me?

When she inserts the ultrasound wand, I'm pretty sure I have a mini orgasm.

"All right, Brooke, everything is looking great. Your uterus lining is beautiful."

Dr. Yang removes the wand and switches off the machine. Boo. I sit up on the exam table, the paper crinkling with my movement.

"So, when am I getting knocked up?" I know this is a serious matter, but my hormones are all over the place. The quicker this thing happens, the less likely I am to lose my mind. I think this might be like sky diving, where you either jump from the plane quickly or you chicken out.

Ellie exchanges a look with Dr. Yang.

"The original plan was to do the procedure next week. But, I've spoken with Ellie and Josh about the status of their remaining embryos, and after some discussion we determined that the surrogacy would have a higher rate of success if Ellie undergoes another round of egg retrieval."

I try not to zone out while Dr. Yang explains science to me. Ellie and Josh used the most viable embryos during their IVF attempts and their remaining embryos, while healthy, have a lower success rate for implantation. Dr. Yang advised them to consider doing another egg retrieval, which compared to the cost of IVF and surrogacy, is minimal.

"The egg retrieval process will take about three weeks. Ten to twelve days of injections to stimulate the ovaries, then after the egg retrieval procedure, another week to develop and fertilize the embryos. When the fertilized embryos are ready, we'll schedule the embryo implantation procedure. In the meantime, Brooke, you will continue to take the hormones."

She must see the look of panic on my face because she follows it up with, "It's completely safe."

Is she sure about that? I wouldn't say anyone who comes in contact with me during the next month is going to be safe.

But, I keep those thoughts to myself because I'm here for Ellie and she needs to know I can do this. I can totally do this. I will just need to factor in a pillow hump every morning and a post-work masturbation session into my schedule and everything will be fine.

Ellie excuses herself to use the restroom.

With Ellie gone, I sit quietly as Dr. Yang writes something down in her file. Or I guess it's my file.

"Brooke, do you have any questions for me? Is everything going well with the progesterone?"

"Actually, I've been experiencing quite a bit of," I search for a word that doesn't make me sound like a nymphomaniac, "sensation down there." I wave my hand over my nether region.

Dr. Yang smiles.

"The hormones can be pretty intense." She smiles again and lets out a laugh. "I did IVF for our twins and my husband was thrilled that I wanted to jump him all the time."

I want to let out a commiserate laugh, but in my case, I don't have a willing husband at home to have sex with whenever I want. I've been humping pillows.

Dr. Yang must realize this, the husband thing, not the pillow thing, because her smile turns sympathetic, and she leans closer to me.

"Brooke, as long as you're using protection, you can still have sex." She reaches for a drawer, pulls out a thin foil packet and rips it open. She unfolds a thin, clear film that looks like one of those breath strips that dissolve on your tongue. "These are spermicidal films. They are a great second form of contraception, to be used with condoms." She places her finger in the middle of the film. "You just insert it into your vagina fifteen minutes before sex and it dissolves."

Yup, it's a breath strip for my vagina.

Dr. Yang reaches back in the drawer and hands me a stack.

Ellie pops back in, "Sorry, too much coffee this morning, I guess."

I use my hand to conceal the spermicide films Dr. Yang gave me. I don't need Ellie questioning why I need spermicide. We usually talk about everything, even sex, but the emotional rollercoaster that Ellie has been on since the last round of IVF, and now she needs to do another egg retrieval procedure, I don't want to add any extra stress or worry to this process. Dr. Yang leaves to call in Ellie's hormone prescription, then I climb down off the exam table.

"Are we on for movie night tonight?" I ask.

"Yes, but Josh reminded me this morning that it's his turn to pick the movie." She's rummaging in her purse for her car keys so she doesn't see me make a face. Josh isn't known for his great taste in movies, and he'll probably choose something gory with a war time back drop, as payback for my last pick, the eighties dance movie *Girls Just Want to Have Fun*. It'll be a good time to paint my nails and drink wine.

Ellie finds her keys and gives me another quick hug. "Love you."

Once I'm alone in the exam room, I hurry to get dressed. I attempt to wipe up the wetness between my legs with a tissue, but I'm still wet and the friction is starting to make me even wetter. I adjust my boobs in my bra, they're achy and tender. At this point they're basically beacons searching for touch, preferably a sexy doctor with a warm mouth. Grrr.

I need to focus. Not only on the surrogacy for Ellie, but on my job. I've been so distracted at work, last week I hung the wrong art work in the wrong rooms, which wouldn't have been a big deal except they were on the wrong walls, too, so I had to do some patch work, which is never a good thing to do in a brand new condo. And yesterday, I had furniture delivered to the wrong place. It was super embarrassing discovering I had made the mistake after I threatened the moving company manager to never use their company again. How am I going to be able to get any work done if I can't stop thinking about sex, Cole, and sex with Cole?

Especially now with the implantation being postponed for Ellie to do another egg retrieval. I totally get that they want the best possible embryo for success but now I'm thinking I jumped the gun on having one last hook-up.

My body is dying for a release. One that isn't at my own hands. I've already tried that and it hasn't helped quench the raging hormones inside me. It's Friday, I could rally Sam for a happy hour and try to find a hook-up. But the thought of putting forth effort to find a guy to satisfy my needs makes me exhausted. I got really lucky with Cole, a sexy doctor with a big dick, who gave me mind-bending orgasms.

Now, my mind is back to replaying images of said dick. How he thrust into me, the delicious burn when he filled me, and how hard I clenched around him when I came. The ache between my thighs returns. I groan inwardly as I think about how distracted I'm going to be all day.

Sue wants me to assist her in a meeting with a potential contractor client and I really don't need visions of Cole's dick floating in my head.

I manage to make my way out of the doctor's office and into the elevator bank without humping anything. I stab the down button and wait.

The elevator dings its arrival and I step on. I stare at the buttons. The L for lobby should clearly be my choice, but along with my mind, the hormones have taken over control of my fingers, which illuminate another button. Before I can even come up with a game plan, the elevator opens on the third floor and I step out.

## 21

## COLE

My morning has been hectic. I've just sat down in my office, hoping to take a few minutes to make lab results calls from my office, when there's a knock on my door.

"Come in." I continue to review the file in front of me.

Usually Lois just starts speaking, so when the silence continues, I finally look up.

Standing in the doorway to my office is Brooke.

"Hey." She waves at me. Her teeth capture her lower lip as her expression turns uncertain. As if she's realizing the fact that she's run off, unexplained, the last two times we've seen each other could be a reason I don't want to see her.

"Hey." I release the file in my hand and lean back into my chair and really look at her. She's dressed in black pants and a sleeveless blouse. My chest tightens as I take her in. Not because of what she's wearing, but because I'm happy to see her. The date with Lori, which included some easy conversation and a shared appreciation for cooking, but absolutely no spark, only made it clearer that I have an undeniable connection with Brooke.

It's been two weeks since I saw her. Fourteen long days since I touched her. Weeks of thinking about her and wondering what the hell she wants. When she disappeared after our night together, I was disappointed that it was just a one-night thing, and when I saw her up on five, I couldn't stop myself from bringing her down to my office and touching her. My dick twitches now with the anticipation of what could happen. Its only action since I slept with Brooke is from my own hand, jerking off while thinking about her.

"Listen, I'm sorry about rushing out of here before." Brooke's eyes shift in the direction of the wall where I fingered her. My fingers flex at the memory of how amazing she felt, and my dick jerks in response.

"Okay."

Brooke slowly walks toward my desk, until she reaches the corner and sits facing me, her animal print flats dangling off the ground.

Her green eyes lift to mine, she looks uncertain, but her words say something else.

"I wanted to see you."

Her tongue darts out to lick her lips, and my dick continues to swell beneath my zipper. I don't say anything. I take in the sight of Brooke's cleavage in her low-cut blouse. How her chest moves up and down with every breath. My body rises out of the chair of its own volition and I find myself standing in front of her. Brooke's legs part until I can move between them. Stepping in closer to her, our centers align. Brooke's fingers lift to my tie. They linger there, lightly stroking. Her green eyes are fixed on her fingers, watching her slow, even strokes on the silk of my tie, then slowly, they lift to mine. I think she knows that

I'm hesitant to touch her, but it's not for the reasons she thinks. I'm not upset with her. I've never been more intrigued by a woman in my life. It's really my desire to sit back and see what she comes up with. I've trapped my hands in my pants pockets because fuck knows what I'd do if I let myself touch her. That's when I feel the tug. She wraps her hand around my tie and slowly pulls me toward her.

Her eyes are hooded, long dark lashes lowered toward her cheeks. It's like torture waiting for the contact. And then, her soft lips press into mine. She tastes sweet like cherries.

What starts out slow and languid turns hot and heavy quickly. Brooke releases my tie, then both hands slide up my chest, over my shoulders and into my hair. I pull back slightly from her kiss, and am punished with a firm tug on my hair. My greedy hands don't last long in my pants pockets. They're moving up her thighs, sliding over her hips and waist to pull her in closer until my quickly growing erection is pressing into her center. Our mouths release on a gasp, and I kiss up her jaw until my lips are right next to her ear.

The noises she's making are driving me crazy.

"Fuck, Brooke."

We're practically dry humping. This is insane. Anyone could walk in right now and catch us, which makes what we're doing feel illicit, and completely unprofessional. When I fingered her against the wall, it was more my ego than anything that wanted to prove to her that she shouldn't have snuck out that night. Temporary insanity after spending three nights replaying our night together. But, I've got my head on straight this time. Don't get me wrong, I still want to bend her over my desk, maybe smack her ass for sneaking out on me twice, but I can be patient.

She gasps, then whispers, "I want you to fuck me on your desk."

Her words are both insanely arousing and exactly what I need to put a stop to what we're doing.

I could bend her over my desk, just like she's requested. She could straddle me in my chair. But then she would probably run afterwards. No, I want to pin Brooke down for more than a quick fuck. I want a date. Dinner, then dessert, all night with her in my bed. I want to know how she takes her coffee. Fuck, if she even drinks coffee. All I know is she likes peach pie and orgasms. She hates expensive smoothies, especially if they're green, and made with kale.

I pull back, sliding my hands down Brooke's arms in a soothing gesture. She still has her eyes closed and when she opens them, she looks drunk.

"Why'd you stop?"

"Because I don't want to fuck you on my desk."

Her eyes narrow and her mouth drops open slightly.

"What?!"

"At least not today," I preface, because she looks pissed, and I don't want to get kneed in the balls. "I want a date. You and me. Dinner. Conversation." I lean in to her again, my lips finding that tender place on her neck before I whisper in her ear, "Then, dessert."

"A date?" She says it like it's a four-letter word. Maybe it is and maybe I'm crazy for pursuing her, but I don't really want to waste my time doing what we've been doing. I already know we have chemistry and I want to find out if there's more to it than that. I'm not going to wait another week or two until she randomly shows up again.

I'm taking a gamble here, but something has to be done. She might just stand up and walk out, but I'm banking on the look of lust in her eyes to be the reason she doesn't. If that's what gets me her number then I'll take it.

Brooke still seems in a daze, like she can't believe this turn of events, so I walk her through it.

"Hand me your phone."

She finds it in her purse and unlocks it for me. I start a text message to myself then hand her the phone. "Put in your address."

"Please." Her narrowed eyes are practically slits now as she stares me down.

"Put in your address, please."

She types it in and hits send, almost begrudgingly.

"I'll pick you up at seven."

I help her off my desk, steal one more kiss, then pat her on the ass as she walks toward the door. Before she reaches the door, she turns her head back, her expression one of confusion, before she gives me a small wave and reaches for the door knob. I get it. I'm still a bit confused as to why I halted what could have been really hot desk sex. But, that will come later. I got what I really wanted from Brooke— her phone number.

## 22

# BROOKE

The rest of my day was a disaster. When I was supposed to be taking notes at the new client meeting, Sue had to stop and catch me up because my mind kept wandering and thinking about my interaction with Cole. And our date tonight. Then I wondered what the fuck must be wrong with him that he turned down sex on his desk for a dinner date. Like what screw must he be missing? Pun intended. Later, I googled lady blue balls to see if it is an actual thing. It is. And I have it.

Sue knows I haven't been myself lately. When I told her about my plans to be Ellie and Josh's surrogate, she was nothing but supportive. She understands what I'm going through. Her daughter and son-in-law did IVF for her two grandsons, so she gets it. But, at the same time, I know I'm still fairly new and I still want to prove myself.

By the time I got home, I was so worked up, I decided that it would be best to use my vibrator, hoping to take the edge off before I see Cole again, lest he think I might be a sexual deviant. But it stopped working halfway through and I couldn't find any extra batteries. My fingers didn't get the job done and for a good three minutes I cried in frustration on the floor of my bedroom. Then I picked myself up and got in the shower.

An hour later, Sam calls while I'm getting ready.

"How'd the appointment go?"

"Good. I'm moody and horny so the hormones are doing their job. The doctor told me my ovaries were fluffy, that's a good thing, but Ellie needs to do another egg retrieval so now I'm just going to be hanging out for a month until there are better embryos to put inside me."

"I thought she already had embryos."

"They used the best ones with their last round of IVF. The doctor thinks to give it the best shot she wants a new batch. More viable she called them?" I just know there's at least another three to four weeks before the embryo implantation procedure, so as Dr. Yang instructed, I'm just going to live my life until then. My swollen, achy, hormonal life. The future isn't really clear, but my current mission is to have sex with Cole tonight.

"You headed to Ellie and Josh's tonight?"

I told Ellie I was going to skip movie night tonight. I didn't go into detail as to why, and she didn't ask. She knows I've been tired and hormonal lately, and to be honest I am tired. Tired of feeling like a walking hormonal mess. Selfishly I'd rather be getting some action from a hot guy than be a third wheel with her and Josh for movie night in. I'll have months and months of that coming pretty soon.

For a moment I think about lying to Sam. It's not like she's going to check up on me. But, why would I lie? I'm not doing anything wrong. I'm an adult, Cole's an adult. We are going to have dinner, then sex. It doesn't have to be complicated. Besides, Dr. Yang gave me the go ahead for sex. I've got at least a month before anything with the surrogacy plan moves forward. That's like a year in single girl time. Knowing all this, and feeling confident about it are two different things.

"No. I'm going on a date." I lower my voice to a whisper, because it feels like a secret. "With Cole."

"I'm sorry, what?"

"I said, I'mgoingonadatewithCole."

"Huh. It sounded like you said you were going on a date. With Cole?"

"Yup. That's what I said."

"Okay. Wow."

"Wow, what? I can go on a date." My defenses are up, these hormones are making me a moody bitch. "Besides, it's only because he's withholding sex. He wants a date, I want sex. We're both going to get what we want."

"Sure. That sounds great."

I don't like her easy response. Part of me is hoping she'll talk me out of it, remind me that I don't need to be dating right now. That I don't date, period. That I was supposed to be done with Cole after the first night. And my focus should be on making my body a cozy, loving place for Ellie and Josh's embryo. I tell her as much.

"I'm not going to tell you not to go. Maybe this is what you need right now. Distraction from the process. Have fun. Enjoy the sexy times, because it's not going to be the same eight months from now when you're sitting on the couch massaging your perineum."

"What's my perineum? Is that part of the baby?"

"Nothing you need to know about tonight."

"Hmm."

After a little more catch up about how Sam's week has been going, we hang up so I can finish getting ready.

I pick out a white off-the-shoulder sundress with a

floral pattern. It's short which shows off my legs, and the short sleeves are off the shoulder which exposes my décolletage. The perfect dress to torture Cole throughout dinner. Hopefully he'll realize his mistake and not turn me down in the future. But *what future* am I even talking about? We're having dinner, I'm getting orgasms, then I'm out. For good. I mean I have to be regardless of what I want. Right?

I'm still wondering, what does he think he's doing with this whole date thing? I just need a few mind-blowing orgasms to tamp down these hormones. I'll just have to make that clear—that we're friends with benefits minus the whole friends thing. So, we're just benefits. Two people mutually benefitting from the orgasms we give each other. Sounds like winning to me.

A simple chain necklace and heeled sandals complete my outfit. There's a knock on my door at five 'til seven, just as I'm throwing my lip gloss, wallet and phone into my purse. Deciding to make him sweat it out for a minute, I run back into my bedroom for an extra pair of panties to bring along as well. I'm thinking the Niagara Falls situation between my thighs calls for bringing a backup pair.

By the time I get to the door, my heart is racing wildly. That's not normal. It's barely twenty feet to my bedroom, I guess I need to work on my cardio. I take a few deep breaths and open the door.

Standing there in dark jeans and a striped button-down shirt is Cole. His sleeves are rolled up, exposing his tan, muscular forearms. Yum, my favorite. My heart beat is thump thump thumping at the sight of him. Apparently it hasn't gotten the memo that I'm not being chased by a wild animal.

He smiles when he sees me. I watch the whole transition from neutral face to lips parted, then teeth appear, and finally it reaches his eyes and wow. I think that's my favorite thing. I wonder if I could video Cole smiling and watch it over and over in slow motion.

"You look gorgeous." He leans in to kiss my cheek, his masculine scent washes over me and fuck, my panties are wet, again. My clean underwear supply is dwindling, and Cole is not helping the situation.

"Thanks." I feel my cheeks heat. What the heck is wrong with me? It's just a compliment on my dress, which I picked out for the very reason he's complimenting me. I don't think I even blushed when he licked my pussy. I've got to get it together.

"Where's your bag?"

I look down at the small crossbody purse in my hand.

"What bag?"

"With your stuff to spend the night." Cole looks at me pointedly to emphasize his requirement that I spend the night this time.

"I don't really need anything. You've got an extra toothbrush, right?"

"You'll need a change of clothes, unless you want to wear that all day tomorrow, too." He shrugs like it wouldn't bother him one bit, but I'm more focused on this change of events.

"All day? I agreed to breakfast, that shouldn't last all day."

"I amended our date. I need twenty-four hours. I'll bring you home tomorrow evening."

"You can't just demand I hang out with you all day. What if dinner is miserable? What if we have nothing to talk about? What if the sex is bad?"

Cole's eyebrows shoot up at that last one. Okay, I don't think that is even remotely possible based on our track record, but who knows, maybe I'll get to know more about him and he'll become less attractive. Now I'm just being delusional but this guy is nothing like I'm used to. He's a lot of work.

It's a standoff at my door, while I weigh my options. If I refuse his twenty-four-hour date demand and he walks away I'm left with zero orgasms and a dead vibrator. A trip to Target for batteries would take thirty minutes, likely two hours if I browse. But, who am I kidding? My vibrator has nothing on Cole's magic fingers.

I could call his bluff, or negotiate, but I'm pretty sure Cole isn't as horny as I am. His refusal to fuck me on his desk this morning is a perfect example of his annoying restraint. I, on the other hand, might go blind if we don't have sex again soon. In the end, I decide that the more time I spend with Cole can only increase the potential for more orgasms, so finally, I step aside, and let him into my apartment.

I watch him taking in the small space that is my living room. Knowing what Cole's place looks like makes me wonder what he thinks of my apartment. It's small, especially in comparison to his spacious two-bedroom condo, my decorating style with its eclectic, bright colors whereas his apartment is decorated in neutral hues and modern style furniture.

"I'll be right back."

I don't think Cole even hears me as he crosses the space to the dining room wall where I have a photo gallery wall display. I leave him there and rush to pack my overnight bag. I don't even know what I'm packing, I just start throwing things in, uncomfortably aware that Cole is in my apartment looking at my stuff, and the fact that my apartment isn't exactly clean. After filling my bag with a random assortment of clothing, I stop by the bathroom to collect makeup and toiletries. At least he hasn't seen the twenty-seven hair products and lotion containers on the bathroom counter. I tell myself not to stress, it's not like I'm auditioning to be his live-in girlfriend. Then, I manage to pare down my ten-step nighttime facial care routine to three items.

Once I'm ready, I return to find Cole still studying the pictures on my wall.

"You have a twin?" He motions to a picture of Ellie and me at the beach when we were sixteen. It was a family vacation we took for spring break our junior year in high school. Ellie and I were signed up for surfing lessons and the instructor was a really hot college guy. I remember being mortified when my dad asked if there were any other instructors, a woman perhaps. My mom had to distract him with a round of golf at the resort or he likely would have been glaring at our instructor from underneath an umbrella for the duration of our lesson.

"Yeah. We're identical."

"Is she as easygoing as you are?"

I laugh. "We're nothing alike. She's a middle school math teacher, married to her college sweetheart. Her house is clean and she doesn't show up unannounced."

On our way out, my bag knocks over the pile of home décor magazines by the door. Cole helps me pick them up, his large hands easily wrapping around the entire stack.

"I didn't have time to clean. This was so last minute. I was going to clean tonight, but then this came up and now my whole schedule is off." My overnight bag swings from the crook of my arm as my hands gesture wildly.

"I apologize for the lack of notice." Cole holds the door open so I can exit. "I myself was surprised by this turn of events." He raises his eyebrows and looks pointedly at me. Yes, I know I showed up at his office unannounced and then practically begged him to fuck me on his desk but really, he chose this.

I narrow my eyes at him as I pull the door shut and lock my apartment. We could have avoided this whole thing if he just would have had sex with me in his office.

We exit my building and I follow him to his car which is parked on the street. He drives a luxury SUV which seems a little large and unnecessary for a single guy. I glance toward the back seat, both of them, then turn to Cole.

"Your car is very roomy." It's also spotless and smells dreamy, but I choose to focus on the former.

"We're not having sex in the car." He starts the car and pulls onto the street, a playful smile on his lips.

I scoff and pretend to be offended, even though the thought did cross my mind. "That's not what I was getting at. Why do you need such a big vehicle? Do you enjoy carbon emissions?"

Cole shrugs, "It's great for hauling gear up to the mountains. For skiing and camping. Do you ski?"

I lift my hand and rotate my wrist, giving him the universal signal for kinda. Growing up in Denver meant learning to ski when I could walk, we skied as a family for years, but I haven't been since my parents died.

"And someday for ki—" Cole clears his throat. "A dog. A big one that needs space."

I could have sworn he was about to say kids.

"What kind of dog?"

"I've always wanted a Bernese Mountain Dog, but I've been working a lot and haven't had the time to devote to a pet. My sister and her husband have a Goldendoodle, so I live vicariously through them."

"Does she live in Denver?"

"Yeah, south suburbs. She has two girls, a baby boy due in a few weeks. My parents are here, too. They're retired, they still ski and travel, but they live for their grandchildren." Cole signals and turns onto Speer Boulevard. "What about your parents?"

The question doesn't cause the anxiety that it used to. I'm accustomed to the question and my canned response that follows.

"They died. Car accident, eight years ago." Don't get me wrong, it still hurts but I can contain the hurt much better now.

Cole's head does a quick turn in my direction, he looks stunned, like he wasn't expecting that at all.

"Brooke…I'm so sorry."

He reaches his hand over to cover mine resting in my lap and rubs his thumb across my knuckles.

"It happened when we were in college, just after junior year."

"I can't even begin to imagine how hard that was for you and your sister."

"Yeah. It was."

In a couple weeks it will be the nine-year anniversary. I don't share that information. What's the point? In a few weeks Cole and I won't be a thing. The less I get into it the better. I'm sure the last thing he wants is to cloud our evening with the discussion of death.

We turn onto 32$^{nd}$ Avenue and Cole pulls into a small parking lot next to a brick building. After he cuts the engine, he turns toward me.

Cole's hand moves from where it was rubbing my hand, up to cup my jaw. His touch is gentle, too gentle, as his thumb caresses my cheek and he looks me straight in the eye.

"Thanks for sharing that with me."

I swallow over the lump in my throat, as Cole leans in and kisses me on the nose. I sit there stunned as he moves to get out and comes around to my side of the car to open the door. What the fuck is happening? Did he just kiss me on the *nose*? Maybe Cole's awkward car talk is all I need, we don't need to have sex, he just squashed my libido buzz with all the deep eye contact and weird feelings.

When Cole opens the door, I nearly spring out, dying to get out of the car, and away from all the yucky stuff that just happened in there. I liked the knuckle rub, that was nice, but everything else has got to go. I don't want Cole to feel sorry for me, like he thinks I need attention or love because I don't have parents anymore. I'm doing fine. Great, even. I'm about to do the most adult thing I've ever done, help my sister and brother-in-law have their baby, and I don't need Cole messing with my emotions. They're already out of control.

Cole extends his hand to me, but I pretend to be searching for something in my purse so I don't have to take it. Enough with this hand holding stuff, dinner and sex— that's what I signed up for. Cole is starting to try my patience. First, he demands a date, now he knows my phone number and where I live then extends our date to tomorrow, too. What's next? Monogrammed pajamas? I think I need to remind him what is happening here. I thought it was pretty clear when I asked him to fuck me on his desk that I don't need to be wined and dined. We could skip all the get to know you stuff and just keep this purely physical.

I know I'm being a bitch, but that's just me, I guess—I can't even blame it on the hormones. When I see where we are headed, I soften a bit. Barcelona. I've heard of this place. I've been dying to try it. It's a new Spanish tapas restaurant everyone is raving about.

Cole holds the door open for me and I'm excited about what greets us. This place is definitely my vibe. Small and cozy, no wonder it's hard to get in, there are like twelve tables. The lighting is low, almost an amber glow, from pendants hanging from the stamped ceiling. The floors are dark wood, and the walls are exposed brick. There's no need for any wall décor, the hundred-year-old brick speaks for itself. There's a small bar toward the back of the room, separating the dining room from the kitchen. I love all the historic charm.

It's cool we got in, but now I'm curious to know how he got a table here on a Friday night, when he just demanded we go on this date eight hours ago.

The hostess motions for us to follow her to our table. Cole places his palm at my lower back, but his fingers are long, so I can feel the tips of them extend over the curve of my ass. As we walk, I can't tell if his palm has moved lower or if it's because I'm moving, but the way his fingers are gliding up and down on my ass is...everything. And there it is. One touch later and the primal need for me to slide his hand down and under the hem of my dress is back. The hostess shows us to our table, a two-top in a quiet nook by a window. In my lusty state I still manage to notice that every woman in the restaurant watches us walk by, and it isn't because they think my dress is cute.

Once I'm seated, I immediately cross my legs, giving friction where friction is desperately needed. The hostess hands us the menus, and I immediately start looking for the drink section.

She knows what's up and kindly hands me a separate small cocktail and wine menu.

"Thank you."

"Of course." She smiles, then sneaks one last glance at Cole before beelining it back to the front of the restaurant.

Our waiter appears, his name is Charlie and he highly recommends the special, which I don't catch because while he's talking, Cole is listening and I'm staring at Cole. Whoops.

I can't remember the last time I went out to a restaurant with a guy. My casual hook-ups are more relegated to Netflix and chill. Maybe drinks out and then heading back to his place.

We order drinks, a rosé for me and an old-fashioned for Cole.

"What sounds good to you?" he asks.

The way he rubs his jaw with his thumb while he studies the menu is so fucking hot. I squeeze my legs tighter. What sounds good is Cole's head between my thighs, but I think he's talking about dinner.

My eyes scan the menu, because I need to make food choices, not just because it's a way to avoid looking at Cole. The printed paper menu is an indication that the menu changes frequently, or at the very least seasonally. My suspicions are confirmed when I see 'week 6' printed in the upper right-hand corner of the menu.

"Everything."

The menu is set up as small plates, which I love, because I like to try a bunch of different things and not have to commit to one entrée. But there are no prices on the menu which bothers me because this isn't a date-date, like there's a future here…I don't want Cole to be confused. I'll have to explain to him later why I'm not a good investment. And it's not just because of the surrogacy. I'm a wild card, and not the good kind, like in Uno where you can change to any color you want and it saves you from the draw pile.

"Have you been here before?" I ask.

"My buddy, Evan, is one of the owners. I was here for a grand opening cocktail party about two months ago."

"I was wondering how you pulled off a reservation with such short notice."

"Evan's a good friend, we went to high school together. He went out east for culinary school, but came back to Denver to work his way up to executive chef at Rioja. Then decided to start up his own restaurant."

"Wow. That's impressive."

Charlie returns with our drinks. I take a sip, hoping the chilled wine will help ease the fire burning in my lower region. Cole tells Charlie that we want his recommendation for selecting our dishes. Charlie lists off his top choices and Cole looks to me to approve.

"Sounds great." I smile. I have no idea what we just ordered. Charlie's reaching for my menu now, but I'm having trouble parting with the only thing shielding me from Cole's intense gaze.

"Did you want to keep a menu for the table?"

"Um, no, I'm good." I finally release the paper menu.

Now that we're seated, I'm realizing we've never just sat across from each other and stared. At the diner we were side by side, at his place he was on top of me, a lot, which warranted some face to face action but I did have my eyes closed for a good amount of it. His office, both times I was more focused on trying to feel him rather than see him. Yeah, this is the first time I've sat across from Cole where I can see all of him. And he can see me. Indigo blue eyes that pierce straight through me. Chiseled jaw line that has a hint of dark stubble lining it. But there's more to it than that. Cole is gorgeous, but there's something in his mannerisms that really suck me in. The way his long fingers curl around the lowball glass before he lifts it to his mouth. The way he leans back in his chair, studying me.

Eating dinner with Cole is a bad idea. First of all, there are his lips, and his mouth, and he puts things in it, then he chews. Like, what the fuck am I supposed to do but squirm in my seat? After his old-fashioned he orders a glass of wine, and if I thought his grip on the lowball glass was revving up my engine, the way his fingers pinch and slowly rotate the stem of the wine glass is like dining table erotica.

I think he knows something is going on with me. He's asked me twice if I'm okay. I uncross and cross my legs again, trying to get more pressure on my clit. If I could just slip my fingers under the table without anyone knowing I'd be okay. We've eaten two of the six dishes that we ordered and there's no way I'm going to make it through the rest of this dinner without losing my mind if I don't take care of this. I wonder how long it's going to take me? Will Cole be sitting here wondering if I snuck out the bathroom window? The bathrooms are on an interior wall so that's not even possible but I have run off before so he might get the wrong idea. Or, he might think I'm sick. Or having explosive diarrhea. Or both.

What's the worst that could happen? He thinks I'm a nut job and leaves me at the restaurant? Then there'd be no sex and this would all be for naught, but he also seems kind of used to my straightforward behavior and maybe he won't think I'm too much of a weirdo.

I'm staring at him trying to decide what to do.

"Brooke, is something wrong?"

"I'm sorry." I shake my head. "Um, I'm kind of having a hard time focusing."

"Oh?"

"I'm really wet."

"Did you spill something?"

Cole's gaze drops to the table where he observes all of our perfectly upright glasses. He looks confused.

"I'm going to go to the ladies room and take care of it. It might be a little while, but just know I didn't leave."

Cole is beyond confused. "Take care of what?"

"Um, I'm just having a lot of sensation…down there." I use my finger to point under the table. "I just need a release and I'll be better."

It sounded perfectly normal in my head, but it sounds a lot worse when I say it out loud. Cole doesn't say anything. He just stares at me for a moment, his blue eyes taking in every inch of my face, before dropping lower to my neck and chest.

He takes a sip of his wine. I'm about to scoot my chair back when he pushes back from the table.

"Excuse me a moment."

Cole stands and walks toward the back of the restaurant, toward the kitchen. Okay. Now I'm not sure what is happening. He's probably decided that I'm too much for him and he's canceling the rest of our food order, then he's going to get the hell out of here. I really can't blame him. I'm normally so even keel, go with the flow, and although I typically have a healthy appetite for sex, the fertility hormones have my libido in overdrive. I'm really trying to focus and have a nice dinner with Cole but this is out of my control, and sitting across from Cole is not helping. So, really, it's his fault. If he would have fucked me on his desk this morning, we wouldn't be in this situation.

Cole reappears and I've managed to go from embarrassed to pissed while he was gone. He stands next to my seat and offers his hand.

"Let's go."

"Fine," I huff, grabbing my purse. I don't really want to hold his hand but the way he squeezes mine and starts pulling me along, I don't really have a choice. We're heading toward the back of the restaurant. Geez, he's so embarrassed we can't even leave through the front entrance? I'm totally calling an uber, I refuse to get back in a car with a man that can't sympathize with my situation. Oh wait, I guess he doesn't really know the whole situation.

Okay, maybe it's not exactly his fault, but he's a fucking gynecologist, so he should be all up to date on the shit that women go through. Oh, and my body didn't get the memo that Cole is acting like a dick. It thinks this rough hand-holding thing is really hot. I see the exit sign and can't wait to get there so I can pull my hand away from his, but then we're turning and Cole is opening a different door. One that opens to a small room with a desk and a guest chair facing it. The desktop is clean with the exception of a closed laptop in one corner.

Cole ushers me in, then shuts the door behind us. The click of the lock startles me and I turn around to face Cole.

"What—"

"I asked my buddy if I could use his office."

He starts to move toward me. The space is small, only three feet between the door and the desk, so it only takes a few steps before my butt hits the edge of the desk.

"There is no way that I would sit out there while you touched yourself in the restroom." Our bodies are so close now, almost touching. Cole's hands reach for my waist and lift me onto the desk. "If you come in this restaurant it will be under my tongue, with my fingers inside you."

"Oh," is all I can manage, because his words have just completely liquified me. I'm a puddle on this desk. A puddle with an ache between its thighs.

Cole's palms slide up my thighs, inching my dress up with them.

"Lean back."

I slowly lower down to my elbows, the hard wood of the desk cool beneath my arms. Cole lifts my dress up past my waist. It's like torture waiting for him to touch me.

Finally, a palm slides along my inner thigh until his thumb is there rubbing up and down the crotch of my panties.

"Jesus, Brooke. You're soaked."

I whimper. I need more than his feather-light strokes. I need sucking and licking and penetration.

"I know." I groan. Reflexively I reach one hand toward my center, determined to get something started, but Cole intercepts and presses me back onto the desk. He hooks his thumbs into my panties, pulling them down my legs and over my sandals. His thumb is back now, sans panties, and it's sooo much better.

"Yes."

I'm watching Cole as his eyes are fixed on where he's rubbing my clit with his thumb. He looks wild. Like a man ready to eat. He probably is hungry. I did interrupt our dinner. In case we forgot where we are, I hear the noises of a busy restaurant kitchen just outside the door. The clink of glasses being stacked, the sizzle of oil in a pan, and voices.

"Do you know how hard I am right now looking at you spread out on this desk? Your gorgeous pussy wet and swollen. Ready for me. How turned on I am by the fact that you can't even make it through dinner without needing me to touch you."

I like Cole's words, but I really want his mouth doing something other than talking.

"Cole. Please, I need you to…"

I trail off when Cole lowers to his knees, his warm breath against my wet center causes a cool sensation and now I think I might come before he even gets his mouth on me. Then he's there. Exactly what I wanted. Needed. Long strokes down the center followed by a swirl and a suck on my clit. My arms are shaky, and I'm fearful that when my orgasm hits they'll give out and I'll bang my head on the desk, so I let my arms slide to the side so I can lower the rest of my back and head onto the desk.

There's another sweep of his tongue before one long finger slides into me. I nearly weep with joy. The sensation is overwhelming. My whole body is like a live wire, every nerve alert, every muscle tense with anticipation of release.

It's sensation overload as Cole adds a second finger and sucks on my clit. I know I'm making noise. Groans and moans, mostly incoherent sounds, but I'm still aware of where we are. My hips buck and I cover my mouth with my arm so I don't scream. When my orgasm rips through me it's an intense tidal wave of sensation. My muscles pulse around Cole's fingers, trying to suck them in further, and if I thought I was wet before, that was nothing compared to the mess between my thighs now.

Once my orgasm subsides, I remove my forearm from my mouth and blow out a breath. My eyes reopen and I can't help the ear-to-ear smile that takes over my face.

"Holy shit."

Cole is standing over me now. He pulls the hem of my dress back down and reaches for my hands to help pull me up. It does occur to me that although we both got off the first night when we had sex, I've been greedy, and this is the second occasion where I've come without even touching him. The goal had been my orgasm, but with that accomplished, I want to touch him.

My hand reaches out to palm Cole's hard length, but he gently guides my hand back to my side.

"Don't worry, I'll have you on your knees later."

His words come out in a husky growl, and my mouth waters with anticipation. He's such a gentleman. I don't know if I should swoon or pout. I barely got to suck his dick the first night. I only got in a few licks before he took control and then he was inside me. It's something I'm looking forward to. Also, I'm excited that he still wants to have sex later. That he wasn't completely freaked out by my need to get off in the middle of dinner.

"Our food should be out shortly. Why don't you go clean up in the ladies room and I'll meet you at the table?"

I nod. "Okay."

I grab my purse off the chair and reach for the doorknob.

"Brooke?"

When I turn back Cole has my underwear in his hand, extended out to me. "I won't be able to focus at dinner if I know you're not wearing any underwear."

"Oh. I actually have another pair in my purse."

But then I take the underwear, because they're expensive and because I don't think Cole wants my wet panties in his pocket at dinner.

## 23

### COLE

After a few minutes in the office alone, thinking about my Grandma Ruth to calm my erection, I use the men's room to wash my hands, then make my way back to our table. That was certainly a first. I've never had to stop mid-dinner to pleasure my date because she wasn't going to make it through the date without an orgasm. Then again, I don't think I've ever met a woman like Brooke. And the fact that she said she had an extra pair of underwear in her purse? Is that a thing? Women do have a different anatomy than men that requires different hygiene practices. She was so wet; it had been difficult to not pull out my dick and rub all over her. If I didn't have any self-control, I would have let her suck me off in the office, but I want to wait until we can take our time. We've got all night. And tomorrow. And any other day I can pin her down for.

While I wait for Brooke, my thoughts return to weeks ago when I ran into her at the fertility clinic. After I fingered her and she ran off again, I hadn't given much thought to why she was there that day, but more that I couldn't figure out what she was about. While it's an ego boost that she is always wet and needy around me, my experience with women with elevated hormone levels tells me that it's highly possible that Brooke is on hormones for one reason or another. That her need for me to touch her in the middle of dinner is less about me and possibly more about hormones coursing through her body. I could ask her about it, but I don't want to scare her off. Reproductive health isn't always the best topic for a first date, and I don't want to throw a wrench in our evening by making her uncomfortable. I want to enjoy our time together and get to know her better. Hopefully to the point that she will share something like that with me on her own.

I watch as Brooke makes her way down the corridor by the kitchen and back toward our table. I enjoy watching her approach, noticing every little detail. Her wavy brown hair cascading over her bare shoulders, her long, toned legs striding out, and the way her dress swings around her hips as she moves. Expressive green eyes, sweet pink lips and the tiny freckle near her mouth all make me realize that I'm the one who is going to be uncomfortably shifting in my seat for the rest of the meal. If Brooke's dress was meant to torture me, it's doing its job. Even the delicate chain around her slender neck seems strategically placed to make me think of kissing her in that tender spot along her collarbone. And now, maybe only because I know what I did to her in the office, I notice a flush of color in her cheeks, a post-orgasm glow, and the expression in her green eyes is relaxed, content, sated. At least for the moment. I keep my focus on her face, knowing that thinking about anything below her neck might have me pulling her into the back room again.

She slides her purse on the back of her chair, sits and takes a sip of her wine all in one swift motion.

"Are you good?"

She smiles then sweeps a stray hair out of her face, and fuck me, she's perfect.

"So good."

Since I notified our waiter that we were ready to continue our meal when I finished in the men's room, the next course arrives shortly after Brooke.

As we eat, the conversation flows from jobs to school, hobbies to favorite places to work out, restaurants that we've tried and ones we want to try, where we've traveled and what's on our bucket list. Brooke likes the bacon-wrapped dates, and I like the calamari. We both love the spiced beef empanadas, so we battle it out to see who gets the odd third piece. Brooke snatches it up while I'm telling her about med school. I mean did I even stand a chance?

I can tell Brooke is more relaxed after her mid-meal orgasm. She's more at ease, less anxious.

At the end of the meal, Evan stops by our table to say hi.

"Brooke, this is Evan, my friend, and the chef and owner."

Knowing what I've told him about my interactions with Brooke, I hope that Evan is going to play it cool, but with the way he's looking between us and smiling, that hope is quickly lost.

He shakes Brooke's hand and smiles, "Well, Brooke, I'm glad you finally put my buddy here out of his misery."

Brooke's eyes go wide. "What do you mean?"

"Oh, he was pretty bummed that you kept running out on him." Evan pretends to whisper behind his hand to Brooke. "Between you and me, I think his ego could use some deflation."

When her gaze moves from Evan to me, her lips pinch together, doing that thing she does when she's thinking.

"Good for you, man." He squeezes my shoulder, then returns to the kitchen. I can't even be embarrassed, it's all true. Nothing I wouldn't tell Brooke myself. I want her to know that I like her. That I want to spend time with her and get to know her.

Our waiter brings out dessert, Spanish flan, on the house. Brooke takes a forkful in her mouth, licking the caramel sauce off her fork before resting it back on the plate.

"Well, you've got me now," she smiles seductively, "what are you going to do with me?"

## 24

## BROOKE

W hen we get to Cole's place, we're not even two feet in the door before he drops my bag and pulls me to him. A second later, his lips are on mine. My body immediately lights up with his touch. I love the way his firm hands grip my hips as he steers me backward toward his bedroom, his mouth never leaving mine. Yes. This is what I've been waiting for.

We're all groping hands and fevered kisses until the backs of my legs hit the bed and I drop to the mattress. My purse falls off my shoulder and hits the floor. Cole has my dress off a minute after that. I'm learning that the speed with which he takes my clothes off is not indicative of his pace during foreplay. He is impatient with clothing, but very patient and attentive once I'm naked. Almost painfully so. When Cole's mouth covers my nipple and he adds the slightest amount of suction, it's a straight shot to my clit.

"Ahhh." The sensitivity in my boobs is unreal. They're achy from the hormones and when Cole touches them, it feels like I want to slap his hand away while simultaneously pressing further into it.

"I remember how much I liked playing with these." He circles my hardened nipple with the pad of his thumb.

That's when I remember the spermicide film that Dr. Yang gave me. The second form of birth control I need to use. Ugh. Lying on this heavenly bed letting Cole have his way with me, I almost forgot. When Cole is touching me it's easy to forget about everything else.

I press up into him, our lips tangle for a hot second before I break the kiss.

"I need to use the bathroom real quick."

"Sure." He helps me up, and I grab my purse off the floor. I'm naked except for a lacy thong, and Cole watches me, unabashed from the bed with hungry eyes the whole way to the bathroom.

The bathroom feels ten degrees cooler, whether that is because of the tile floor, my lack of clothes or the loss of Cole's delicious body heat on me, or maybe all three. I'm about to search for a towel to cover up with when I spy Cole's bathrobe hanging on a hook by the glass shower. It's gray and soft and smells like Cole's aftershave. I wonder if I would be able to fit it in my bag.

Cole's bathroom is huge. I could probably fit half of my apartment in it. It has a large, glass walk-in shower and a separate soaking tub. The toilet is separated from the rest of the room with a pocket door. The vanity lights are square, opaque glass in a row of three above each sink. The mirror covers the entire wall, and there are two sinks surrounded by white quartz countertop, with dark wood cabinets beneath. Each sink is designed to have a cabinet and three different sized drawers in the middle of the vanity.

I roll up Cole's gaping robe sleeves, then get down to

business. After reading the directions, I realize maybe I should have looked at them earlier. It says you should insert it at least fifteen minutes before sex. Now, I'm going to have to sit in the bathroom for the next fifteen minutes and hope that Cole doesn't think I'm taking a shit. Or oral will likely be off the table. That gets me thinking, will this strip make me taste different? I'm kind of curious, but how would I bring that conversation up? Hey, Cole, did you notice any flavor differences between eating me out on the desk in the office at the restaurant and now? Just curious if the spicy beef empanadas added extra flavor.

I should really focus or the fifteen-minute wait is going to turn into thirty. I tear the foil packet at the designated spot and remove the film. It's a small square, but according to the directions, it can be unfolded and then inserted, using clean, dry hands. I guess I should wash my hands first. After washing and drying, I find the square film again, which I set on top of the foil packet on the counter by the sink. It's now slightly wet and when I attempt to find a corner to open it, the film sticks to my hands. I decide to start fresh, and wash my hands a second time since they're now sticky from the first film. I get the second film unfolded, after straining my eyes to find the edge and picking it apart with my fingernails, but when I attempt to put it up inside me with my finger, the film sticks to my finger and I can't get it to stay inside. My pile of failed attempts is growing, so I pull out my phone to Google it. I find an article that says to insert it quickly because it will stick to your finger, especially if you are well lubricated, it tends to slide right out. Finally, third time is a charm, and I successfully open the film and insert it quickly.

I set a timer for fifteen minutes, just as I hear a knock on the door.

"Brooke? Are you okay?" Cole's voice is deep, but gentle.

"Yes! I'll be out in a minute." Fifteen to be exact but hopefully Cole doesn't notice those extra fourteen minutes.

"Okay. I'm going to grab a water. Do you want one?"

"Sure. That would be great."

While I wait, I use the mouthwash that I find under one of the sinks. It's obviously the sink Cole uses. His electric toothbrush is plugged in next to it, along with his razor and shaving cream. The cabinet and drawers for the other sink are completely empty. If this were my bathroom, I could probably fill up both cabinets and all six of the drawers, no problem. There would be a single drawer designated to makeup and one just for face mask products.

I poke my head in the linen closet to find white and gray towels neatly rolled and sorted by size. Everything in its place. My phone timer goes off and I nearly jump. I put the unused films in my purse and head for the door.

I enter the bedroom to find Cole shirtless and under the covers, reading a book, and I think it might be the sexiest thing I've ever seen. He smiles when he sees me and my stomach clenches.

"Come here."

I set my purse on the chair nearby then move to straddle him on the bed. Cole leans in to give me a soft kiss on my lips. I anticipate the kiss to deepen, but instead he pulls back, his eyes searching mine.

"Everything okay?"

It's a simple thing to ask someone who has been in the bathroom for over twenty minutes, but for some reason, the way he's looking at me, like he actually cares, makes my heart squeeze.

"Oh, yeah. I just wanted to freshen up." I smile, then lean in toward him until our lips meet again, the slide of my tongue against his bottom lip letting him know that we can pick up right where we left off.

Cole's blue eyes are on mine as he undoes the robe ties, revealing me. I didn't bother putting my underwear back on after I inserted the spermicide film, so I'm completely naked underneath. He slides the robe off my shoulders, I help by freeing my arms, then the soft gray material pools around my hips. A second later, I'm flat on my back with Cole hovering above me. He lowers, and our lips meet in a soft, sweet kiss. I let my hands wander up the length of his muscular arms, over his broad shoulders, and down his firm chest, feeling every inch.

Cole breaks our kiss to reach over to his nightstand and pull out a condom. Seconds later, he's covered and right there. Exactly where I want him. This is what I want, what I've been daydreaming about for weeks. One more night with Cole. Yet, when he slowly thrusts into me in one perfectly-angled stroke, I realize there's no place I'd rather be right now, and that scares the hell out of me.

## 25

## COLE

When Brooke snuck out after our night together, I didn't know if I would get this again. Now that I'm on top of her, her dark hair spilled over my pillow, her green eyes looking up at me, I want to savor the moment. I love how expressive her face is. Brooke's eyes widen with anticipation of what's to come as I hook my arm under her leg to spread her farther open. When I nudge at her entrance, her lips part on an exhale as I slowly press into her heat. She's so wet, which helps me move, but it's still a tight fit. I slide in deeper, watching her face as I stretch her. Her eyes narrow and she inhales sharply, a slow thrust of my hips and I'm all the way in. So deep inside her it feels amazing. Warm, wet perfection. A whimper escapes her throat, so I pause for a moment, letting her adjust to me.

"You feel amazing," I tell her as I lower down onto my forearm, use my other hand to cup her ass, and pull her leg up to wrap around my hip. Then, I start to move slowly. Brooke lets me choose the pace for a minute, then her hips start to rock, urging me to move faster, along with her words. More, more, more.

Her eyes flutter closed, and I immediately miss seeing them. Brooke arches up into me, and I love the feel of her body flush against mine. Her softness pressed into my hardness. Her hands are everywhere, fingers groping my hair, palms squeezing my ass.

"You are so beautiful."

I snake my hand between us to apply the pressure to her clit I know she desperately needs.

Brooke comes hard, a gasp on her lips right before her body starts to tremble and her muscles clamp down tight around my dick.

I don't give her much time to recover, before I flip us so she's on top.

"I want to come watching you ride me," I tell her.

Brooke's palms press into my chest to steady herself. My hands run over the curve of her waist and up to the underside of her breasts. My fingers grope and knead her before I slide the rough pad of my thumbs over her tight nipples. I pinch and tease then enjoy the vision of Brooke's tits bouncing up and down as she rides me. Brooke's pace has increased, from slow and steady to fast and deliberate.

"Touch yourself, Brooke." I guide a hand from my chest to her clit where our fingers slide together over her swollen bud.

"Did you touch yourself thinking about me? Did you imagine it was my fingers sliding over your wet pussy?"

Brooke continues to stroke herself as my hands move to her hips to take over the pace. I slam up into her, my hands anchoring her hips down so I can push in deeper. I'm about to blow, but I want her to find her release again. The sight of Brooke bouncing on top of me while she touches herself is a goddamn dream. I can't hold off much longer.

My fingers are gripping her hips so tight I'm afraid I might bruise her. I bend my knees, angling her forward, closer toward my body to change the spot where my cock is stroking her inside. A moment later Brooke's familiar breathy pant fills the air.

Her breath turns ragged, followed by a moan that's so sexy, the second I feel her pulsing around me my orgasm hits like a freight train. I pump into her until my orgasm subsides, slowing my pace until I'm completely spent. Jesus, fuck.

Brooke collapses onto my chest, our heavy breathing the only sound that fills the room. I'm still hard inside her.

"You good?"

"Better than good." I can feel her smile on my chest. We lie quietly for a few minutes, then I slide out from beneath her so I can remove the condom. After dropping it in the bathroom trash can, I return to find Brooke snuggled up under the covers. I crawl in beside her, and use my elbow as a prop so I can look at her.

"You're going to spend the night, right? Or do I need to tie you to the bed?" I watch Brooke's eyes light up at the thought. I can't help but chuckle at her reaction.

"Another time." I drop a soft kiss to her lips.

She smiles, then our sated bodies curl into one another and drift off to sleep.

## 26

## BROOKE

I wake up alone, but hear noise coming from the kitchen. I stretch long, then curl up into a ball pulling the covers tight against me. Cole's bed is like heaven, I never want to leave it. But then I smell coffee and it's a battle my caffeine addiction wins.

I feel rested, but I don't know if I can even credit the feeling to sleep. Not sure how much I actually got last night. After our first round, we fell asleep, only to wake up a few hours later for a repeat performance. I'd say I only got five hours of sleep total, but with five orgasms, I think that equates to like eight and a half hours. I'm not exactly sure, math's always been Ellie's thing.

I'm still naked and there's no way I'm putting my dress on again. I'm too bone tired for that kind of apparel. After a perusal around Cole's bedroom for my overnight bag, I come up empty and opt to rummage through his dresser for a t-shirt.

It's soft and smells clean with a hint of Cole's man smell that must be trapped inside the dresser. When I pad out to the kitchen, I find Cole there in running shorts, his hair slightly damp. I watch his back muscles stretch and bunch as he moves his arm to push the plunger on the French press.

He hears me and turns around, a sexy grin on his face.

"Good morning."

If I thought Cole's back was a nice view, I'm completely unprepared for the visual overload I'm presented with when he turns. I know I've seen him naked, twice. And I'm pretty sure my hands were all over the same chest and abs that I'm seeing right now, but it looks different in the daylight than it feels in the dark. He felt great in the dark, but feeling something doesn't show you all its contours. The way Cole's shorts hang low on his waist and expose the indented V on either side of his hips has the ache between my thighs returning. This isn't the plan. I was going to be satisfied after one more night together but Cole's half naked body is fucking it all up.

"Where's your shirt?"

"It was sweaty from my run." Great, now I've got that visual to add to my catalogue. Sweaty workout Cole. He could probably make me take up running.

"Mmm." Flashbacks of Cole's sweaty chest hovering over me fill my mind. "I don't know how you went for a run. I can barely walk."

"That was my plan. So you couldn't escape."

He wiggles his eyebrows, then turns back toward the cabinet to grab another mug.

"Coffee?" He raises it in question.

"Yes, please."

"How do you take it?"

My brain is focused on memorizing the way Cole's back looks without a shirt on, the muscle contraction that occurs with each movement is fascinating, so it takes me a moment to realize he's talking about the coffee.

"With cream."

I move around the island to accept the piping hot mug of coffee. Cole grabs out a container of almond milk.

"This is all I have."

Of course, he doesn't have cream. That's why his body looks like that. I'm sure his fridge is full of egg whites and vegetables, protein shakes and kale. The pie-eating incident must have been a one off, lucky me to have benefitted from Cole's one moment of weakness.

There's a snarky comment on my tongue but I decide the five orgasms Cole gave me should give him a reprieve from my hormone-induced bitchy attitude. I pour the almond milk in until my coffee looks like cocoa, then take a drink and let the warm, rich liquid fill my belly. We stand in silence drinking our coffee. I want it to be awkward, but it isn't.

Because even though I don't relish the morning after, apparently Cole does. He's handsy and goofing around and in such a good mood.

"Oh, lord. Are you a morning person?"

"I started my day with a beautiful woman in my bed and a vigorous run. Wouldn't you be in a good mood?" He winks at me and my insides melt.

Cole fists the front of my shirt, his shirt, pulling me closer to him, then he presses a gentle kiss to my lips.

"I like this on you."

"Oh, I couldn't find my bag."

Cole releases me with a playful grin.

"I hid it."

I'm thinking it's some ploy to keep me naked all day, but Cole walks over to the closet by the front door and pulls out my overnight bag. Darn. Now I'll have to get dressed.

"Your track record isn't great for staying put, so I took

a precaution this time."

I can't really be insulted, so I just take another sip of my coffee.

"Are you hungry?" Cole opens his fridge. "I can make us something here, or we can go out to breakfast?"

"I'm starving, and too lazy to shower."

"Pancakes?"

"Mmm. Yes, please."

Cole nods and starts to place items from the fridge onto the counter. I don't really make pancakes at home, they're more of an eating out treat, but I don't recall ricotta cheese or Greek yogurt being ingredients. I thought it was just a box with dry mix and you add water to make the batter. Cole's version also has a banana and almond flour.

"Are these healthy pancakes?" I ask after he's got the batter all mixed up.

"They're good for you if that's what you mean." Cole pours batter on the skillet, then sets the bowl down.

"Ugh, but do they taste good or am I going to have to cover them in a whole bottle of syrup?"

Cole just chuckles good-naturedly at my snarky attitude. That's what I find most fascinating about him. He's so easygoing with all my moods and antics, only half of which might be the real me, the one not taking hormones in preparation for implantation of Ellie and Josh's embryo.

I eat my words, along with six of Cole's fluffy, nutritious and delicious pancakes. The banana makes them taste sweet; I barely use any syrup.

"Where are you putting all those?"

"My vagina. It needs to refuel."

Cole laughs as I stab another pancake with my fork.

"I mean how many calories does sex burn? And orgasms? As a gyno, I feel like you should know this information."

We finish breakfast then end up in his walk-in shower together where Cole washes me clean, only to make me dirty again with his skillful fingers. I return the favor by deep-throating his cock and swallowing. I give him a sassy smile when he looks at me with adoration and awe.

We dress and leave Cole's apartment.

I'm rested, sexually satisfied and well fed, so when Cole reaches for my hand as we walk down 15th Street it doesn't even phase me. We're technically still on his date, I suppose, so I'm trying to be accommodating. We walk for a while, checking out the shop windows and wandering with no real destination in mind. Since it's a beautiful Saturday morning everyone is out. The sidewalks are filled with runners, couples walking their dogs, women walking with yoga mats into the coffee shop.

We rent scooters and ride them on the Cherry Creek trail until I nearly crash into a railing and decide I'm not only a hazard to the public but myself. We stop at REI where Cole looks at camping gear. I browse the women's clothing section, then remember that there's no point in looking at tank tops because anything I buy now isn't going to fit once I get pregnant. We eat a late lunch at Amato's Alehouse, a brewery that took over an old fountain shop that overlooks downtown. I order a mimosa because it's Saturday and Cole orders a beer. He's such a guy. I watch him take a sip. I feel more relaxed with him now than I did at dinner. I feel less on edge, more at ease. The hormonal assault on my body must have decided to take the weekend off. It's been years since I've shared a meal, let alone multiple meals in the same day, with one man.

"So is this how you normally spend a Saturday?" I ask.

"I'm on call one Saturday a month." Cole takes a sip of his beer. "The night I met you at the diner, I had just gotten off a shift at the hospital. But, when I'm not working, I usually go for a run, maybe meet up with some buddies to play golf or tennis, or depending on the time of year catch a Buff's game in Boulder. There's a group of us that tries to go to every home game."

Last night we discovered that we both went to the University of Colorado in Boulder. Cole was years ahead of me, graduated and on to medical school before I was even out of high school. I'm not really into football, and I haven't been to a game since I was a student, but part of me wants to sign up for this weird Saturday tradition of tailgating and team spirit just to hang out with Cole. I don't normally take interest in the extra-curricular activities of the guy I'm fooling around with, and I definitely don't do any of them with them, so I'm not sure where this strange desire is coming from. I remind myself that I'll be pregnant and he'll likely have moved on to a former Miss Colorado contestant by the time football season comes around.

"So, you play golf?" I ask.

"Yeah, do you?"

"Not really, but I like the cute skirts. And I like balls."

Cole's lip does that smirk where one side lifts up. The one that makes my panties melt off.

"We could play some time. I could teach you."

I'm envisioning Cole behind me, his muscular arms over mine as he shows me how to swing the club, me in one of those golf skirts that would provide easy access if he wanted to, and that's all the visual I need to agree.

"Yeah, we should do that," I tell him, but then realize my baby bump will likely object in a few months.

All these tentative plans Cole is suggesting are not pregnancy friendly. Hmm, I guess we'll just have to stick with sex and eating pancakes.

## 27

## COLE

While we finish our lunch, I tell Brooke about my sister and parents. She tells me a few stories about her and Ellie growing up. She doesn't mention her parents much. I can tell after the way she reacted last night that it's still hard for her to talk about. I don't want to press her on it, knowing she'll tell me about them when she's ready.

After lunch, we pass by the farmer's market at 15th and Boulder. I've never been before. Most of the vendors are packing up for the day, but we manage to snag two donuts from the Doughnut Club truck. Brooke is in awe when she discovers that they top the donut with the donut hole, like you would put a cherry on top of a sundae, and both are covered in frosting and sprinkles. I can't see her eyes behind her sunglasses, but the little hum she makes when she takes the first bite lets me know she's enjoying it.

On our way out Brooke buys the remaining flowers from a floral vendor. They're an assortment of pinks, purples and oranges, with greenery added in for filler. They remind me of Brooke's apartment. I attempt to pay, but the vendor is cash only so Brooke's twenty-dollar bill wins. After her purchase she hands them to me.

"For you."

"Aren't I supposed to buy you flowers?"

She shrugs. "Your apartment needs more color."

I pull her in for a kiss. "Thank you." She tastes like chocolate, and I wonder if I can convince her to spend another night. Then, I look at the flowers, and know full well I don't have anything but a drinking glass to put them in.

Later, we're walking along Platte Street when Brooke pulls me into a small home furnishing store. It's mostly kitchenware, vases, pillows and throws. I follow her around the store as she points out different pieces that she likes, mentioning a townhome she just staged and how perfect that pillow would have been. She stops in front of an assortment of ceramic vases, and I pause beside her, shifting the flowers into my other hand.

I glance around the store and catch the eye of another guy holding who I presume to be his girlfriend's purse while she examines a set of dishes. He lifts his chin in acknowledgment.

"They've got us trained, huh?"

I nod and lift the flowers. "Yeah."

Moments later his girlfriend mentions she's ready to leave and takes her purse back as they exit the store.

Is it odd that something as mundane as following Brooke around a home goods store gives me the most satis-faction? Imagining this is our usual Saturday routine, the farmer's market and picking out home décor. Is it crazy that I want it to be? After just one date? To hell with golf and beers with the guys, listening to them grumble about their wives and children. This is what I want.

"This one is perfect." Brooke lifts a small white vase

with gold edging up to me in victory. She has no idea I was thinking the exact same thing about her. I pay for the vase, and we leave.

We spend the rest of the afternoon walking around near downtown's Union Station, then we cross back over the Millennium pedestrian bridge, a cable-stayed bridge that connects downtown to the Platte River North neighborhood where my condo building is located, and decide to grab a spot under a tree in Commons Park to people-watch. Commons Park is a large open-space area that draws in people playing kickball or soccer, catching frisbees or throwing balls for their dogs. I love the fact that Denver is an extremely active city. Couples walk by with strollers, dogs leap for frisbees and a rowdy group of guys in camp chairs drink their beers. Usually I'd post up with some friends to play catch and toss a few back. But, just sitting here with Brooke, I am completely content.

I've got my back against the tree, and Brooke is in between my legs, the back of her body pressed against my front. I smell her hair and can't resist pressing kisses against the back of her neck. Fuck, I've never wanted to defile anyone in a public place as bad as I want to Brooke right now. Getting to know Brooke today has made me exponentially more attracted to her, if that was even possible considering before she just had to walk in the room and I got a hard-on. Our sexual chemistry is off the charts, but now I know there's more to it. We can talk nonstop for hours, or sit in quiet contentment. She's a breath of fresh air in what has been a stagnant personal life.

After last night and our entire day together, I've gotten a better understanding of who she is. She loves her job, shopping, reading mysteries and thrillers, and watching 80s movies. When she's excited, she talks with her hands. Between the carefree moments of laughter and teasing, there's the vulnerability that I didn't understand before. She's guarded with good reason. I can't imagine how I would have coped if my parents were taken from me at such a pivotal time in my life. I have a strange desire to console her, to take care of her...be her protector.

I've always been protective of my sister, but this safeguarding is different, more primal. I've never had a connection like this with any of the other women I've been with. I cared about them, but those relationships were surface level. A quick 'how was your day' tossed out before we hopped in bed.

I run my hands up the length of her bare thighs, letting my fingers roam underneath her cut-off jean shorts. I can feel her arch back into me, and I groan when her ass presses into my dick. I want her again.

"I think we should go back to my place before we get ticketed for indecent exposure," I whisper in her ear.

"We're still clothed." She cocks her head with a twinkle in her eye as she whispers back.

"I know, but I'm seconds away from stripping you down naked, and I think we should be in private for that."

Brooke laughs, then lets me pull her up so we can race the few blocks back to my place.

## 28

## BROOKE

"**D**o you know where my bra is?" I pull my tank top over my head, without the missing garment.

Cole lowers the glass he was chugging water from to respond.

"It might be in the couch."

He smiles as he watches me pull on my shorts and zip them up, eyeing me hungrily, like a man who didn't just bend me over his couch. I move back toward the living room, but Cole quickly intercepts. Wrapping his hands around my waist, he lifts me onto the kitchen counter, next to the flowers I painstakingly arranged for fifteen minutes while Cole begrudgingly watched. I was waiting for the spermicidal film to take effect, and needed to buy myself some time. I don't know exactly why I bought the flowers. Cole's apartment needed more color. Flowers are always nice because they only last a few weeks and can easily be changed out. They're temporary.

He's still shirtless and I'm forced to palm the warm skin covering his muscular shoulders to balance myself.

"We can grill steaks, or do you want to order in? No

bras required." Cole winks and my stomach does that jittery somersault thing that's usually reserved for the first drop on a rollercoaster or the last twenty-five percent of a John Grisham thriller, but I'm also starting to associate with Cole looking at me.

"Dinner? I feel like we just ate lunch."

Cole laughs. "That was five hours ago."

I glance at the clock, and am shocked to see it's already seven o'clock. I don't know when it happened, but somewhere between Cole's healthy banana pancakes, our aimless wandering around the neighborhood, and lazy afternoon in the park, I forgot to be disgruntled by all the time we were spending together and started enjoying Cole's company. That's when it hits me. All day with Cole, I haven't been feeling like a horny, sex-crazed maniac. He can still make me wet with a single look, but my hormones must have leveled out with all the stimulation my body has received courtesy of Cole. I smile, knowing that I've gotten exactly what I came for. Hot, toe-curling sex that I will be able to fantasize about when I'm pregnant with Ellie and Josh's baby. I feel like a new woman. I'm a genius. Everything is working out perfectly.

But when my gaze returns to Cole's to find his intense, yet comforting blue eyes scanning my face, a knot forms in my belly. Okay, maybe genius isn't the right word. In the midst of seeking relief for my overactive libido, my brain didn't exactly think through this whole thing. I agreed to Cole's date request with the sole focus being to have sex with him, but didn't think about the implications of getting to know more than his body. The sex last night and today was amazing, but more than that, I found myself really liking him, as more than a giver of orgasms.

And there lies the problem. I don't want to like him. I've got plans that don't involve a sexy doctor. My life right now is a bit complicated, nothing like Cole's put together one. If I stay, we'll eat steak and snuggle on the couch, and have more amazing sex, and then I'll never want to leave. But, I have to leave. I got what I came for, and Cole seemed to enjoy himself, too, so I can't really feel bad for him.

So, when he's staring at me now, massaging my thigh with his thumb and waiting for my answer, I think of the only logical response.

"Actually, I can't stay." The second the words leave my mouth, they feel hollow, forced, like I didn't really plan to say them. But they're out there now and it's for the best.

Cole opens his mouth to say something, but stops short, then nods. "Okay."

He moves back a little, so I can slide off the counter, then I head for his bedroom to get my stuff. Cole follows.

"Yeah, I've got some stuff I have to do." I make a non-committal shrug because keeping things vague is always best. "Some stuff around my apartment…I've been putting off for a while and, um, need to get done."

Vague is one thing, but lame is another. My rambling excuse is completely unconvincing. I half expect Cole to push back and persuade me to stay. If he only knew that it wouldn't take much convincing. I gather my bag from the chair in the corner. When I turn around Cole is there with my missing bra. I almost expected him to hide some of my stuff or some cute shit to get me to stay. Maybe I even wanted him to in some way.

"Thanks." I take it from him and toss it in my bag. There's no way I'm going to attempt to put it on right now. With my warring thoughts and uncertain emotions, I just need to get out of this place.

It takes me a moment to realize that Cole is fine with me not staying. He even retrieves my makeup bag from the bathroom and hands it to me. I don't know why, I guess I thought there would be more of a resistance. He doesn't have to drop to his knees and beg, but a simple 'I'd really like you to stay' would have been sufficient. It's the hormones, I convince myself. They're making everything feel off balance. Making me think I want things that I know I really don't.

The truth is I'm a liar who lies. I don't have anything to do at home, but I don't like what it means if I stay the night with him again. It means I like him. That I've been with him for twenty-four hours. In. A. Row. Which is a really long time to be hanging out with someone, and still want to continue hanging out with them. Besides, I'm not some needy girl who attaches herself to a guy and lets him become the only thing she cares about. We went on one date. I've got a life and things to do. I'm keeping it cool, casual and easy breezy as usual. So why am I feeling off about all of this…

———

On the drive to my apartment, Cole chats about all the construction going on in the Highlands neighborhood, how nice the new bike lanes are. I can't even focus on the conversation, my head is a mess of contradictions, as I convince myself that if he really liked me he'd try harder to spend time with me, but I'd still have to turn him down because this is all for the best. He doesn't say anything about seeing each other again, he just opens the passenger door and gives me a kiss on the cheek, which is fine, because that was my plan anyway. I'm glad that I didn't have to deal with any of the awkwardness of making future plans that I don't intend to keep. As I key in the code to the building, I hear him drive off and turn to see him rounding the corner. So what? That's what I wanted—what the hell is wrong with me? In my apartment, I head straight to my bedroom to unpack my bag, hoping to dispel any remaining evidence of my date with Cole. Once the contents of my bag are dumped onto my bed, I move quickly, tossing shoes into my closet, putting toiletries back into my bathroom, and throwing dirty clothes in my hamper. Finally, I'm done. Except there's one item that doesn't have a place. Cole's t-shirt. It must have gotten tossed in my bag when I changed out of it this morning. Before I can fight against the urge, it's in my hands and I'm holding it up to my nose. It smells like fresh laundry with Cole's masculine scent and a hint of pancakes. I shove it under my pillow, after assuring myself I will not sleep in it tonight.

With all my baggage unpacked, I head to my tiny kitchen to make a cup of noodle soup for dinner, then plop down on my sofa to read a book.

But, I can't get into it, I'm not feeling the reading vibe. It makes my apartment too quiet. It's a mystery and the hero happens to be described just like Cole. I set it aside and turn on the television, scrolling through Netflix, hoping it will set me into a binge-watching mood, but it doesn't work. Even a *Love It or List It* marathon on HGTV can't keep my attention.

I decide reading or TV watching isn't going to cut it. I need something to keep my hands busy. Since I missed movie night with Ellie and Josh, where I had planned to paint my nails, I decide that sounds like the best way to be productive. I also apply a hydrating face mask before I paint my nails, because aging, dry skin is no joke. See, I did have things to do tonight. Then I have to sit still while my nails dry, and that's when my mind starts to wander. I check my phone. Nothing. From Ellie or Sam or anyone else. The feeling of disappointment is unusual. I check my social media, all of them, hoping something will lead me down a time-sucking rabbit hole. It doesn't work. I just end up stalking Cole, who doesn't have any social media accounts, except for LinkedIn, so all I find is his work history and school degrees. Everything he already shared with me last night. And his work head shot. He looks hot, in a professional way. It's better than nothing, but nevertheless unsatisfying. Most of the guys I've hooked up with usually have a plethora of thirsty workout selfies on Instagram to peruse. Or the highlight video from their band's latest gig.

Ugh. I feel restless. Why do I feel restless? I'm a single woman and it's Saturday night. It shouldn't be hard to enjoy it. I love down time. Down time is my jam. Two minutes later, I check my phone again. Nothing. I text Ellie to confirm our dinner plans tomorrow, then I text Sam to see what she's up to. Ellie sends a confirmation with a smartass remark about bringing good wine. Minutes later, Sam replies to my message saying she's getting drinks at Tavern Uptown with her fashion merchandising friends, and asks if I want to join. I've been out with them before, they're a fun group, but I don't know if I really want to get dressed and go out. She also asks how my date with Cole was. I spend a good fifteen minutes trying to word and re-word my response, not sure exactly what to say or how to describe our time together, until I finally give up and send her an eggplant emoji. That sums it up, right?

Speaking of eggplants, I'm kicking myself for not buying batteries when Cole and I passed the Target downtown today. I wasn't thinking about my vibrator then because I had Cole, the real thing. It wasn't at the forefront of my mind anymore because I didn't feel like I was going to hump a lamp post or spontaneously combust from lack of penetration. Instead, I had Cole pulling me into random shops and making me laugh.

I just feel off, and I can't quite pinpoint what I need. Sitting on the couch is not doing it for me. With my nails now dry, I decide to do some push-ups because Cole's hard body made mine feel soft, and maybe getting my blood pumping will move this funky energy I've got. I'm in the middle of my third push-up when I start to wonder how his dinner was, if he grilled a steak out on his balcony, or if he decided on takeout. I'm guessing he didn't eat a cup of noodles. Push-up five gets me wondering what he's going to do the rest of the night. The two nights I spent at his house, we were in bed the entire time, so I wonder what a night in with Cole is like. Does he watch sports? Home renovation shows? A special on the history channel? Or maybe he reads? He said he likes suspense thrillers and I wonder if he's read Dean Koontz's latest. I just finished it last week. I could text him to see if he wants to borrow it. I'm mid-push-up when it hits me. What the hell am I even talking about? I'm not going to text him. I'm not going to call him and I'm most definitely not going to see him.

It's Cole. This funky feeling is about Cole. My arms are shaky, and I collapse onto my living room floor, then roll over to stare at the ceiling. I don't want to think about what he's doing. This is exactly the distraction I didn't need. He tricked me into a date so I could get sex; now I know more than just how his dick feels when he thrusts into me, he's got hobbies and thoughts and jokes. He's a person, one that I kind of like to hang out with, and that's annoying. The sexually frustrated, hormonal mess I was just days ago is nothing compared to the emotionally conflicted person I've become in a mere twenty-four hours. This is not good.

My fingers feel for my phone on the couch. Once I have my phone, I type out a quick text, then pull myself off the floor to go shower. Apparently, I need a distraction from my distraction.

———

By the time I shower, get ready, and call an uber, Tavern Uptown is packed. I can tell this by looking through the window, from outside the bar, in the line I'm waiting in to get in. I text Sam to let her know I'm outside and will be in soon. Everyone around me is chatting with friends or their significant other, or the date they're with. Three twenty-somethings in front of me debate which filter to use on the selfie they just took. I don't know if it's the selfie talk or the young couple making out behind me, but I'm feeling awkward and out of place. A few people leave so the line shifts.

Finally, I make it inside. It's crowded, and lively. Odd as it sounds, the upbeat dance music and the loud chatter around me make me feel more relaxed. A girl nearly runs me over with two beers in her hand, but I can't be too mad because I manage to snag the coveted spot at the bar that she just exited. I decide to order a drink before I look for Sam. I'm sipping my cocktail, waiting for my tab when the guy on the stool next to me bumps his elbow into me.

"Oh, shit. I'm sorry."

"That's okay." I wipe up the spillage with the bar napkin under my drink.

"I feel bad. Can I buy you a drink?"

My eyes lift from the soggy napkin to him. He's cute. Brown hair, brown eyes, a small smattering of facial hair that gives him a rugged bad boy kind of vibe. Ripped jeans and a band t-shirt complete his look. He seems like the type of guy I would normally go for. A perfect night of fun that wouldn't call me the next day, or withhold sex in order to take me out on a date. He's more my speed. Fast lane, going nowhere.

I smile and lift my drink. "How about the next one?"

We chat as I finish my drink and let him buy me another. I'm taking a sip of my second drink when Sam finds me at the bar.

"Sam!" My hug is more like a tackle. "There you are!"

"Hey. I didn't know you were in yet. I thought you'd come find our table." She looks from me to Dex. That's his name. Yup, just change one letter and you get the word *sex*. He said his real name is Dexter, but that he doesn't go by it because it doesn't fit his image. I get it. I'm also getting that he is not the brightest bear in the woods. He'd hurt himself taking a selfie at the gym.

"Hi, I'm Dex."

In case she missed it, I follow up.

"This is Dex."

Sam shakes his hand.

"Excuse us a minute," she says as she pulls me to the side, away from Dex.

"Sure." Dex doesn't seem to be too bothered by Sam's curtness. He's a pretty chill guy. I actually think he might be high.

"What are you doing?" she asks.

"I'm having a drink. Dex bought me a drink."

"I was surprised you came out. I thought you were still with Cole."

"No, I jumped that ship." I mean for it to sound casual, but my flippant comment about Cole makes my stomach twist with regret. "He's an amazing guy, he's just not for me."

"Why? What happened?" Sam presses.

"Nothing. Everything. He's hot and smart and funny and gives me lots of orgasms. He's not what I was looking for." I can't meet her gaze, so I reach for my drink instead.

"What were you looking for exactly?"

"You know. One night. A fling. Sex to tide me over while I pursue the surrogacy."

Sam's eyes narrow at me.

"It sounds like you two had a good time, but now you're just done with him?"

"Oh. We had a fun date and I had like six orgasms. He made me pancakes, and we walked around downtown and people-watched in the park. He asked me to stay the night again but I just thought that wasn't for the best..."

Sam's eyebrows are at her hairline.

"You're batshit crazy."

"Hey!" I exclaim, knowing full well she's right. I'm feeling it, too.

"If your friends can't tell you, who can?" Sam shakes her head and rolls her eyes. "Why are you out here chatting up Dex with the weird sideburns when you could be in Dr. Hottie's bed?"

"Because..." I know there is a whole list of reasons. I reminded myself of them before I came out tonight.

"Because the whole point of hooking up with the doctor was to have some good sexy times before you get pregnant with Ellie's baby?" Sam finishes my thoughts for me.

"Exactly." See, she does get me.

"So why not keep having those sexy times? Especially now that you have to wait another month for Ellie's egg retrieval thingy."

"Because I can't be in his bed every night that I want to or I'll never leave!" The panic I felt earlier is back. Feelings and emotions I'm not used to dealing with are flooding my body.

Sam smiles, and raises her eyebrows at me pointedly. I feel like I've been caught. I'm a helpless fly that's wandered into her sticky web.

"What?" I ask, calmer now and hopefully cool.

"I just wanted you to admit that you like the doctor. That's all."

"There, I admit it. I like him." I take another sip of my drink. "It doesn't mean anything. We're not a thing. We're not together. It was just sex. And one date." I firmly hold up my index finger in hopes that the reminder will sink in. It was just *one* date. I mean, what's all the fuss about?

"Uh-huh." She smirks at me. Her eyes wander to the back of Dex's head. He's talking to his buddy who's wearing a SpongeBob SquarePants shirt. Weird. Suddenly I'm wondering why I was talking to this guy. Maybe if I finish this drink Dex's appeal will return.

"How about you kiss Dex and if he is a better kisser than Cole, then I won't mention Cole's name again."

My eyes narrow into slits. This feels like a trick.

"What if he isn't a better kisser?"

Sam laughs. "Then you know what you need to do."

I side-eye her as I move past her to get closer to Dex.

"Hey. I'm back."

I waste no time.

"We should kiss."

He looks shocked for a second, but then starts to lean in. "Wait." I hold up a hand. Dex looks like he might need some coaching. Cole would never need coaching, damn it. This feels like a futile effort. "Don't just kiss me. It's got to be your best effort. This is important. Lives hang in the balance."

Dex's eyes go wide, and I get the distinct impression that he's not a good performer under pressure.

Sam just shakes her head and rolls her eyes behind

him. Dex makes a show of moving his head side to side, like he's trying to loosen up before a workout. Oh, man. This isn't going to go well. He leans in and then his lips are on mine. It's...nice. His lips are soft, and I'm pretty sure I feel a tongue ring, but it's nothing compared to the way I feel when Cole kisses me. The way my whole body lights up. The way I can't make it through dinner without him touching me.

With Cole, when he pulls back, I want to lean in. When Dex pulls back, I just sigh in defeat.

"How'd I do?"

"Uh, it was nice." I shrug.

"Cool." He doesn't seem to get that nice isn't enough, it's not Cole.

I want to feel bad for Dex, but a busty blonde is already moving into my seat at the bar, so I think he'll be all right. I turn to Sam who is already handing me my purse when I tell her, "I gotta go."

## 29

## BROOKE

The drink and a half I had at the bar gives me enough courage to get me in the uber and to Cole's building. Once I'm there, standing outside, I start to freak out. What was the reason I decided to come here? Because I realized that Cole makes me feels things that no one else does? Was that what Sam convinced me of? I guess I didn't take much convincing, I only kissed one guy, I could have taken more of a data sample to argue my case. That I'm just a woman on fertility hormones that can't get enough sex. This doesn't mean Cole and I are together. It just means I really like his dick and he's fun to be with. Right?

Okay. Maybe those drinks were stronger than I thought. I check the time on my phone, it's ten-thirty, not really that late for a Saturday night. What if he's not even here? Maybe he's forgotten about me and he's out in a bar kissing a random woman. I send him a text.

**I'm here.**
**Where?**
**Your building. Outside.**

He doesn't respond again, which has me wondering if he thinks I'm a complete wackadoodle. Maybe he's calling security to haul me away. A large man in a suit approaches and opens the door. I brace for a stern lecture but he smiles and holds the door open.

"Miss Ryan?"

"Yes."

"I'm Robert." He extends his hand and I shake it.

"Brooke."

I recognize Robert from the night I came home with Cole after the diner, he had been sitting behind the concierge desk and Cole had said goodnight to him. I wonder if he recognizes me, and also if he thinks I only frequent Cole's place for late-night booty calls.

"Dr. Matthews requested I send you up."

"Oh, okay."

He motions me inside. I follow him through the lobby and to the elevator bank where he calls the elevator for me, then swipes a key card and selects Cole's floor.

"Have a good evening."

"Thanks. You, too."

I have an urge to ask Robert how many times he has to escort women up to Dr. Matthew's condo, like is this a typical Saturday night? I know Cole was on call the Saturday I met him at the diner after his hospital shift, but if he hadn't met me would there have been another woman on her way over?

The elevator ride is quick, so I'm pondering this when the elevator door opens, and I step off to find Cole standing in the doorway to his condo.

He's in a soft gray t-shirt, similar to the one I have stashed under my pillow at home, and jeans, his bare feet make his casual look even sexier. I don't have a foot fetish but there's something about a man in jeans and bare feet that really does it for me.

"Oh, hi." I'm a little caught off guard that he's right here. That I didn't have time to check my hair in the elevator wall's reflection or reapply lip gloss. And that I didn't have at least ten minutes to pace in his hallway before I talked myself out of knocking on his door.

He smirks at me in that way that tells me he knows all of this.

"I was just in the neighborhood and wanted to say 'hi.'" I move closer to his door, closer to him. "And let you know I have your shirt. I need to return it. It's at home, though." I have no game plan, which is clear from the ramblings coming out of my mouth.

Cole's standing in the doorway, hands braced against the door frame, which makes his arms flex and his biceps strain against the soft cotton of his shirt. His stance isn't exactly welcoming. He's taking up the entire doorway, not making a move to let me come inside.

"Did you have a good night?" He takes in my appearance. A black spaghetti-strap romper and wedge sandals, my hair is curled and I'm in full makeup. "Did you get all your 'stuff' done?"

Oh yeah. The stuff.

"Yes. Very productive evening." I clear my throat and try not to sway. I'm not really drunk, more intoxicated by Cole's presence. I wait for him to bust me on my little white lie. Make me feel silly for showing up here after I ditched him earlier. But he doesn't. Instead, he pins me with his gorgeous blue eyes, and my heart starts beating a mile a minute.

"Here's the thing, Brooke. I like you."

I can't quite get a read on his expression. It's not exactly inviting, but not quite hostile. A little intimidating and a lot sexy alpha male confidence. While he's exuding confidence that somehow knew I'd be back, my legs feel weak and shaky.

All he said was that he liked me, but the way his blue eyes are staring at me so intensely, it sends a wave of heat up my neck and across my cheeks. There's really no point in mentioning what his stare is doing to my lady parts, that's always a given. Wet and needy. That's the state I am constantly in around Cole, and right now is no exception.

"I like you, but I don't like playing games." His gaze lowers to my romper, then the expanse of bare leg I'm currently sporting.

"Games?" I question.

His eyes flick back up to mine.

"I don't like when you run. You don't have to tell me anything you don't want to. If you want to talk, I'll listen. That can be on your terms." He continues, "But there are things I want from you. I want to take you on dates, hold your hand, and watch movies on the couch with you."

He looks so earnest that my heart cracks open a little bit. Cole's hand moves from the door frame to my shoulder. When his thumb slides the thin strap of my romper over my shoulder until it falls loosely down my arm, my whole body starts to vibrate. Just his thumb grazing my skin makes my entire body light up.

"I also want you in my bed every night."

His fingers gently drag over my exposed collarbone, downward toward my chest. I wonder if he can feel my heart racing. I think I might be having a heart attack. I know his specialty is vaginas but I hope he can at least administer CPR before the ambulance arrives.

I'd wonder if I was still breathing, but it's actually the loudest sound in the hallway, so I know it's still happening.

My thoughts are scattered, my sole focus on where he is touching me. Where he's drawing me in.

"We don't have to label it if that's what you want." Cole's thumb slides over my nipple, the fabric of my romper still between us, covering me, yet I feel completely exposed. "But that's what I need right now."

I focus on the words 'right now' because all the other words he is saying are so foreign to me. Right now means in this moment, for the time being, temporary. That's something I'm familiar with. I can do that.

I exhale a slow, shaky breath.

"Okay."

As soon as the word leaves my lips, Cole's arms are around my ass, lifting my legs until they wrap around his waist. He backs us into his condo, then kicks the door shut. There are no more words after that.

## 30

## BROOKE

I would have to say that even though I was originally against the whole dates and hand-holding stuff, now that I'm getting off on a regular basis, I feel more human and less like a walking hormonal bitch. So, it's a win-win.

It's only been two weeks since our date, yet we've managed to fall into a steady routine. Either Cole cooks or I pick us up takeout on my way to his place, we have sex, reheat the food and eat while watching a show, have sex again then read before lights out. It's a nice routine. I'm like a squirrel collecting nuts before winter, except in my case I'm racking up orgasms before a dry spell.

Ellie had her egg retrieval procedure this week. Josh went with her for that and I have to admit I was glad to not make an appearance at the clinic. I don't have any more appointments until the bloodwork before the actual embryo implantation procedure in two weeks. I don't really get the process, it's a lot of timing and hormones and science that I just don't understand. I've decided to not worry about it and just do what they tell me to. And, until then, I'm going to live my life.

Which currently involves sitting in Cole's bed together reading. Well, Cole's reading and I'm watching him read. The romantic suspense novel I'm attempting to read isn't holding my attention as well as Cole is. He's very distracting. The way his brow furrows when he's concentrating, and of course there's the fact that he's shirtless.

I pull the covers back and move to straddle him. "What part are you on?"

The book is a mystery by an author we've discovered we both like. I've already read it, so I gave it to him. He sets the open book down on the bed to mark his spot. He smiles, his blue eyes focusing on me.

"Mmm. The good part."

Cole runs his hands up my thighs. I'm wearing one of his t-shirts and conveniently no underwear. Because what's the point? I've started putting the spermicidal film in right after dinner to decrease wait time. I really can be a planner when I want to.

Cole's grin turns devilish when my shirt reaches the tops of my thighs and he exposes me.

I know I'm already wet, but I'm trying to play it cool, so I'm attempting to not sit directly on him, and it's a hell of a thigh workout, let me tell you. But then it's all for naught because Cole grabs my hips and presses me down onto his lap, where I can feel his growing length beneath me. I bite my lip, stifling a groan. The pressure on my clit feels amazing. Cole's eyes are fixed to where he's moving me over his length, his black boxer briefs the only thing between us. When I look down I can see where my slick-ness has left the material shiny and wet.

"I want to feel you on me," he says before lifting me up

so he can slide down his boxers. "Is this okay?" he asks before he settles me back on top of him.

I nod. It's more than okay. Sitting on top of him with nothing between us is fucking awesome. Feeling his bare, warm skin underneath me makes me wild. Cole's so rigid now, that every time I slide back his dick lifts up in response. I shift my hips forward again, this time sliding all the way to the crown before retreating. Cole sits forward, his dick now sandwiched between us. His hands move to the hem of my shirt to lift it up and over my head.

He sucks a nipple into his mouth. The sensation travels all the way down to my clit. My hands roam over his back, dig in his hair, then move down his arms, wanting to feel all of him. It feels like we're teenagers dry humping, but without clothes, and I'm so wet I slide right over him. It's wet humping, I'm sure that's a thing. Or maybe that's just called sex.

I'm so into it, I don't even realize that when I slide back down, the tip of Cole's dick nudges inside me. All I know is it feels amazing and I don't want to stop.

"I should get a condom." Cole's mouth rains wet kisses along my jaw and down my neck.

"I know."

I slide over him again, the width of his crown spreading me open.

"Fuck, Brooke. Do you know how good this feels?"

It feels so good, it takes two more strokes for my brain to catch up and for me to remember that this is how people get knocked up without medical intervention. I pull back.

"Shit. We need a condom."

Cole's eyes are filled with lust as he holds my hips in place, not entering me, but just sliding me along his length.

"Right." He quickly lifts me up and away from his bare cock.

I lean back on my hands while Cole retrieves a condom from his bedside table. He makes quick work of ripping open the package and rolling it on. Then, he's nudging at my entrance, and I slide down onto him, his hips meeting mine with one delicious thrust. It's so good. I can only imagine how it would feel to have him bare inside me.

I'm lazily riding him now, letting him lift me up and down by the hips.

"You are so beautiful." The adoration in Cole's eyes makes my stomach flutter and my heart race.

Cole grips my hips, his fingers digging into my ass as he angles me to find that sensitive place inside.

My orgasm hits suddenly, and seconds later Cole's release follows.

————

I've been really into my skincare routine lately. Tonight, I'm trying another face mask. It's anti-aging and is supposed to tighten your face until you look old and wrinkly. Seems counter-intuitive, but I saw it on an Instagram ad and it got great reviews. Plus, I've got to stay on top of my appearance, lord knows it's going to start going downhill once I'm pregnant. I'm glad we already had sex because Cole seeing what I might look like in forty years probably isn't going to be a turn on.

It's a clear gel type mask that comes with a small brush to paint it on with. I dip the brush in to the jar and start to apply it to my face.

Cole enters the bathroom. He's shirtless, a pair of cotton pajama pants hanging low on his waist. I'm painting on my mask as I watch him splash his face with water then pat it dry with a hand towel. The difference in our facial routines is not lost on me. Annoying.

He turns to lean against the counter and watch me.

"I've got a work event on Saturday night."

"Oh, okay. Maybe I'll get dinner with Sam then. Or see if Ellie wants to catch that new romcom," I muse out loud while I continue slathering it on until I'm well coated.

"No, it's Rose Medical Center's annual fundraising gala. You'll be going with me."

"Shoot. I already have plans." I fake pout like I'm sad to miss but Cole just shakes his head.

"Nice try."

The cool gel felt so good going on, but it's drying now and starting to tighten my skin. It feels like someone is turning a crank behind my head, pulling everything tight, and making it hard to move my face. Making a facial expression is absolutely impossible, which may be a good thing since I feel like I would either have a look of horror or panic on my face. Hospital gala? Would any of the doctors that I've seen be there? Would they recognize me? Maybe I can fake an illness.

My face is so tight that I can't fully move my mouth, making it difficult to form words. It says to not talk during the thirty-minute drying process, it didn't say that you physically won't be able to.

"I don haf anyting ta wear."

Cole kisses me on the head, "We'll go shopping," then moves to leave the room.

"Ey," I call after him, out the side of my mouth because that's all I can manage to move, but he's already gone. I'll have to hand it to him, Cole picked an opportune time to bring this up, one where I can't speak for thirty minutes. Now all I can do is wait patiently until everything starts to crack.

## 31

## BROOKE

If I thought the white doctor coat was hot, Cole in a tux is downright lethal. He's already dressed, and I'm lagging behind. I got distracted watching him shave, so I had to nix the fake eyelashes. Because, priorities. I'm pulling on my dress in Cole's walk-in closet when he strides in and leans on the closet door frame. He glances at his watch.

"Do I need to fuck you before we go? Or will the two orgasms from this morning hold you over?" There's a smug grin plastered on his face. "I'd hate to miss the entrée."

Smug bastard.

I narrow my eyes at him. "You better watch what you say or you're not going to get any action tonight."

Cole chuckles, and I hate that I can't even threaten to withhold sex because he knows that it would not just punish him, but me, too. Jerk.

He watches me step into my dress; his eyebrows raise in surprise.

"You're not wearing any underwear?" Cole's voice is

husky, and I notice the way his lustful eyes follow the dress as the fabric moves over my ass and up my back.

Okay, maybe it's not a surprise, but more like wariness at the idea that I'm going to be completely naked under my dress all night and he won't be able to touch me. He thinks I'm the sex-crazed one, but I know he's just as affected.

It's strange how we've just entered this compatible living situation. I've rarely spent any time at my place. Only to pick up clothes, check my mail and water the plants. I even brought a few of them over to Cole's because he doesn't have any greenery and I can't live anywhere that doesn't have plants. Not that we're living together, but proximity is a requirement for sex and foot rubs. And Cole is excellent at both.

I'm starting to wonder if things with Cole could work out even when I get pregnant with Ellie and Josh's baby. He's a gynecologist, he can't be that adverse to pregnant women, he's around them frequently. Not that it means he wants to date one, and have sex with one that isn't pregnant with his child, but it's a starting point, right?

I've thought about telling him multiple times. Just last night the words were on the tip of my tongue. We had just finished Chinese take-out when he refilled my glass of Bread & Butter rosé, my favorite kind, which he now has stocked in his wine fridge, then he brought up a newly recorded *Love It or List It* from his DVR, pulled my feet into his lap and started massaging them. I was speechless. Literally no words. He told me I seemed stressed out lately and he wanted to help me relax. It would have been a perfect opening for the surrogacy conversation if I wasn't blissed out by his thumbs finding all my pressure points. And later when Hilary knocked the remodel out of the park, but the owners were still convinced by David to list their home, I didn't even care. I was too preoccupied with Cole sliding my panties down my legs, a mischievous grin on his lips. Just thinking about it makes my insides clench.

I know I'm being selfish. The past three weeks have been amazing with Cole, and I'm afraid he won't want to be with me, almost as much as I'm afraid he will. What would that even look like? I haven't ever been in a relationship that lasted longer than a few weeks before the lust settled and I moved on. With Cole, I don't know how I could ever look at him and not want him. But I don't even know if he feels the same way. I already know what it feels like to lose people I love. Not that I love Cole. That would be way too soon. I've only known him for two months and we've only been seeing each other half that time.

I don't even know what I'm talking about. This whole thing has been confusing. One minute I'm convinced that I'm going to stop whatever it is we're doing, the next I'm texting him a sexy pic or picking up his favorite pie from the diner.

Like he said he would, Cole took me dress shopping last Sunday. This was the first dress I tried on and I fell in love with it, but still proceeded to try on another ten dresses. Cole said he was happy to view all of them. It did need to be altered, the straps tightened and the hem raised slightly, but while the alterations lady sewed it, Cole violated me in the private dressing room under the pretense that he was trying on pants, and therefore needed to take his off. It was a women's dress shop. So, yeah.

I slide the dress straps over my shoulders, gather my hair to one side, then turn for Cole to zip me up. Did I mention my dress is gorgeous? And wearing it makes me feel like a princess? Not a Disney one with a puffy tutu dress, but more like Grace Kelly, one that is elegant and sophisticated. From my breasts to just past my butt it's tight against my body, showing all the curves of my hips and butt, hence the lack of underwear, then fans out at mid-thigh. It's off-white, which I was unsure about at first, but the saleslady convinced me it looked amazing with my dark hair.

Sam came over earlier, under the pretense that she was going to help me do my hair and makeup, but we both know she lives in ponytails and Chapstick and only wanted to meet Cole and see my dress. With no help from Sam, I styled my hair in waves, and swept it to the side to give myself an old Hollywood glam look. I don't look like me. I look like the girlfriend of a doctor going to a hospital gala. How did this happen? It's my vagina's fault. Guys get a bad rap for making decisions with their dicks, but really my slutty vagina has been the root cause of this whole thing.

Cole moves into position behind me. We're now facing the full-length mirror that's hanging between two sections of built-in drawers. The sight of Cole in his black tux and bowtie standing behind me in my off-white dress is over-whelming. Until this moment I hadn't considered how we would look together. Cole in a tux and me in an off-white gown. Like bride and groom. With that thought, I feel my chest tighten. Or maybe that's just the dress material constricting my boobs.

"Did your boobs get bigger?" Coles asks as he works to pull the zipper past my upper-back. "They look amazing in this dress."

"Ha! I wish." I attempt to suck in, but the area that he's struggling with isn't really suck-in-able. Shoulder shrugs are my attempt at helping him pull the material together. It does feel tighter in the chest than it did a week ago, but it may have changed with alterations and I'm just now noticing it. Finally, he closes it.

"Your breasts are fucking perfect." Cole palms me over

my dress, then presses a kiss to the back of my neck. The soft press of his lips sends the most delicious shiver down my spine. I'm immediately regretting the fact that this dress doesn't have easy access. Sex right now would be the perfect distraction for my overactive brain. Cole takes a step back, clearly indicating that he doesn't plan to undo his handiwork and we should get going.

I do one last scan of myself in the mirror, smoothing out the material over my stomach. When I look up, my gaze locks with Cole's in the glass. His appreciative grin tells me he likes what he sees, but there's something else in his eyes that stops me in my tracks. I'm afraid to put a name to it. What acknowledging it could mean. Everything I had planned to avoid, feelings and attachment, I see in his eyes. And it makes me wonder, what does he see in mine?

He breaks eyes contact to grab his phone out of his pocket.

"The uber's here."

---

The gala is taking place in the Grand Ballroom at the historic Brown Palace Hotel downtown. The hotel is known for its Afternoon Tea which is served every day from noon to four in the hotel atrium with grand piano accompaniment. It's a frivolous affair that my mom brought Ellie and me to a few times when we were kids. Getting dressed up like we were princesses going to have tea with the queen. The same atrium is decorated to the nines for the holiday season with tourists and locals alike stopping in just to take a look. The hotel has several restaurants including Ellyngton's, where I've accompanied Sue before to meet with a client. For all the times I've been here for one reason or another, I've never been to the Grand Ballroom. Everything about the Brown Palace is regal, and richly decorated. From the gold chandeliers hanging from the coffered ceiling to the ornate crown molding and rich velvet curtains. The vibrant colors of the plush carpet are laid out in an intricate circular design that is entirely custom. The architecture is vintage and the upkeep is flawless. There's no need for additional decorations at the gala. Everything speaks for itself. Anything added to the work of art we're surrounded by would just look like gaudy prom décor.

And we haven't even made it into the ballroom yet. We're gathered in the reception area outside the ballroom for a cocktail hour. The gala attendees are an older crowd, with a few young faces here and there.

I really can't complain too much. I'm in a gorgeous dress, on the arm of the sexiest man here, who is currently getting me a drink at the bar. I'm posted up at a high-top table checking my phone when I hear a woman behind me.

"Ellie?"

When I turn toward the woman's voice, I find a curvy blonde in a red dress.

"No, I'm Brooke. Ellie's sister," I correct her.

"Oh, sorry. I'm Kara Summers." She extends her hand to me, and I take it. "I work with Dr. Yang at the fertility clinic. I've seen Ellie a few times when Christine was out of the office."

She eyes me curiously.

"I'm particularly interested in your surrogacy case, with you and your sister being identical twins and all. I find the whole thing fascinating and such a selfless thing for you to do."

She obviously doesn't know how selfish I can be.

"How are things going?" she prods.

I can't tell if she means in general or if she's talking about preparing for being Ellie's surrogate. I scan the room for Cole. I don't really need him walking up to this conversation.

"Good. Great. Wonderful." Maybe a bit of an oversell. I can tell my voice is a little pitchy, as I feel a rising panic at the thought that Dr. Summers might mention the surrogacy in front of Cole. I want to be the one to tell him. I plan to tell him. Soon. The last thing I need is her mentioning it now.

"Who are you—" She doesn't even get to finish her sentence. Cole steps up to my side with a glass of champagne in one hand and an old-fashioned in the other.

He hands me the champagne, then leans in to give Dr. Summers a hug. Now that I'm holding the champagne glass, I notice that my hand is shaky. I watch as Dr. Summers smiles, almost seductively, then presses her body to Cole's. It only lasts two seconds but I can tell she made the most of her time.

"Kara, good to see you."

She smiles at Cole, her eyelashes lowering in a subtle, yet flirty gesture, but when she looks back to me with Cole by my side, her smile isn't as warm as it once was. They both seem comfortable being close to each other and I'm a little confused. It's hard to get a read on their relationship. They work together in some capacity obviously, but it feels like something else. Like they have a history, a past relationship that was romantic, or in the very least sexual.

My stomach churns. Gross. I've never really thought about Cole's past. I'm more of a live in the present kind of girl, so I shouldn't be surprised that he didn't go from losing his virginity to fucking me, there'd be no way he would have the skill set that he does, but I don't really want it right in front of my face. That makes my stomach drop again, thinking of Cole with Dr. Summers. Did they fuck in his office? Has she been in his bed? The same one that I'm currently spending every night in? Even in my head, I hear how possessive I sound. Why am I feeling like this? Like Cole belongs to me?

They're talking about something at work and I'm trying to pay attention but my nerves have taken a front seat, so I slam back my champagne, hoping it will help calm me and whatever else I'm feeling. I don't really like to label things, but I think it's manic jealous rage. Or something along those lines because I've never been the jealous type.

Kara finally turns to me, all her pearly whites on display. "How did you two meet?"

Cole slides his arm around my waist, which she does not miss. If Kara's eyes were laser beams, my waist and Cole's hand would be burning right now. For a moment, I think my stomach is burning, but that might just be the champagne.

My eyes flick up to Cole's face. He's got the biggest smile on his face, he might be a second away from laughing.

"We kept running into each other. She finally let me take her out on a date."

Yeah, that's definitely the PG version of our story. Kara smiles sweetly, which I can tell is completely fake.

"That's sweet," she says. "I was just asking Brooke about—"

Kara doesn't get to finish that sentence. I'm saved by the bell. More like a chime and a man announcing that dinner is being served in the ballroom, but I'll take it.

"Oh, what table are you?" Kara leans into Cole, and

places her hand on his arm, like she needs to touch his body to glean this information.

Cole reaches in his pocket for a card.

"We're seven."

"I'm four."

"Oh, darn." I give my best pouty face, but I think Kara and I both know it's fake.

Cole is holding my hand so I should feel like the winner here, but Kara gets in one more dig.

"Are we still on for coffee on Monday?"

"Yeah."

There's that ugly feeling again. My emotions war and I can't tell what bothers me more, the thought that she might tell him about my plan to be Ellie's surrogate or the idea that Kara and Cole are spending time together, and she's obviously got a thing for him. I watch as Kara makes her way toward her table, hips swaying in her tight red dress. She's got a nice ass. Bitch.

Cole places his hand on my lower back, which is just skin due to the backless nature of my dress, to lead me into the ballroom.

With his warm hand on my flesh, his mouth lowers to my ear, "Have I told you, you look absolutely gorgeous tonight?" His words give me butterflies, but I refuse to be distracted by his sweet gesture. I already know that Kara and Cole have a work relationship. She's a fertility specialist and Cole works with high-risk pregnancies, sometimes referred to him by her. He knows I know this. Asking him anything about their working relationship will likely open up the conversation of why I was at the fertility clinic, one I have avoided and Cole has not directly asked about, so I have to use a different tactic.

I stop moving and turn to Cole.

"So, coffee on Monday, huh?"

Cole lifts his low-ball glass to his lips, taking a long sip. I'm sure it's just coincidence that he chose that moment to take a drink, but it's hard not to read into. Maybe he's concocting an excuse, trying to cover up their secret workplace romance.

Cole lowers the glass until it's by his hip. My eyes catch on the way his long fingers grip the glass, then flick back up to his because I need to stay focused. I can't let Cole's sexy glass grip distract me. Cole's free hand slides to my hip, pulling me closer. His voice lowers as he looks straight into my eyes.

"Brooke, ask me what you want to ask me."

"Have you and Kara slept together?"

"Yes."

I don't know why it surprises me that he's so forthcoming. That's one thing I know for certain about Cole, he's always honest with me. So, why does it feel like I just got punched in the gut? I feel like I already knew the answer, but I was hoping I was wrong. Hoping I could erase the visuals in my head of them together, knowing it never actually happened. But it did happen.

"We had a romantic relationship in the past. We're just friends now. That's all."

I think I growl. Or maybe that's my stomach. The champagne is doing funny things to my body, I need sustenance. The look on my face must match my grumpy stomach.

"How can you be mad about a woman I slept with years before I even met you?"

"I'm not mad." Not mad, just jealous, whispers a voice from somewhere in the deep dark place where feelings live. Feelings that have been resurfacing since I've met Cole.

"Everyone has a past." He says it softly as his face searches mine, and I know he's talking about more than just previous lovers. He wants me to let him in, tell him more about my family. But there's no way I can do that right now.

"Yeah, but you see her every day and get coffee, I don't do any of that with guys I've slept with."

"The coffee is a group thing."

"Like an orgy?" I'm ridiculous but I just can't help myself. Emotionally stable Brooke has left the building.

Cole takes another drink of his cocktail. And rightly so, he doesn't give a response to my absurd question.

"How long were you together?"

"I don't know, like a year. I don't even know if you could call it dating. We were just fucking. It was during a time where all I was doing was working and I didn't have time for anything more. She fulfilled a need."

I don't like the way Cole said fucking. It sounds dirty, and hot, like what we're doing. Are we just fucking? I don't even know now. We went on a date. We're here at the gala together. We sleep together practically every night. Would he consider us friends with benefits? That would normally be fine with me, but I'm not feeling normal. Everything with Cole feels magnified and it's hard to tell if I'm just emotional because of the hormones or if there's something else going on. Something dangerous to my heart.

"Does she know it's over? She was practically humping your leg."

"Can we discuss this later? We should sit down for dinner." He looks annoyed and I should have just dropped it but my jealous side pushes on.

"No. I want to talk about it now."

Cole sighs. "Brooke, we were together for a year. It's been two years since we were anything more than friends."

"Why'd you stop?" I have to ask because sex with Cole isn't something you give up easily. Trust me, I would know.

And I'll likely be going through my own withdrawals soon enough.

"We wanted different things. Kara wanted to get more serious. She wanted to get married, start a family, and I didn't. We stopped seeing each other. That was two years ago."

I don't know what stops me from asking any of the obvious follow-up questions. You didn't want those things with her? Or at all? Do you want those things now? It's likely because I don't want to know the answers. Because suddenly, I feel like I could have it all with him. And that thought freaks me out.

I feel like I'm going to pass out and I'm not sure if Cole notices the sweat on my face but he quickly leads us to our table. He greets the people that are already there and makes introductions. There's Jen, the newest OB at Cole's practice and her partner, Corinne, Alex, who went to med school and started the practice with Cole, and his wife, Michelle, and their good friends, Rajesh and Amy. We sit down, a plated salad already in front of us. A server comes by offering red or white wine, and I choose white. Cole passes, he's still got half his cocktail left. There's light conversation around the table as everyone starts to eat their salad. It's a pear, walnut, goat cheese salad, which normally I would find delicious, but my stomach is a wild tangle of knots.

We're not the last people to our table, a few minutes into eating our salad, the empty seats to my left are filled by a couple in their mid-fifties. Cole stands to hug them both, then he introduces me to Mark, and his wife, Patricia.

We all sit back down to start eating, but then Cole is pulled away by a phone call.

Patricia turns to me.

"It's nice to see Cole with a lady friend. How long have you two been together?"

Her smile is friendly. She has short, dark hair and the most gorgeous pale skin, both accentuated by her bright red lip color.

"It's new. A month, maybe?"

"Well, it's good to see Cole happy."

"How do you know each other?"

"Mark," she leans to her left to indicate the salt and pepper-haired man wearing dark-framed glasses, "was Cole's mentor in the fellowship program when Cole first started at Rose Medical."

"Oh, that's nice."

"I don't think I've seen Cole with anyone since Kara." She leans closer like she's telling me a secret. "I know she's an excellent doctor, but between you and me, I never really cared for her."

I like Patricia. She's my kind of people. I want her to tell me more without seeming too eager.

"Oh, really?"

"She's a bit pushy. It always felt like she had an agenda."

I couldn't agree with her more. That's exactly the vibe I get from Kara. And it feels like her current agenda is to get Cole back. Patricia tells me about her work as the philanthropic chair for the hospital and I tell her about my job with Sue.

Cole returns from his call.

"Sorry about that. The on-call doctor wanted to consult with me about her patient."

We finish our salads and the main course is served shortly after. I do my best to eat, my stomach feels unsettled, but nothing sounds appetizing. When the paddle raising starts for the fundraising part of the evening, our table becomes quite lively. I'm surprised when Cole is announced as the silent auction winner of the vacation for two to Hawaii. I didn't even see him bid on it.

Patricia leans into me. "That'll be a fun trip."

She's assuming I'm going to Hawaii. That the romantic getaway for two is for us. She has no idea that this, whatever this is between Cole and me, has an expiration date, and it will likely be before we're sunning on a beach in Kauai.

I raise my eyebrows, but Cole just smiles. "Guess I'm just a lucky guy."

"You didn't win a raffle. It's not luck. You are paying money for the trip." I shake my head, but laugh when he winks at me.

He shrugs. "It's for a good cause." Then he leans in close so only I can hear. "And fucking you on a private beach in Hawaii will be worth every penny."

Warmth creeps up my neck, then spreads to my cheeks and ears. Holy shit. I've created a monster. It's not an official invitation but the idea that Cole is thinking about taking me on a trip that is months away makes me breathless. It's unnerving how giddy that makes me feel. It also aids in putting manic jealous Brooke back in her box, or wherever she came from.

The announcements continue, as I excuse myself to use the restroom. I exit the ballroom and find the ladies' room just off the main corridor where the cocktail hour was held. After I pee, I wash my hands, then pull my lipstick out of my clutch. The door swings open just as I start to reapply. My eyes shift toward the door, where they land on Kara. Our eyes meet in the mirror. She doesn't move toward the stalls, but instead in my direction. I continue my application, trying to ignore her presence without being obvious.

"Brooke."

I rub my lips together, then turn to face her.

"Kara."

"I think we both know this is a little awkward."

"Why is it awkward?"

"Cole and I have a history."

"I know. He told me." I don't mention that it was only twenty minutes ago. Those are details she doesn't get to be privy to.

"Does Cole know about your surrogacy plans?" she asks. But, when I don't respond, I think she already knows the answer. She nods thoughtfully.

My defenses are up. I'm anticipating a cat fight, whatever that may be. Honestly, I've never been in one before because I've never cared enough about a guy to be jealous about ex-girlfriends or scorned lovers. While I'm contemplating challenging her to a duel, something changes in her expression.

"I'm sorry for how I acted before. I think I was just surprised to see him with someone. And," she pauses, "when I saw the way he looks at you, I realized, I can't compete with that." Kara breaks eye contact for a moment, turning in the direction of the sound of the door opening, and a woman in a black gown going into a vacant stall, before she turns back to me. "He never looked at me like that."

With Kara's admission, all of the witty, snarky comebacks I was preparing die on my tongue. This is not what I was expecting. I've got nothing now.

"Cole is a great guy. An amazing doctor, he's kind and honest and sweet and attentive," she clears her throat, "as I'm sure you know. But, he's married to his career, so enjoy it while it lasts."

She gives me a tight smile, then moves toward a stall.

Our interaction leaves me flustered and confused. While the part of me that was jealous about their past relationship and current working one has calmed, there's a part of me that wonders if Cole and I are the same thing that Kara and him were. Just fucking. Friends with benefits. I know exactly what that looks like, it's what I've done with every guy. Just sex. No feelings and emotions. That's what I wanted with Cole, right? But now it terrifies me that I've taken it too far with him. What if I'm having feelings and Cole just wants it to be casual?

## 32

## BROOKE

W hen I hear a phone ringing, I groan and roll over. The bed shifts and I hear Cole talking in a low voice. My eyes pop open to see the bedside clock, it's barely seven. Too early for a Sunday morning.

"Good morning, gorgeous," Cole says as he returns to bed and pulls me close. My brain is awake, but my eyes are slow to open.

"Mmm." I stretch long in his arms, then press my lips to his neck. "Good morning. Did you get a call?"

"Yeah. That was my mom. My sister had the baby early this morning."

His news perks me up. I haven't met his family, but he's told me so much about them, and I knew his sister would be having her baby any day now. Obviously, today was the day.

"Oh, wow. That's exciting. How are they doing?"

Cole's hand slides under my tank top, his fingers start to lightly trace circles on my back.

"Everyone is doing well. His name is Jack."

"Cute." I smile.

"I thought I'd visit them later this morning." He searches my face. "Do you want to come with me? We can get brunch after."

The prospect of meeting Cole's family is not new. He's asked me to join him for their family dinner twice already. I've conveniently had my own dinners at Ellie and Josh's to attend. He seems so casual about it, maybe I'm making it into a bigger deal than it is. I immediately wonder if he ever introduced Kara to his family. Did they like her? Do they miss her? Is she on their Christmas card list?

"Your sister just had a baby; I doubt she wants to meet new people right now."

"You don't know Carrie." He laughs. "She's dying to meet you."

"You've told her about me?"

"My entire family knows about you. If I don't produce you soon, they're going to think I'm making you up to avoid their setups."

I've never felt the need to be the girl that guys tell their friends and family about. There's never been a desire to lay my claim to someone. At least not until Cole came along. This feeling is new and scary and it makes me feel vulnerable.

"What did you tell them?" I whisper, not sure I want to know the answer.

"That you're the most alluring woman I've ever met." He kisses my collarbone.

"Um. I have brunch plans with Sam at noon."

"I can drop you off after." He kisses his way down my jaw.

Cole is pretty persuasive. Somewhere between his hand in my sleep shorts and his tongue on my breasts, I agree to go to the hospital with him.

After we shower and get dressed, Cole makes fried eggs and avocado toast, but it doesn't sound appealing to me, so I grab a banana from the kitchen on our way out. I don't manage to eat much of it on the car ride. I can't tell if I'm just nervous to meet his family or if last night's conversation with Kara is the reason my stomach feels unsettled. After dinner, we danced for an hour before going home. Cole managed to fall asleep right after we had sex, but I lay awake for hours. My body was tired but my mind couldn't relax. It was focused on replaying my conversation with Kara, dissecting what Cole told me about their casual relationship, and debating when to tell Cole about the surrogacy. I finally drifted off around three. Now, my whole body is achy and tired.

I yawn.

"Do you want me to stop for coffee? Or there's a Star-bucks in the hospital lobby."

My head says yes, but my stomach says no.

"I'll be okay. I'm just really dragging today."

"You are quite the party animal." He winks at me.

I just shake my head and can't help but smile, his sarcastic comment is ironic, seeing that he was the one asleep at eleven o'clock last night.

When we get to the hospital, Cole gets a coffee, and while I can't commit to my own cup, I do take a few sips of his, and it makes me feel a little better. On our way to the elevator, Cole steers me into the hospital gift shop, which I would imagine to have overpriced teddy bears and baby onesies with hospital logos on them, but the shop is actually a satellite location for a local flower shop, The Perfect Petal, and it has the most gorgeous arrangements. I help Cole select one for his sister and brother-in-law, then we take the elevator to the postpartum floor and check in with security.

I wasn't sure what to expect, I'm not really prepared to meet his entire family, but when Cole leads me into the hospital room, I'm put at ease when we find his sister alone nursing the baby. Though I haven't met Carrie, it's safe to assume she's the one in the hospital bed with a baby attached to her boob. She looks a lot like Cole, same dark hair and piercing blue eyes. Her complexion is flawless and glowing. I've never seen a woman hours after she's given birth, but I can't imagine this is normal. This is her third child so she's likely a professional, regardless, she's stunning.

When Carrie sees Cole, she smiles. When he moves to set the flowers on the table and she sees me, her eyes widen with curiosity.

"Brooke, this is my sister, Carrie."

"Hi." I give an awkward wave because a handshake or a hug are clearly not appropriate at this moment. I get the feeling that if she hadn't just pushed a baby out of her vagina eight hours ago, she might have a question or a thousand for me, but to my advantage she is a bit preoccupied right now.

"It's great to meet you." Although I can tell she's tired, her smile is genuine. "This is Jack."

Cole moves around the side of the bed to get a closer look. I'm trying not to stare at Carrie's boob, which is nearly the same size as the baby's head. Bigger boobs had been something I was looking forward to with pregnancy, but the hard, veiny breast that is currently on display isn't exactly what I imagined.

"Where's Kyle?" Cole asks.

"He's grabbing a coffee downstairs. You must have missed him on your way up. Mom was with us in the delivery room, then went back to our house. Dad stayed with the girls. They'll both bring them over after lunch."

I watch, fascinated, as Carrie easily maneuvers Jack from one breast to the other. Carrie's husband returns with his coffee, and after Cole gives him a congratulatory hug, he introduces me.

We get a detailed account of Jack's birth, it was quick and easy, then Carrie asks Cole about the gala. I wonder which part she wants to hear about. How Cole and I were dressed like it was our wedding day, which makes me feel nauseas but in a terrifyingly good way? Or that Kara, Cole's ex-fuck buddy and work associate, was there and knows I'm going to be my sister's surrogate, that I haven't told Cole yet, and that I'm afraid she might use that information against me to try to get him back?

So, I just smile and say, "It was fun."

Cole talks with the doctor when she stops by. It sounds like everything has been smooth sailing with both mom and baby, but I'm sure it's Cole's natural protective big brother instinct that has him checking all the paperwork.

Kyle offers me a seat, and I'm thankful. I'm feeling a little lightheaded, and wishing I had the rest of the banana I left in the car. A moment later, the door to the room opens and two little girls wearing swimsuits under tutus burst in the room with an older couple, who I imagine are Cole's parents, following in their wake.

"Mommy! Mommy! I drew baby Jack a picture!" the older girl shouts. The younger one twirls around aimlessly, almost crashing into the bed tray. Both of them attempt to climb up into the hospital bed to see the baby, but need to be assisted by their dad in order to reach.

"We tried to hold them off as long as we could. They were really excited to meet their baby brother."

Carrie smiles knowingly, "Yes, I'm sure you weren't hurrying their breakfast along so you could rush back over here."

Cole walks over to give his mom a hug, then turns to me to introduce us. Before I even get a 'hello' out, she envelopes me into a hug.

"We're so happy to meet you," she says warmly. Again, I think under other circumstances there would be more conversation, but the focus of the day is baby Jack and I'm grateful for that. Introductions continue with Cole's dad and nieces. His dad is kind and easygoing, I can see the similarities in Cole's personality. The girls alternate between staring at their baby brother and asking me if they can play with my hair. Cole's mom brings out a sticker book and some paper from a bag and sets them up at the table.

The baby keeps moving around the room, everyone eager to hold him. I have yet to be asked, and I'm okay with that. I'm not the most confident baby holder, especially when they're so tiny and can't hold their heads up. I don't think Carrie wants her baby's head to snap off. I don't think they actually do that, but I've been party to an awkward baby hold once or twice, and it wasn't pretty.

The girls lose interest in stickers, and start doing spins around the room.

Finally, Annie sits on the couch, holding her baby brother while Sophia leans over them. Sophia looks confused, like she doesn't quite know what just happened and what it all means. The adults snap pictures of this tender moment until Annie loses interest in holding her baby brother and nearly rolls him off her lap in order to get up. Four sets of hands rush in to snag a chance to hold the baby.

The baby is passed again, and he's getting closer to me. My anxiety about Cole and his family watching me try to hold a baby is growing. Or it could be that I'm warm and hungry. Any of those things really.

I excuse myself to use the restroom, and ask the nurse in the hallway for directions. Once there, I splash my face with water. I didn't bother with makeup, which I'm thankful for when I pat my face dry with the paper towel. I'm just feeling off.

When I return, Cole's at the foot of the hospital bed, talking to his mom. They're both looking down at Jack who is securely snug in the crook of Cole's left arm. The girls skip over to him. They must have a homing signal for where their brother is at all times.

"UnCole!" Sophia squeals as she grabs his leg. "See Ack!"

"You trying to eat into my time?" Cole laughs, then relents by crouching down so both girls can see the baby. This results in a full-on view of Cole as he lovingly cradles Jack, with both girls swarming him.

"Gentle," he tells Sophia, and redirects her hand that was aiming for Jack's face toward his feet. I'm taking in the scene, completely captivated by watching him with all these tiny humans, so when Cole looks up at me and winks, I'm not prepared for the explosion in my ovaries. Pow! Right in the uterus.

I've never been that into men holding babies, but Cole does it for me. He makes holding babies look like porn. Is Daddy porn a thing? I don't really know if that's what it's called, but I'm into it, whatever it is. It's my new favorite visual. Then it occurs to me that I didn't have the same reaction when Kyle was holding his son. It's not just any guy that can elicit that response from my ovaries. For a moment, I forget that Cole is cradling his nephew, and let myself imagine what it would be like if that was his baby, *our* baby, that he's holding. Realization hits me like a ton of bricks. I want those things. With Cole.

———

I'm thankful that Sam has a lot of venting to do about her contractor, because after the revelation about my feelings for Cole, I'm not a great conversationalist.

After we left the hospital, Cole dropped me off at Sarto's, a modern Italian eatery in Jefferson Park where Sam was waiting for me. He didn't really drop me off. He parked, opened my door and gave me a hot, possessive kiss against his car before smacking my butt and telling me to have fun, and he'd see me later. I basically floated into the restaurant. But now I'm back to thinking about what I felt at the hospital. It had nothing to do with Cole's steamy kisses, or sex at all.

Sam snags a bite of my blueberry pancake.

"What's going on with you?" She waves a hand to get my attention. "I saw Dr. Hottie dropped you off." She raises her eyebrows. "What's happening there?"

Sam is too intuitive for her own good.

"What do you mean?" I'm thankful for this sunny patio and my dark sunglasses.

"You two seem cozy," she says in a teasing voice.

I might be able to convince Sam it's just casual, but after my realization at the hospital, I really need someone to talk to.

"Sam, I'm so confused. I think I have feelings for Cole, but I don't know what to do. Do I tell him about the surrogacy? Should I still go through with the surrogacy? Ellie and Josh will be crushed if I don't. But, if I do, what does that mean for Cole and me? I don't even know what we're doing or what he wants. Somewhere along the way my plan to just have sex with him completely backfired. I think it might have been the moment I met him."

Sam is up and around the table in two seconds. It's not

until she wraps her arms around me that I realize I'm crying.

"Do you want to be with him?" she whispers.

My throat is tight, so I just nod.

"You've got to tell him."

"About the surrogacy? That I want to be with him?" I search Sam's eyes for the answers.

"Everything."

## 33

# COLE

I t's Monday, and I'm on my way back to the office after a lunch meeting with a pharmaceutical rep. When my phone buzzes and I see Brooke's name on the screen, I can't help but smile.

"Hi, beautiful."

"Hey." Her voice is low and sultry. "What are you doing?"

"Just got back from a lunch meeting."

"Ugh. I didn't even have time to eat lunch. I've got a staging and two properties that sold so I need to be there for the furniture removals." She sighs. "I wish I could come to your office for dessert."

Brooke's office visits are always full of surprises and there's nothing I would enjoy more right now than giving her that desk fuck she requested weeks ago.

"I wish you could, too. I missed you last night." After we stopped by the hospital, Brooke went to brunch with her friend, Sam, then said she was going to spend the night at her place. It made me realize we have slept in the same bed every night since our first date. Last night felt odd without Brooke there. I've easily grown accustomed to her soft breathing beside me, the way her sleep-warm body cuddles up next to mine during the middle of the night. And nothing beats the sight of her first thing in the morning, bright green eyes, wild dark hair and her sleepy smile.

"But I'll see you tonight?"

"Yeah, I'll pick up dim sum on my way over."

"Sounds great."

That's when I see her familiar shape standing by the elevator bank. She's got her phone to her ear while waiting for the elevator. I chuckle at her telling me she's busy at work, her attempt at throwing me off her trail.

I walk up close to her back and lower my head toward hers.

"Well, this is a nice surprise."

She startles, whipping her body around to face me and when her green eyes meet mine, I can't miss how her brows knit together in confusion, and her lips tighten into a thin line as she side-steps in the opposite direction from me. She moves her phone, which she still appears to be on, away from her head.

"Excuse me?" She looks pissed.

It only takes me a second to notice the absence of the freckle that Brooke has above the right side of her lip, and moments later when I see the ring on her left hand, which is still clutching her cell phone, I know that she isn't Brooke.

"I'm sorry, I thought you were someone else." I clear my throat and take a step back from Brooke's twin sister. "I thought you were Brooke."

"Oh." Her eyes are still wary as she looks me up and down. She hits a button on her phone and drops it in her purse. Either she was listening to voicemails or she just hung up on somebody.

Brooke has told me a lot about Ellie, but we've never actually met, so the moment feels a little odd. I extend my hand out to her.

"I'm Cole."

"Ellie."

"Nice to meet you."

Ellie's death stare finally relaxes, but she still looks confused. Her eyes drop to the credential badge clipped to my pants' pocket.

"Oh, are you a doctor here?"

"Yes. Maternal-Fetal Medicine, my office is on three."

The elevator opens, and we both stand back to let people out before stepping in. She punches the button for floor five on her side of the elevator, while I punch three on mine. I don't want to stare, but it is uncanny how much they look alike. From the back it was hard to tell the difference. Watching Ellie now, I see similar mannerisms to Brooke, but I can also see their differences.

"I'm sorry, but how do you know my sister?"

"We've been seeing each other." Even though we haven't met yet, I'm surprised Ellie has no idea who I am. Brooke and I are together, we have been for weeks now. In my eyes, it's a committed relationship. I'll admit, I haven't told Brooke exactly how I feel. That I'm in love with her. I know my feelings for her are real, but I'm also afraid it's too soon. I've thought about telling her, but am afraid of scaring her off.

She considers this for a moment before responding, "Huh. She didn't mention she was seeing anyone else besides Dr. Yang. Is an MFM specialist typical in surrogacy cases?"

"Dr. Yang?" Now I'm confused.

"Well, she's my fertility doctor, but for the surrogacy she's Brooke's doctor, too."

"Whose surrogacy?"

"I thought you said she was seeing you. Isn't it about her being my gestational surrogate?"

I don't know if it's the confusion on my face, but understanding finally hits Ellie that when I said we were seeing each other I meant as man and woman, not as doctor and patient. With that realization her eyes widen.

"Oh."

Ellie looks at me with new interest, like she has so many questions she wants to ask, but all I can do is replay her words and try to make sense of them. Brooke has mentioned Ellie's fertility issues, but had I completely missed her telling me she was preparing to be Ellie's surrogate? Not possible.

My floor arrives. I manage a smile and a 'nice to meet you' before striding out. I walk to my office in a daze. Once there, I drop into my desk chair.

My mind is a fucking mess trying to piece together what Ellie just revealed and the last six weeks with Brooke. Our first night together, running into her at the fertility clinic on five, our first date, her insatiable appetite for sex, her tender breasts, and sometimes overly dramatic emotions. I thought that was just Brooke, but now that I have more context, it makes complete sense.

I reach for my phone to call her, but stop myself. This isn't a phone conversation. Besides, I know she's got a busy day at work and I will be seeing her tonight.

## 34

## BROOKE

"I got the dumplings from Star Kitchen." I let myself in to Cole's place but pause halfway to the kitchen when I see him sitting on the couch. His hair is wet, likely from a shower after his workout. "Hey, how was your day?" I continue to the kitchen, where I place the takeout bag on the counter, then move toward the couch and slide into Cole's lap. "Do you want dinner or dessert first?"

Cole's eyes finally lift to meet mine and I can tell something isn't right. He looks pensive. His hands find my hips, but he doesn't pull me in for a kiss.

"I met Ellie today in the hospital lobby."

I don't know if it's the intense way he's looking at me or my own guilt for not telling him about the surrogacy, but alarm bells start going off in my head. I move to slide off his lap, but his long fingers wrap around my hips, holding me in place.

"Oh, yeah?" Surprisingly, my voice sounds calm. It doesn't give away the dread that has settled into my stomach.

"At first, I thought she was you, surprising me with a

visit." He has a faraway grin that doesn't quite reach his face.

I immediately wonder if I have any unchecked messages from Ellie. A message that would have given me a heads up as to what I would be walking into. I'd been busy all afternoon at work, gone straight to pick up the food, and then come over here. Of course, the one day I don't check my phone twelve hundred times.

My mind is racing with all the possible scenarios that could have played out between them. Cole knows about Ellie, but Ellie has no idea Cole even exists. I kept them separate at first because Cole was temporary, I had no idea that we would turn into this. I still don't know what *this* is, but I know it's more than a one-night stand or casual fling and it scares the hell out of me. I know I should tell him about the surrogacy, I just haven't found the right time.

"Were you ever planning to tell me about the surrogacy or just wait until you started showing?"

I cringe at Cole's words. I hate that he found out this way. It's exactly what I didn't want. I know I messed up, but I can't go back and change it. And I had my reasons.

"Of course, I was going to tell you, but nothing has happened yet." As I say it, I realize he deserves more than this.

Cole slides me off his lap onto the couch, then stands and starts pacing. My stomach drops as I feel the tension radiating from his body. He's usually easygoing and approachable, the way his jaw is clenched and his arms are crossed over his chest are anything but. His body language suddenly puts me on the defense. I spring up from the couch.

"I mean, what was I supposed to do, walk up to you that first night and say by the way, I'm going to be my sister's surrogate, do you want to have sex before that happens?"

"I understand why you didn't tell me right away, but Jesus, Brooke, it's been over a month since we were first together. I wish you would have found another time to tell me."

"I wanted to, I just couldn't find the right time."

"The right time was any time before I found out from someone other than you. I should have heard it from you."

"Look, I'm already being a total bitch and I'm not even pregnant yet. You're going to be so tired of me. I'm going to be moody and emotional, and I'm going to get huge." My hands move apart to demonstrate a size I don't think I could even be if I was having octuplets.

"I'm well aware of what pregnancy entails. But it's my decision, not one for you to make for me." He runs a hand over his face, before meeting my eyes again. "And those aren't reasons to walk away from you."

His response should make me feel better, but it only makes me feel worse. Hadn't I planned to walk away? I was certain that I had to focus on being Ellie's surrogate, that I didn't want marriage and kids for myself. But everything has been changing since I met Cole. And now, he wants to support me? That's what he says now, but there's no guarantee he'll feel the same when everything starts to change. I'm not sure I can handle it when Cole does walk away.

"What about sex? I've read that some women have no sex drive while pregnant, just because I've been horny on the fertility hormones doesn't mean I'll want to do it, it can flip like that." I snap my fingers.

Cole's brows knit together in confusion before he levels me with a hard stare.

"Because sex is the only reason we're together?"

"I mean it is…or was…I don't know." My bent arms lift above my shoulders, palms to the ceiling. I'm literally the shrugging emoji.

"Wow."

Cole just stares at me, then shakes his head, a sad smirk on his face.

"So, I was just your fuck toy and then you planned to walk away when you were done?"

"I don't know, I didn't plan any of this!"

"You're using being a surrogate for your sister as a reason to not have feelings for me. That's bullshit." I've never seen Cole mad and I'm not seeing it now either, it's more of a disappointment and that's worse.

"It's not bullshit, it's how life works. There are no guarantees." And just like usual, I dig myself deeper into a hole.

"You just assumed I'd walk away as soon as I found out about the surrogacy?"

He looks incredulous, it's hard to look him in the eye.

"It doesn't matter what I say. You've already made up your mind."

What I hate more than anything is Cole isn't angry. He just looks sad…disappointed. But I remind myself that I'd rather go through this now than lean on him during the pregnancy and then have him decide he's not interested in sticking around. After my realization at the hospital yesterday, it would be heartbreaking. I don't want to deal with either of those things.

"I'm sorry." I gather my purse from the kitchen counter and move toward the front door.

"Yeah, me, too."

After I leave and take the elevator, I'm hoping he runs to stop me. But it doesn't happen this time either.

I think I've just messed things up for good.

## 35

# BROOKE

W hen I get to my car, I check my phone for messages from Ellie, and am surprised to find nothing. On the drive to her house I analyze what that means. Could she be mad that I was seeing someone? Or more upset that I didn't tell her? I focus all my energy on thinking about Ellie, because if I let my mind think about Cole, and what just happened back there, I don't know if I'll be able to drive.

Ellie answers after what feels like a full minute of urgent knocking.

"I can explain," I say by way of greeting, then I'm already moving past her into the house and toward the living room before she can respond.

Ellie follows.

"About?"

"Cole." I take a seat on the couch, next to a blanket that Ellie must have been snuggled up in a minute ago, because it's still warm. "I know you ran into him today at the clinic. I'm sorry I didn't tell you about him. But really, there was nothing to tell. I hooked up with Cole before we even started looking into me being your surrogate, but then my hormones were kind of crazy and I wasn't ready to give up sex, which I know we didn't exactly discuss the whole thing about me dating or having sex, but I thought I would just continue to have sex with him until we did the embryo implantation thing so that I could have the most sex before not being able to have sex for a while. But then I liked Cole, for more than just sex, and I was afraid he wouldn't want to be with me if I was pregnant with your baby, so I didn't tell him about the surrogacy. He found out today, when he ran into you." I pause. "Not that it's your fault, it's my fault. I should have told him. He actually took it well, but then I was an idiot and made him feel like I was just using him for sex. Which I was, but I shouldn't have said it like that. He was hurt, and I got angry because I didn't mean for any of this to happen." I finally let the tears that I've been holding back escape. Ellie wraps her arms around me. I didn't think I would fall for him. That was never the plan. I didn't even think it was possible. I've been so guarded since my parents died, not letting anyone close enough to care about them. Keeping my relationships casual, and with guys that would never want more from me, because I didn't want to know what it would feel like to want more from them. Until Cole.

"Oh, Brooke." She envelopes me in a hug. "I'm sorry. I wish I had known."

I hadn't noticed before, but her face, which is normally full of color and rosy, looks pale, and her green eyes have bags under them. Because of the egg retrieval procedure, Josh had postponed their Glenwood Springs trip, and they just got back from four days relaxing in the quiet mountain town and hot springs resort. Ellie doesn't look relaxed. She looks exhausted.

"Not to change topics, but you look terrible. I thought

the trip to the mountains would be relaxing and restorative. You don't look restored. You look like death."

Ellie had texted me when they arrived safely in Glenwood Springs and to let me know she was surprised and appreciated me packing her nothing to sleep in. I think she was being sarcastic with that last one, but it was hard to tell via text.

Ellie bites her bottom lip.

"Brooke, you're not going to be my surrogate."

"What? Because of Cole? I don't think—"

She cuts me off.

"I'm pregnant."

I nearly fall off the couch. Surely, I didn't hear that right. "How?"

She shakes her head and smiles. "I don't know. We were all set to do the egg retrieval. I hadn't been feeling great, but I just chalked it up to the hormones. But when we went in for the procedure, they were unable to do it because I was already pregnant."

"Holy shit," is all I can say. Then I hug her tight. "This is incredible news."

I can feel years' worth of emotion and stress being released from Ellie's body as she clings to me. It's emotional for me, too. I want her to be happy. That was the reason I offered to be her and Josh's surrogate. I've watched them struggle for so long and now Ellie is pregnant. I'm amazed at how my heart manages to simultaneously break and feel love in the same day. When we pull back, we're both crying.

"We couldn't have done it without you." Ellie wipes at her tears.

"What are you talking about? All I did was take hormones and act like a weirdo."

"Brooke, you offering to be our surrogate was the most

amazing gift. It let Josh and me relax, have fun with each other again, and not be so stressed about the process. You took that burden from us, even for a short while, and I just know that's how this pregnancy happened."

"You're giving me too much credit. Were you able to have fun on your trip, or did you feel sick the whole time?"

"Even if I don't look like it," she laughs, "I did relax by the pool quite a bit. We couldn't do the hot springs because of the water temperature. Josh hiked on his own when I wasn't feeling like it and we had some nice dinners out even though food that I would normally enjoy sounded awful. And I couldn't have any wine at the winery or get a massage. So, there's that." She smiles ruefully and I can't help but let out a small laugh.

"How ironic that Josh planned a trip with activities that you can't do while pregnant, thinking there wouldn't be any chance of you being pregnant after all this time."

"I'm sorry I didn't tell you sooner. I just didn't know what to expect. It's still early times, but I feel like shit, so it's encouraging that the hormones are doing their job. That's why I was at the clinic. I was doing a blood test to check my hormone levels, to make sure they're still on their way up, as expected."

"And that's when Cole saw you." My heart does that squeezing thing again when I think about Cole. How he's been so patient with me, and I've been so careless with him. I'm a complete idiot.

Ellie nods. Her eyes are hopeful. "But you can fix it, right? The surrogacy isn't an issue now."

I sigh. "I don't think it was ever an issue. At least not for Cole. He was shocked, rightly so, but he didn't care. He still wanted to be with me."

And I was using the surrogacy as a reason to not be with him. Just like he said. To keep him at a safe distance.

Like all the other guys before. But, really, I knew it was different with him from the beginning. That's what kept me running. Then, when I thought it would just be temporary, I gave myself permission to keep seeing him, never thinking about the consequences of developing real feelings for him.

Now, I don't know what to do. Not telling Cole about my plan to be Ellie and Josh's surrogate was the reason for our fight, even though those plans have changed doesn't mean Cole will want me now. I hurt him. There's still the issue of me running and pushing him away whenever I feel overwhelmed.

Even though Ellie is the one who really needs to rest, she covers me with a blanket, and I lay my head down in her lap. The feeling of her fingers combing through my hair is soothing. I offer to make her tea or lemon water, but Ellie just shakes her head.

"Ellie?"

"Yeah?"

"You're going to be an amazing mom."

## 36

# BROOKE

"I'm finished downstairs. Do you need any help up here?"

I turn to find Jake standing in the doorway watching me as I arrange a set of four art prints on the floor, trying to remember what order I wanted to position them on the wall.

Jake's in his usual white t-shirt and worn jeans, hard muscles and sexy smile on full display. He looks exactly the same as he did the first day we worked together, but I can't even get excited. I'm tired, and there's nothing I want to do on this bed unless it's crawl under the covers and take a nap.

With Ellie's pregnancy and the embryo implantation put off indefinitely, I stopped taking the oral progesterone, and although Dr. Yang told me my body might take a month or two to regulate its hormone levels, I just feel off lately. The last ten days I've been a zombie. Going through the motions of my job, then falling into my bed with a cup of noodles every night. I know this isn't normal.

When I started spending every night at Cole's, I

stopped reading the pregnancy and surrogacy books. I couldn't exactly curl up next to him with *What to Expect When You're Expecting*, but I gathered enough information in the early days to understand pregnancy symptoms that are common. I'm starting to wonder if the way I've been feeling has less to do with Cole and more to do with things happening inside my body. But, I can't get up enough courage to take a test. I'm in that sweet spot of denial where I know exactly what could be happening but am too scared to face it, hoping maybe I'm wrong. Because what the hell would I do if my suspicions are correct?

I haven't heard from Cole, but I haven't reached out either. Without the surrogacy to hide behind, being rejected by Cole would be too hard. He'd be rejecting me, not just my situation. I don't know if I can handle that.

"Um, what was the question?"

Jake chuckles at my distracted response.

"Do you need help hanging those?"

I shake my head. "No. I'm good. Thank you."

I wait for him to leave but after a few seconds I turn to find him still standing there watching me.

"Do you want to grab a drink later?" His lips curve into a sexy grin. My eyeballs are the only part of my body that register his appeal. It's purely an observation, with my body having no reaction to it. My libido must be broken. *Or*, a little voice whispers, *you're in love with Cole*. Part of me wishes I could easily accept Jake's offer, go back to impromptu flings and casual sex, but I'm not the same woman that lusted over his hard abs and sweat-clingy shirt a few months ago.

I shake my head. "No, thanks. I'm seeing someone." Which is not technically true. I haven't seen Cole in nine days, four hours and twenty-seven minutes. But Jake doesn't need to know the details.

"Okay." He shrugs, his confidence unshaken. "See you next week."

When I'm finished at the condo, I pack up my stuff and head to my car. Sue is on a remodel project and won't be by to check out my work until tomorrow. Before I drive home, I text Sam to see if she wants to come over to watch a movie. She responds quickly letting me know she's tied up at the boutique and will call me tomorrow. Ellie and Josh are on a date tonight. She had excitedly told me that Josh finally got reservations at Barcelona. My thumb hovers over Cole's name. I could text. Or maybe call? What would I say? I drop my phone into the console and drive. I'm just not ready for that conversation yet.

———

For the past nine years, August twenty-third has been the same. Ellie and I take flowers to our parents' grave. This time of year, the weather is typically sunny and warm, but we've had a few rainy years that required an umbrella. We sit for a while, talking about favorite memories. Trips we took to Disneyland and the Grand Canyon. Mom's affinity for tube tops in the 90s. The time Dad burned his eyebrows off trying to repair the furnace himself. We laugh. We cry. When we are done, Josh drives us back to their house where we grill steak kabobs, my dad's favorite, and eat the strawberry rhubarb pie that Ellie made, mom's recipe. It's been nine years since my parents died. It feels like forever.

So much has happened in those nine years, it feels like we've been missing them for a whole lifetime. Each year gets easier, yet harder. Easier because it's another year that we've lived without them, but harder for the same reason. It's another year that life has moved on. And now with

Ellie pregnant, I feel that life change even more. Every year I'm reminded that life keeps moving on, whether I want it to or not.

After dinner we settle onto the couch to watch old family movies. Since we grew up before capturing every moment on video or in photos on your phone was possible, our selection is limited. But video recorders were a thing, and lucky for us that when VHS went out of style, my parents had all the video tapes transferred onto DVD.

We've done everything the same, but I can't shake the feeling that something is different this year. Like, the weight of loss feels heavier somehow. But, I chalk it up to this funk I've been in since Cole and I broke up. Or just stopped talking, I'm not even sure what to call it.

When the last video ends, I excuse myself to use the bathroom. I have a headache, not sure if it's from the wine I had earlier or from the emotional toll of the day. I find the ibuprofen in the cabinet and take two with a cup of water. When I set the bottle back in the cabinet, I notice a box of pregnancy tests. They must be left over from Ellie's last round of IVF. I've taken one before, not because I actually thought I was pregnant but because I wondered what it was like to pee on a stick and have it tell you something important about your life. Baby or no baby. It was in the midst of Ellie and Josh's fertility woes, I was trying to give moral support to Ellie. The ever practical and financially responsible Josh was annoyed that I used a perfectly good test for no reason. You basically peed on a five-dollar bill, was his response. I hadn't thought about it like that before.

I peek in the box. There are two tests left. Ellie won't be using them, she's already pregnant. I pull one out but hesitate for a moment, wondering if now is really when I want to put my suspicions to rest. Ultimately, I unwrap the test, follow the directions and wash my hands. This is nothing like the commercial where the couple sets a timer to wait the requisite three minutes, then they pace around the house until finally ending up back in the bathroom for the big reveal. I'm alone, and I've got results in fifteen seconds.

Two unequivocally dark lines.

## 37

# BROOKE

**B**ack in the living room, I start to fold up my blanket. I feel the need to escape. I need time to think. Time to process all the feelings that positive test is stirring inside me.

Ellie looks up at me from where she's snuggled with Josh under a blanket.

"You okay?"

I could tell Ellie. She would be supportive, giddy even, I'm sure. But I'm not ready for that yet.

"I'm going to go home," I say.

"Really?" Her surprise is evident.

"Yeah, I'm just tired."

"You can sleep here," she offers.

"I know, but I think I'll sleep better in my own bed." I usually spend the night, and this year would be easy to do especially since it's a Saturday. "Is that okay?"

"Of course. I just want to make sure you're okay. Are you sure you want to be alone?"

"Yeah, I'm good. Just been a long day. It's always a lot."

I lean in to give her a squeeze. "I love you."

"I love you, too."

I give Josh a quick hug, then head for the door.

At home, I get ready for bed, brush my teeth and put on pajama shorts and a tank top. I respond to all the text messages I've received from Sam, my Aunt Margaret, Carla, and a few other friends that managed to remember the date and what it means to Ellie and me.

I will sleep to come but my exhausted body is no match for my racing mind. Holy shit, I'm pregnant. How crazy is that? I smile. Then I think of Cole, and telling him about the baby. It makes me excited and anxious at the same time. An hour goes by and my sheets are a jumbled mess. I can't sleep. Maybe I should have stayed at Ellie's. My phone sits silent on my bedside table. It's nearly midnight now. After putting on a sweatshirt and flip flops, I grab my purse and head out the door. Sam's still up, she told me to come over. And Ellie texted me three times to make sure I am okay. She's right, I really don't want to be alone tonight. I'm driving on autopilot, my body taking over for my overloaded mind. I park and walk up to the building. I still have the key card in my purse so I use it to get in the main door and then into the elevator. When the elevator opens, I hesitate to get out, but finally I move my feet. They smack all the way down the hallway in my flipflops. I knock and wait. It's excruciating. My thoughts are still running wild. It's late, I shouldn't have come. What am I going to say? Sam and Ellie are great for talking and listening and giving hugs, but I need more. I want more. If today has made me realize anything, it's that I don't want to stay in the same place I have been for the last nine years. Paralyzed by the fear of loving someone and having them taken away.

There's no answer. I'm feeling vulnerable now and my

body's reaction is to sweat. Only a lump in my throat that's threatening to break down the wall that I've built. The wall that I've been laying for nine years, keeping me protected from caring about anyone else that could be yanked out of my life in an instant. I slowly back away from the door, and finally turn toward the elevator, back to where I came from.

"Brooke?" I hear his deep voice behind me, husky, and laced with sleep. I turn around to find Cole there shirtless with gray pajama bottoms on. His dark hair is mussed, he even makes bed head look good. He's Cole at his sexiest. The one my body can't get enough of. But it's not my body that reacts to seeing him now. That's there, of course, because I don't think that is ever going to go away, but it's my chest that tightens, my heart that squeezes at the sight of him. He's my person, the one that despite my defenses, managed to crack my hard exterior and steal my heart.

And now more than ever, after seeing that positive test, the worry that I fucked it all up, that Cole could be done with me, is beyond heartbreaking. But I owe it to him to be honest and put myself out there, knowing that he could walk away.

Cole rubs his eyes again, trying to clear what was obviously a peaceful sleep until I started banging on his door.

"I'm sorry. I…" I shake my head. I don't even know where to begin. As usual, I didn't think about what I was going to say.

"Brooke. It's late." I can hear the wariness in his voice, and it kills me.

"I know. It's just…" My voice cracks as I search for the words to tell him. "I wanted to tell you…" I take in a ragged breath.

"Hey, what's wrong?" Cole's eyes are so gentle,

concerned, that I can't hold up the pretense that I'm okay. The tears that I've been fighting back finally start to fall.

A second later Cole's arms are around me. His sleep-warm skin encircles me as he pulls me in close. His arms wrap around my back, my head presses into his chest, and I just lose it. I don't cry often, but when I do, it's not pretty. Red puffy eyes, salty tear streaks down my face, and snot, lots of snot.

On this day, when I'm missing my parents the most and thinking back on their life, our life as a family, I realize that for the first time I've found a man I want to build a future with. Cole's the one I want to be with. He's my person. I love him, and it absolutely terrifies me.

## 38

## COLE

My thumb brushes her cheek, then I tuck a strand of hair behind her ear. I never want to see Brooke in pain, but I do want to be the person there for her when she's hurting.

Brooke smiles through her tear-stained cheeks. She's so fucking beautiful.

"The worst part for me was just the fact that we were older, in college, out of the house. I mean it would have been horrible if we were little kids losing our parents, but there's something about having a last moment before someone's gone. It was the weirdest feeling, not knowing what they did that day, what they had eaten for breakfast, where they were going, and then they were just gone."

I don't comment. I don't think she needs me to. She keeps talking.

"At Ellie's wedding, I walked down the aisle with her. It was one of the hardest things I've ever done." Brooke blinks and another tear falls. "It felt like she was leaving me, too, that day. I know it's silly. I love Josh like a brother and they're perfect together, but it was a sad day for me.

Seeing her be so open to something I couldn't even imagine having. I think that's when it really set in that we ultimately give love to those that can hurt us the most. It's ironic. Why would you give someone that power? It's scary."

She inhales deeply, her breath shaky on the exhale. "You know?"

Fuck yeah, I know. I'm staring at the most vibrant, beautiful woman, she's everything I want and the fact that I don't know if she could ever feel the way about me that I feel about her scares the shit out of me. I know now isn't the time to tell her. She came to me tonight because she needed someone to listen. There's so much I want to tell her, but not tonight. The last thing I want to do is scare her off, again. I've learned that I need to be careful with her, and now that she's letting me in, I don't want to risk her pulling back.

Her hand lifts to my chest, her fingertips flex, and her palm spreads over my skin. Her roaming fingertips lightly trace my collarbone. My eyes are fixed on her. Her eyes are focused on where she's gently stroking me.

I had no intention of touching her. I'm content to hold her. Listen to her. Watch over her until she falls asleep.

But, when her eyes lift to mine and she asks, "Will you touch me?" I know that I'll give her anything she wants. "I need to feel your skin on mine."

My lips gently brush hers, tasting the saltiness from her tears as well as the sweetness that is all Brooke before I roll her onto her back.

She lifts her arms up as I lift the hem of her tank top and pull it over her head. My fingertips are light when they skim down the middle of her body, trace her belly button, then pull her sleep shorts down and off. She watches me, our eyes meet in a knowing glance right before my mouth closes over her hardened nipple.

Brooke gasps, then arches her back to press further into me.

I spend a few minutes licking and teasing her before I trail my lips upward, kissing her neck, her jaw, her lips. Our mouths meet with a soft kiss that takes my breath away. Our kiss is hungry, but in a different way than I've felt before. Brooke's mouth opens to mine, letting me be in control. It feels like she's giving me a gift. She's letting go, trusting me to give her what she needs.

My palms move over her body, fingertips lightly trailing over her skin. Touching, caressing, loving every inch of her before I reach my destination and slide a finger into her slick heat. I spend a few minutes rubbing her clit and pleasuring her with my fingers.

"Cole, please." I pump two fingers into her. "I need more."

She's ready for me. I reach into the nightstand for a condom. Once it's on, I lower myself over her, my forearms bracketing her head.

"This okay?"

Brooke nods, her green eyes locked on mine. In one slow thrust I'm inside her. Fuck, it's been a long ten days without her beneath me. She bends her knees to wrap her legs around my waist. Our rhythm is slow. One thrust in, one long drag out. Her hips rock up to meet me on each thrust. Her arms are around my neck, our chests pressed together. I'm surprised when I feel my orgasm approaching. The heat of it crawling up my spine. Normally slowing down would be the solution, but I don't think I can go any slower than we already are.

Brooke's breath is heavy now, her little sounds telling me she's close. I snake a hand between us and apply pressure to her clit. Then I take in one of my favorite sights, Brooke's expressive face as her orgasm hits full force.

Her chin lifts as her eyes widen, a small O forming at her lips. She's fucking amazing to watch. I wait for her eyes to close, but she keeps them open, fixed on mine. I stop moving when her muscles squeeze me tight, and just enjoy the feeling of her milking my cock deep inside her. It's enough to send me over the edge. Seconds later, my release follows.

## 39

# BROOKE

I couldn't sleep, so I left Cole's place and walked to the diner. It's early, six-thirty on a Sunday, so the diner crowd is mostly white-haired octogenarians here for the breakfast special. Carla isn't here, according to the waitress behind the counter, whom I don't recognize because I've never been to the diner at this hour on any day, but she did inform me there are a few slices of pie left from yesterday. I'm posted up at the counter, and I've already reserved a slice of peach pie for here and a slice of French Silk to go, for later.

The waitress sets the plate of scrambled eggs down in front of me, then slides a roll of silverware across the counter. I want pie for breakfast, but from what I've read, a baby needs protein so we're compromising. Eggs, then pie.

When the waitress looks behind me to address another customer approaching the counter, I turn to find Cole standing there, his blue eyes locked on me. He's in a t-shirt and shorts, his hair still a little rumpled from sleep.

"Coffee, please," Cole responds to the waitress, then turns to me and smiles, "I got your note."

He's referring to the takeout napkin I wrote on with a Sharpie. It wasn't the most romantic gesture but it's what I had to work with.

"I couldn't sleep."

Cole nods, his hands gripping the back of the stool next to mine. "Thank you for telling me about your family last night. I know that was hard for you."

The waitress brings a cup and pours the piping hot coffee from the pot. Cole thanks her then trains his eyes back to me. "There's still a lot we have to talk about."

I can still see the hurt in his eyes. I know last night didn't erase our fight about me keeping the surrogacy from him. I swivel on my stool to face him.

Cole slides into the stool beside mine.

"Brooke, I'm sorry for the way I reacted last week. I was completely caught off guard, and that's what bothered me the most about it. I think it's great what you're doing for Ellie and Josh, I just thought we were at a place where you would share something like that with me." He pauses, running his hand through his hair. "After I thought about it, I could see why you didn't tell me immediately, but after we had been together, shared intimate moments, I thought that we were more than just fucking around."

"We were." I study his handsome face, his brows drawn down in concern. "I'm sorry I didn't tell you about the surrogacy. I should have, I just didn't see the point at first, then when I knew things were getting more serious," I take a breath, "when I started falling for you, I was afraid to tell you. Because I don't love people easily. And when I realized I loved you," I swallow thickly, my nerves making it difficult to speak, "I wanted to hold onto that as long as I could. Not knowing if you would still want to be with me. But then I was freaking out about my feelings for you and trying to pull away so even when you said the surrogacy didn't matter, I just couldn't get past the idea that you might walk away, and how badly that would hurt."

I lift my eyes from where they've been glued to Cole's collarbone to find him grinning ear to ear.

"What?" I ask.

"You love me?"

"Yeah." I smile, too, the words feeling less foreign now. "I love you."

"Do you have any idea how happy that makes me?" Cole reaches a hand to palm my cheek. "I want you to know that I completely support you. You having your sister's baby was never a deal breaker for me. I do want to have a family of our own someday, but there's plenty of time for that. Brooke, I love you, too."

Those three words, and the mention of *our* own family someday make my eyes fill with tears.

Cole's eyes sweep over my face and I can feel the love pouring out of them. My tears threaten to spill over. I want to bottle this moment and keep it forever. My throat is so tight I can barely get the words out.

"I'm pregnant."

Cole's smile is genuine as he lifts me off the stool and pulls me into an embrace.

"That's great, Brooke. I'm so happy for Ellie and Josh."

I sink into Cole's embrace, letting his strong arms hold me. I love the way he makes me feel safe and protected, secure and content. The way I'm sure he will make his son or daughter feel. For once I don't want to rush things, or be impatient to move on to the next thing, I want to savor this moment.

I don't want to leave his arms, but I pull away so I can meet his eyes.

"The baby isn't Ellie and Josh's. It's yours."

## 40

## COLE

B rooke's words hit my ears but it takes me a minute to understand what she is telling me.

"I haven't done the embryo implantation, and I stopped taking the fertility hormones, because Ellie and Josh are pregnant, on their own, by some miracle. I have been feeling really tired and my stomach has been unsettled, so I took a test last night at Ellie's and it was positive."

Her green eyes are shining with tears, and it takes me a moment to realize I haven't said anything.

"I don't know how it happened. We used condoms and I was using spermicidal films Dr. Yang gave me. Except that one time I was sliding on top of you and you slipped inside me for like five seconds. Okay, maybe ten…"

"Brooke."

"You probably think I'm a crazy person and are a little stressed about creating offspring with me that might share these traits as well, but I think it might just be a personal issue and not necessarily DNA, because Ellie is my twin and she seems normal. I know you only met her briefly and under odd circumstances, but she really is a stable, organized and rational person. And with you contributing fifty percent of this baby's genetic material, I think we have a solid shot at creating a normal human being."

"Brooke."

"What?" Brooke finally pauses from her ramblings to meet my eyes.

"You are crazy if you think that I wouldn't be the happiest man in the world right now."

I pull her into my arms, her happy tears soaking the front of my shirt as she half laughs, half cries, but I don't care. My mind's already filling with visions of a mini-Brooke running around the house, wearing brightly-colored dresses, climbing on the counters and drawing on the walls with markers. Or, maybe it's a boy, with Brooke's green eyes and captivating smile, and my easy-going temperament. That would be fun, too.

I've been a part of so many pregnancies throughout my career, investing in other people's journeys to parent-hood, but nothing can compare to the thought of having my own family, and being on that journey with Brooke. I'm crazy in love with her. I can't imagine my life without her in it.

When I lower my mouth to hers, Brooke's soft lips open up to me and even the fact that we're in a diner at six-thirty in the morning surrounded by people eating break-fast can't stop me from kissing her breathless. We're both caught up in the moment until the waitress stops by to drop off a plate with a slice of peach pie on it. I can tell she warmed it up because the filling is oozing out the sides.

"Pie for breakfast?" I ask.

"It's actually breakfast dessert. I'm going to eat these eggs first."

"Well, I guess *technically* it is a serving of fruit."

Brooke smiles at me in delight. "Exactly."

I've never eaten pie for breakfast but I think this could be the perfect occasion for it.

I signal to the waitress, "I'd like a piece of the peach pie, too, please."

"Sorry, that's my last piece." She nods at the plate in front of Brooke before picking up a coffee pot and moving to the other end of the counter.

When I turn back to Brooke, she's biting her lower lip, trying not to laugh.

"You're going to share, right?" My eyebrows lift in question.

She reaches over the counter to grab another set of silverware, then hands it to me.

"There's no one else in this world that I would want to share pie with."

# EPILOGUE

*Three Months Later*

I place the framed picture on the bookcase, then give it a small shift to the left before standing back to examine it again. Better. I move the lamp on the other end of the bookcase three inches to the right, fluff the pillow and place it in the glider, and refold the cream blanket before hanging it over the side of the crib. I look around the room one last time. It's perfect.

Anticipating my finish, Ellie was folding laundry, little white onesies, in her and Josh's bedroom down the hall. When I appear in the doorway, she's already dropping the laundry and moving to follow me down the hallway. Ellie's white sweater is snug against her small baby bump. I look down at my black sweater dress to see nearly the same sized bump extending from my mid-section. Ellie and I are both due in April, her one week before me. Ever the planners, Ellie and Josh found out they are having a girl. They are over the moon. I'm excited for them, too, and finishing the nursery that Ellie and I started years ago has been the most satisfying project. We decided to go all out girly, pink and cream with gold accents. From the crystal chandelier with a gold chain hanging over the cream glider with a dusty rose cable knit poof to the large pink floral print wallpaper on the accent wall behind the crib. A large script style letter 'A' I painted gold hangs in the middle of the gallery wall of art and photos I assembled above the bookcase. Ellie and Josh are naming their little girl Ava Diane. Her middle name for our mom. She assured me that if Cole and I have a girl we can use the name, too.

When Ellie steps in the room, I immediately know she loves it.

"Brooke. This is…" Her voice catches in her throat. "It's perfect. I love it so much."

I wrap an arm around her back and squeeze her into my side. Ellie does the same to me. We're not even that big yet and front hugs are starting to get awkward.

Ellie's on Thanksgiving break from school and I have the week off from work. I'm still staging homes with Sue, but I've started a side business decorating children's rooms and nurseries and blogging about my projects. One of the kid's rooms I recently designed was for a set of boy/girl twins and it was featured in the design issue of *5280 Magazine*, Denver's local magazine. While I still enjoy picking out furniture and staging entire homes, I have found my passion in creating fun, playful spaces for children.

I'm so happy to be going through this journey with Ellie, talking about our changing bodies, discussing baby names and registering for baby stuff. However, Cole convinced me to be surprised and not find out the sex of our baby. It's driving Ellie nuts, but I'm enjoying imagining both scenarios.

"I've got to run. Cole was supposed to be picking up the pies and I want to make sure everything is perfect for dinner tomorrow."

Cole and I are hosting Thanksgiving dinner in our new house tomorrow. We moved into our modern farmhouse style home three weeks ago and I've been busting my ass to get it decorated and feeling homey for the occasion. It's been a challenging deadline to say the least. Turns out it's a lot easier to stage a home knowing the furniture is temporary and just to give the buyer's an idea of how the space could be used than picking out furniture and art that *I* will be looking at every day.

I'm excited to host Thanksgiving dinner, but It's a lot of people and I'm not really the cooking type, so Ellie promised to come over early to cook the turkey and help with some of the side dishes. Everyone is bringing something, too, so it won't be all on us, but it's still a big undertaking.

Ellie walks me upstairs.

"You're still planning on coming early tomorrow, right?" I ask.

"Of course. I'll see you at ten."

"Sounds great."

———

Later, I pounce on Cole as soon as he walks through our front door. I'm so quick even Murphy, our excitable Bernese Mountain puppy and usually first door greeter, is trailing behind me. With Cole and me it's been a whirlwind. Baby on the way, a new house and then just to make things interesting, we got a puppy, too.

Even though tomorrow is Thanksgiving, I feel like a kid on Christmas as I eye the plastic bag he's carrying.

"Did you get them all?" I say by way of greeting. A month ago, I placed my pie order with Carla and Cole offered to pick them up on his way home from work today.

"It's great to see you, too." Cole smirks as he wraps his free arm around my waist to pull me in for a kiss.

What starts as a gentle press of our lips soon turns into a hot make-out session in the foyer. When Cole kisses me, I completely lose myself in him. His clean, manly scent, the way his strong arm holds me close, making me feel protected, and how even now that I'm pregnant, just being near him makes me wet. I'm about to suggest he toss the bag he's holding so he can lift my leg around his hip so I can get some friction until I remember the precious pies. Also, Murphy is trying his best to wedge his body between our legs.

I break our kiss and seductively whisper in Cole's ear, "Are those pies in your bag or are you just happy to see me?"

Cole laughs into my neck, then places a tender kiss right below my ear.

"Both."

With a chaste peck to my lips, Cole releases me and I follow him into the kitchen. Murphy, sensing that something exciting is happening, is right on our heels. As soon as Cole places the bag on the counter, he moves to the side, knowing I will want to unpack them.

I open the first box to discover a flawless pumpkin pie.

"Yum." I'm actually regretting not ordering two of these. I'm going to be really disappointed if everyone eats it up and there are no leftovers.

I open the second and third containers to find apple and pecan pies nestled perfectly inside their boxes. Cole has been right beside me, watching as I open one box after the other. He usually likes to tease me about my obsession with Carla's pies, but he's being awfully quiet.

When I get to the last box, there's a noticeable difference in the weight of it when I lift it out of the bag. Based off the heaviness of the other boxes, there's no way there's a pie in this box. I turn to look at Cole and he's gone slightly pale, he runs a hand through his hair, then clears his throat like he's about to make a confession, his blue eyes intently fixed on where I'm holding the pie box.

"Oh, no. Did something happen to the cherry pie? Did they forget to give it to you? Was it not ready yet?" I know Carla is a stickler for details and she'd never leave me hanging without a cherry pie. Maybe it got dropped and there were no back-ups?

"Brooke."

"I could probably run out and grab one from the store. It might be frozen if the bakery is out of fresh. It won't be as good as Carla's pie but it would be better than no cherry pie at all."

"Brooke."

"What?"

Cole shakes his head, a small smile pulling at his lips. "Just open the box."

I lift the lid and although I'm not surprised there isn't a pie inside, my eyes do widen with excitement when they land on the small velvet jewelry box. My birthday's not until March and although these pies are putting me in the holiday spirit, it's still a month until Christmas. Is this what I think it is? I reach for the velvet box, telling myself not to be disappointed if it's earrings. Earrings are nice. If Cole picked them out for me, they'll be more than nice. But then I turn to find Cole on one knee in front of me. Okay, it's definitely not earrings.

"Brooke Elizabeth Ryan." Cole takes my hand, the one that isn't clutching the jewelry box. I can see the emotion in his eyes and it makes me tear up, too. Murphy, on the other hand, takes the visual of Cole kneeling on the ground as a sign that he's available for pets and jumps up onto him. Good naturedly, Cole rubs behind Murphy's ears to calm him. "Hey, buddy," he says quietly, "I'm excited, too, but we haven't even found out if she says yes."

Murphy quietly lays down on the kitchen floor and Cole turns his attention back to me.

"Brooke, I'm crazy in love with you. Will you marry me?"

I'm crying, and nodding, then Cole stands up and I jump into his arms.

"Yes!" I finally manage to say when I've stopped sobbing. "I love you so much."

Cole takes the ring box from me and seconds later a sparkly cushion-cut diamond is on my finger. Then, Murphy's back in action, trying to climb our legs as Cole and I embrace again.

A minute later, Cole bends down to pick Murphy up, and moves to leave the kitchen.

"Where are you going?" I call out.

"To get the cherry pie out of the car." He winks, and I can't help but laugh. I still can't believe how lucky I am to have found Cole. He's the best plan I never made.

*Five months later…*

<br>

## WELCOME TO THE WORLD
## JAMES MICHAEL MATTHEWS
Born on April 19 at 9:30 in the evening
7 pounds 11 ounces, 21 inches long
Proud parents,
Cole and Brooke

THE END

# ACKNOWLEDGMENTS

This book is eight years in the making. Not that it took me eight years to write it, but that I've been stumbling around this writing thing for that long, coming up with AMAZING and EXCITING book ideas, just to be frustrated and set it aside halfway through for another AMAZING and EXCITING book idea. Finally, I figured out how to get to the finish line. It feels AMAZING and EXCITING! Thank you for taking the time to read it.

Thank you to my husband and three children for your love and support. Eric, without your encouragement, this would have not been possible. To my children for understanding that when mommy says give me one more minute, it's usually twenty minutes. I love the four of you beyond words.

Thank you to Jenny Hawkins, Erica Scott and Courtney Murphy for being my early readers, letting me complain about my book, and encouraging me to keep going even when I just wanted to bang my head against the wall.

Thank you to Sue Grimshaw for your encouragement during the content editing process. You kept me going when I really wanted to shelve the entire thing.

# ABOUT THE AUTHOR

Best Laid Plans is Erin Hawkins's debut novel. She lives in Colorado with her husband and three young children. She enjoys reading, running, spending time in the mountains, and watching reality TV.

Follow her on Instagram @authorerinhawkins